Sam had made it clear that his son was all that mattered.

There was no room in his life for a woman. Not now, anyway. So she was wasting her time.

They had reached a lookout point and Lauren gasped at the splendor of the azure Pacific. Sam lifted Jamie and held him against his shoulder. With his other arm he instinctively drew Lauren to him to share the moment.

As always when he held her close as part of their charade, Lauren's heart went into overdrive. Only this time it was worse, because there was no one watching them, no one to impress. He was holding her because he wanted to…and because it seemed the natural thing to do.

Daddy, Mommy and son.

If only for an instant, the dream had become reality.

Dear Reader,

September celebrates the onset of fall with a refreshing Special Edition lineup!

We begin this month with our THAT SPECIAL WOMAN! title. *The Secret Wife* by bestselling author Susan Mallery is book two in her TRIPLE TROUBLE miniseries and tells an uplifting tale about an estranged couple who renew their love. Look for the final installment of this engaging series in October.

Travel to the mountains of Wyoming with *Pale Rider* by Myrna Temte—a story about a lonesome cowboy who must show the ropes to a beautiful city girl, who captures his heart. Can she convince this hardened recluse that she loves him inside and out?

The sweet scent of romance catches these next heroes off guard in stories by two of our extraspecial writers! First, veteran author Carole Halston spins a delightful tale about a dad who's in the market for marriage but not love in *Mrs. Right*—book three of our FROM BUD TO BLOSSOM promotion series. And look what happens when a hard-driven city slicker slows down long enough to be charmed by a headstrong country gal in *All It Takes Is Family,* the next installment in Sharon De Vita's SILVER CREEK COUNTY series.

Finally, we round off the month with a story about the extraordinary measures a devoted dad will take for his infant son in *Bride for Hire* by *New York Times* bestselling author Patricia Hagan. And keep an eye out for *Beauty and the Groom*—a passionate reunion story by Lorraine Carroll.

I hope you enjoy each and every story to come!

Sincerely,

Tara Gavin,
Senior Editor

Please address questions and book requests to:
Silhouette Reader Service
U.S.: 3010 Walden Ave., P.O. Box 1325, Buffalo, NY 14269
Canadian: P.O. Box 609, Fort Erie, Ont. L2A 5X3

PATRICIA HAGAN

BRIDE FOR HIRE

Silhouette®

SPECIAL EDITION®

Published by Silhouette Books
America's Publisher of Contemporary Romance

SILHOUETTE BOOKS

ISBN 0-373-24127-5

BRIDE FOR HIRE

Copyright © 1997 by Patricia Hagan

Printed in U.S.A.

Books by Patricia Hagan

Silhouette Special Edition

Bride for Hire #1127

Yours Truly

Boy Re-Meets Girl

Harlequin Historicals

The Daring #84
The Desire #143

PATRICIA HAGAN

New York Times bestselling author Patricia Hagan had written and published over 2,500 short stories before selling her first book in 1971. With a background in English and journalism from the University of Alabama, Pat has won awards for radio, television, newspaper and magazine writing. Her hobbies include reading, painting and cooking. The author and her Norwegian husband, Erik, divide their time between their mountain retreat in North Carolina and their home in Bergen, Norway.

HOW TO BE A BRIDE FOR HIRE:

1. First, decide that love—and *real* marriage— is not for you. One ex-fiancé is enough!

2. When you meet your would-be groom, ignore the fact that he is a totally gorgeous hunk.

3. Remain professional when he kisses you in public. After all, you have to convince the world that you are a real-life wife. Go ahead and kiss him back—but don't you *dare* enjoy it!

4. When you hold his tiny son in your arms, do *not* let him steal your heart.

5. Keep telling yourself, "It's only pretend... it's only pretend." Whatever you do, do NOT fall in love!

Prologue

The engagement party from hell.

That was how Lauren was thinking of the beach weekend Stewart's parents had hosted for the Easter weekend.

And it had been a lovely idea—having the bridesmaids and groomsmen get together to enjoy the holiday while finalizing all the wedding plans—till Stewart invited Sherry.

He had met her the same way he had met Lauren, through his job as a pharmaceutical sales representative, and he said he felt sorry for Sherry because she was new in town and didn't know anyone. It had been only two weeks since she'd been hired as a dental assistant at the Brockworth Clinic where Lauren was a hygienist.

So Sherry had come for the weekend, looking like Pamela Sue Anderson in a swimsuit. Stewart had been playing the role of genial host to the hilt…and Lauren was not a happy camper.

She had gone to bed and tried to sleep but couldn't.

Midge, her roommate and best friend, had sneaked out to meet her boyfriend, Scott, saying they were going to make mad love till the wee hours, and Lauren was tossing and turning and miserable.

She switched on the bedside lamp and raised her left hand to admire the pear-shaped diamond Stewart had given her on Christmas Eve, only three months after their first date, and thought about how Mrs. Hastings had insisted they have a big wedding.

Lauren had explained she could not afford it. An orphan, she had been raised in foster homes and had no family to help with the expense. It was only recently that she had started making a decent salary, she hadn't had time to save any money.

But Mrs. Hastings had waved aside her protests and said she and Mr. Hastings would pay for everything.

Lauren sighed and pressed her head deeper into the pillow as she thought about Midge on the beach with Scott.

And she thought about Stewart, all alone in his bed.

She sat up straight as the thought struck like a sledgehammer.

She could tiptoe to his room like the proverbial mouse. In and out before morning. His mother would never know.

Besides, they *needed* to be together, she told herself excitedly as she bounded out of bed. They needed to make love and feel close, and then maybe they could talk and everything would be okay again.

Padding to the door she eased it open and stuck her head out. All was quiet. The hall was dark.

Stewart's room was all the way at the other end.

Tiptoeing, careful not to make any sound, she hurried to his door. Deciding not to take a chance that someone would hear her if she knocked or called to him, she turned the knob and eased herself into the darkness.

The light of a full moon shone through the windows, illuminating the room so she could move about without bumping into anything.

And it was only when she reached the side of the bed that she realized, to her shock and horror, that Stewart was not the only one in it.

Sherry was wrapped in his arms.

Chapter One

"**W**ant to sneak a peanut butter ball before the party?"

Lauren shook her head at Robin Petrie, the girl who had replaced Sherry at the clinic. The chocolate-dipped delicacies were enticing, and she had to muster every ounce of willpower to refuse. "Thanks, but no thanks. Maybe you can eat anything you want and never gain an ounce, but I can look at food and put on a pound."

Robin scoffed. "With a figure like yours, you can pig out once in a while, and you know it." She took another candy before asking, "What time do you think Midge will be here?"

"She took the afternoon off to go with Scott to get their marriage license, but she said she'd stop by around five to pick up her paycheck."

The room was lavishly decorated. White and silver balloons hovered over the table. The cover cloth, embossed with bells and doves, matched the paper plates and napkins. There were bowls of mints, and the peanut butter balls Robin was helping herself to. But it was the centerpiece that caught the eye—a miniature wedding cake topped with a real orchid, compliments of Dr. Brockworth himself.

"I guess you're sad to see her go, huh?" Robin remarked around a mouthful of peanut butter.

Lauren flashed a grin. "Like they say—we all gotta go sometime."

Robin stared at her, the stab at wry humor going over her head.

"Forget it," Lauren said. "Besides, she's not going anywhere. She's just getting married."

"But she's not coming back to work."

Lauren decided the plastic forks would look better if they were in a straight line rather than in a messy pile, and she began arranging them. "True. She's going to work for Scott as his bookkeeper. You know he has his own electrical contracting business."

"Doesn't sound very exciting." Robin popped another peanut butter ball in her mouth.

Lauren feared if she didn't get her out of there, she would eat them all. "We'd better get back to work."

Robin grabbed another on her way out. "So what are you going to do about a new roommate?"

That was something Lauren didn't want to think about. She was happy for Midge that she and Scott were finally getting married, because they seemed so right for each other, but finding someone as congenial as Midge was going to be difficult. "I'm going to try to find somebody," she said as she hurried to her next appointment. "If I don't, I'll just have to move into something cheaper, because I can't afford the rent on my salary."

As she worked, she thought about how she hated to have to move. The condo was in an ideal location, convenient to work, a huge mall, and situated next to a park where she could ride her bike without having to worry about traffic. And nothing she had looked at so far was comparable.

It was depressing…like her whole life seemed of late.

Ever since Stewart.

Her brow crinkled in a frown. She had loved him, trusted him, and he had betrayed her in the worst possible way. And even though it still needled, she had come to terms with it and rationalized it was all for the best.

She knew now that there had actually been many differences between them that she had been willing to overlook—differences that no doubt would have led to big problems later. So how could she have been so stupid as to think it would ever have worked out?

Desperation.

She had been lonely and wanted to be married and have a family, and had leapt at the chance when Stewart proposed, too thrilled by the wonder of it all to think it through and see what a mistake she would be making.

She had left the beach house in the middle of the night and returned to Atlanta, too crushed to care about the aftermath of her sudden departure.

Midge had arrived at the condo by early afternoon. The party was over. After all, when Lauren had left so abruptly, then Sherry, it hadn't taken a rocket scientist to figure out the reason, so everyone had gone home.

Lauren had dreaded having to face Sherry at work on Tuesday morning, unsure of how she would react, but she needn't have worried. Sherry had already sent word that she was quitting without notice and would not be back.

Stewart called, begging for another chance. Sherry had thrown herself at him, he whined. He hadn't known she was going to sneak into his room, till she crawled in bed with him, and then, gee-golly-wow, what was a guy to do? He was only human and surely Lauren could forgive him, because he really, really did love her.

And Lauren had bluntly, coldly, told him to go to hell.

So he had tried another ploy. Stopping by the office, he

had managed to find her by herself to argue that he would agree to have a baby right away. And, with a big wink— which she had found positively disgusting—he had added they could get started on making one right away if she wanted.

"Remember your own words, Stewart," she had told him coldly. "A baby won't hold a bad marriage together, and believe me, it would *be* a bad marriage."

Finally he had stopped trying. Life went on. Lauren began to go out with other men, even though she had no interest in another relationship.

The truth was, she had decided perhaps she should forget about ever getting married. She could always adopt a baby. Lots of women opting to remain single were doing that. It was no longer uncommon. That certainly beat having her heart trounced on by every man she let herself get serious about.

Finishing with her patient, she walked her to the front desk, where Robin said brightly, "Lauren, I've got the perfect solution for you."

"Solution to what?" She glanced at her watch and wondered where her next patient was. She hated it when someone was late. It backed her up for the rest of the day, and she got the blame. But today was especially important, because it was her last appointment, and she wanted to get through in time for Midge's shower.

"About your condo."

Lauren wasn't listening. She had leaned over the desk to look at the appointment book, and, seeing the patient's name, groaned, "Oh, no. It's Mr. Pollard. That's even worse."

"What's worse? What are you talking about? Are you even listening to me, Lauren?" Robin cried, exasperated.

Lauren whispered so the patients in the adjoining waiting room could not overhear, "Mr. Pollard makes Beavis and Butt-head look like choirboys. You should hear him. He not only complains—he curses and calls me names. I hate working on him. Next time he calls for an appointment to have his teeth cleaned, tell him I'm booked all the way into the next century.''

Robin stamped her foot. ''Will you listen to me?'' she asked in a tone so loud that the patients in the waiting room glanced up from their outdated magazines to stare.

Lauren shook her head, perplexed by her friend's impatience. ''What?''

''I've got a roommate for you.''

Lauren felt herself go into a wary mode. ''Like who?''

''Like me.'' Robin slapped a hand against her bosom. ''I can hardly turn around in that one-room efficiency I've been renting since me and Eddie split.''

Lauren bit back a scream of protest. She had been to that efficiency, had seen what a messy—no, *nasty* was the correct word—place it was. Roaches paraded around in broad daylight. Ants crawled on days-old dishes stacked in the sink. Dirty underwear was piled in a corner in the bathroom, and it looked as if something was growing on the walls of the shower stall.

Robin's sloppiness was probably a major factor involved in Eddie moving out, and Lauren vowed silently that there was absolutely no way she was going to move in with her. It would never work out. Howard Stern and Bob Dole would be more compatible.

''Uh, I've already got some girls I have to talk to first,'' Lauren hedged. ''But if they don't work out, I'll let you know.''

Robin said stiffly, ''Well, I should think you'd give me first consideration. After all, we've worked together for over six months now, and I think we'd get along just fine. But if you don't have as much faith in our friendship as I do…'' Her voice trailed off accusingly.

Lauren had never thought she would ever be glad to see the cantankerous Mr. Pollard, but at that precise moment she was grateful he had arrived.

''I hope you aren't going to make me wait,'' he said by

way of greeting, a scowl on his face. "I don't have all day."

"Right this way. I'm ready for you." Lauren's smile was genuine—not for him but the opportunity to escape Robin while she tried to think of a way to say no and still be friends. Over her shoulder, she called, "We'll talk about it later, okay?"

Robin was momentarily pacified. "Sure thing."

Mr. Pollard grumbled as Lauren clipped a linen bib around his neck, then adjusted the chair. "I hate to have my teeth cleaned. Always have. I brush every day. Why should I have to go through this torture? If it weren't for my wife, I wouldn't. But she nags and nags. Hell, we're both in our seventies. Why should I worry about cavities? My teeth will last longer than I will."

Lauren had cleaned his teeth twice in the year she had been working at the clinic and had learned early on that it did no good to attempt to impress upon him the importance of regular checkups and good hygiene. Instead, she concentrated on what she was doing, hurrying as much as possible.

More and more lately, she had been asking herself if she really wanted to clean teeth for the rest of her life or if being a dental hygienist had just seemed like a good idea at the time.

Like Stewart.

She grimaced at the thought.

Mr. Pollard noticed and cried, "What's wrong? What do you see? Is it bad? Is it going to be expensive? I'm not made out of money, you know, and—"

She struggled for patience. "I don't see anything, Mr. Pollard. I was thinking of something else. Now please, if you won't try to talk while I'm working on you, I can have you out of here that much sooner."

He settled back.

She returned to her musing.

For the past month or so she had been checking the classified ads but was greatly discouraged. She was not trained to do anything except what she was doing, and the thought of going back to school to learn new skills was not appealing. Computer technology and health care were the hot careers for the moment, but she had never been good with computers, and nursing was out. She was up to her eyeballs with having to deal with difficult patients. Nursing would be even worse.

She had thought about merely changing jobs, maybe going to work for a larger clinic on the other side of town. Or perhaps leaving Atlanta altogether. But quitting one job and taking another seemed the same as divorcing one man and marrying another—one set of problems was merely exchanged for another.

So what to do? She had no idea. She felt as if she were in a sea of limbo; Midge marrying and moving out only made it all the worse. Not that she was upset with Midge. Far from it. She deserved her happiness. But it had nudged Lauren into a reality check, which made her wonder where the hell she was going with her life.

"Whatch hid, hew dhewpid bimdo," Mr. Pollard yelped against the water Lauren was spraying into his mouth. "Hew dryin' dew droun me—" He grabbed her hand, which made the nozzle fly out of his mouth to spray him in the face.

"Now look what you've done," he yelled, yanking at the bib to wipe himself off. "Damn it, woman. I've told you I don't like water spewing around in my mouth."

"Please, Mr. Pollard. I'm almost through." She wished she had a fire hose to use on him.

Oh, why did she ever think she was cut out for this kind of career? She could have been a hairstylist, an airline stewardess, a travel agent—anything but this.

"You're rough with me. You always are. I'm going to speak to Dr. Brockworth."

She felt like telling him to go ahead. Why should she be any different from the other hygienists she'd heard he'd complained about in the many years he'd been coming to the clinic?

She was tempted to give his chair a spin that would send him sailing right out the window.

But she didn't.

In actuality, Lauren was being very gentle with the old goat.

She glanced at the clock. It was nearly five, but she was afraid to work any faster for fear she *would* make him uncomfortable.

"I'm really sorry, Mr. Pollard. We're almost through. I just need to take your X rays, and then we're done."

"Well, hurry up."

She slipped a tiny cardboard shield between the teeth she planned to X-ray first and the ones behind it. "Bite down on this and hold tight till I tell you to—"

Before she could let go and get her fingers out of his mouth, he pushed the divider away with his tongue, then bit down with all his might.

Lauren screamed as he sank his teeth into her finger.

"That pinched, damn you," he roared as he shoved her away from him and leapt from the chair. "You did it on purpose. You knew my gums were sore and tender from all your butchery. I don't have to take this!"

Lauren stared in stunned disbelief at the blood oozing through the tear in her rubber glove. Her first thought was AIDS. But no. Mr. Pollard was an old man. He would not be sexually promiscuous. Still...

She ran for the peroxide bottle. Not that it would help if he were, God forbid, infected with the virus, but she had to do something.

She was standing at the sink, squeezing her finger to make it bleed harder to get as much bacteria out as possible, when Robin appeared.

"What's wrong with Mr. Pollard? He just charged out the front door with his bib dangling around his neck, screaming he was going to see his lawyer.'' Her eyes widened at the sight of the blood. ''What happened?''

''Robin, I—''

Lauren never knew what she would have said at that particular traumatic moment, because Greta, the other hygienist, ran in just then to announce, ''Midge is here. I just saw her turn in the parking lot. Let's go. We've all got to be in the lounge when she walks in.''

Robin hurried away to tell Dr. Brockworth.

Lauren wrapped a piece of gauze around her finger, then went to the lounge.

By the time Midge got inside the building, everyone was in place and waiting to leap out at her and yell, ''Surprise!''

She promptly broke into tears, and the next moments were filled with hugs and thank-yous and well wishes.

Lauren was also crying—but on the inside, where no one could see, as she thought about the wedding she might never have.

Punch was poured, the cake was cut, and Midge began opening her presents.

She had just thanked Dr. Brockworth for the lovely silver platter he and his wife had given her when the phone rang.

''Darn. Wouldn't you know it?'' Robin mumbled around yet another peanut butter ball as she went to answer.

She was back within seconds to cast a worried glance at Lauren as she told Dr. Brockworth, ''It's Mr. Pollard. I told him we were in the middle of a private party, but he insisted that he talk to you.''

Lauren felt a chill of apprehension.

A few minutes later Dr. Brockworth came back to frostily say, ''Lauren, I'd like to speak with you in private.''

She followed him into his office.

''Well?'' He glared at her from behind his desk. ''I think you know what that was about. What have you got to say for yourself?''

''For myself?'' she echoed, stupefied. She held up her

gauze-wrapped finger. "What about him? What has he got to say about biting me?"

"He said he was defending himself, because you were deliberately hurting him."

Lauren leaned over and placed her hands, palm down, on the desk and looked him straight in the eye as she said, "Mr. Pollard has been coming to this office a lot longer than I've been working here, and I know his reputation for being a pain in the butt, and you should, too. None of this is my fault."

"That's not what he says."

"I don't *care* what he says. I *know* what happened."

Dr. Brockworth leaned back in his chair and momentarily closed his eyes, then looked at her and said, "It doesn't matter. He thinks you were unnecessarily rough. Now I've smoothed things over, and I think if you call him and apologize, he'll let it go."

"*He'll* let it go? Why, I should have him arrested for assault."

He held up a hand in rebuke. "Now, now. We'll have none of that. I can't have any scandals in my office. You call him and apologize, and the next time he calls for a cleaning appointment we'll make sure someone else takes care of him. You might even send him flowers. Maybe a dish garden.

"You can charge it to the office," he added with a patronizing smile.

Lauren was afraid of what she was going to say if she kept standing there, so she turned on her heel and stormed out.

The party was breaking up. Midge was the only one left in the lounge. The others were loading the gifts in the car while she wrapped what was left. "Oh, there you are," she said when Lauren walked in. "I wanted to especially thank you, because I know this was all your idea."

"Actually, everybody wanted to do it."

"Well, it was really sweet. And you know something?

I'm going to miss living with you. It's been great. You're like my sister."

"I feel the same." Lauren began to clear paper plates off the table. She did not feel melancholy just then. She felt mad, damn it. Mad and dumped on. But there was no need to spoil Midge's glow by crying on her shoulder.

"Hey, I know it's none of my business, but—"

"Did she tell you already?" Lauren spun around, fresh anger churning. She didn't want Robin spreading stories when she really didn't know what had happened. People would think the worse, like Dr. Brockworth, unless she had a chance to tell her side.

"Well, yes, she did," Midge said hesitantly, stunned by Lauren's apparent anger.

Lauren wrung her hands in frustration. "She had no business doing that. I suppose she told everybody."

"Well...yes...they were here. I mean, what's the secret? Robin's okay. Sure, she's messy, but you can straighten her out about that."

Lauren blinked, bewildered.

"Well, golly, Lauren. I don't see why you're so upset. You said you really wanted to keep the condo, that you hadn't found anything as nice that you could afford. But if you don't want Robin to move in with you, why did you agree that she could?"

"I didn't."

"Robin said she was moving in with you. I assumed you told her it was okay."

Dear Lord, it was too much. First Mr. Pollard had bitten her. Her job was on the line unless she got down on her knees and apologized for something she didn't do. And now Robin had backed her into a corner, and she was either going to have to let her move in or make an enemy for life.

Too much. Way too much. Could things get any worse?

Midge's eyes narrowed. "Are you okay?"

"I'm fine," she lied.

"Then why did you turn blue when I mentioned Robin moving in with you?"

"She isn't."

"Then what—"

Lauren threw up her hands. "It's like this. I've had a really, really bad day." She recounted the episode with Mr. Pollard.

Midge gave a low whistle. "That's awful, honey. You know, you've not only had a bad day, you've had some bad *months*. What you need is a new man in your life."

"What I need is a new life, period."

Robin and Greta returned, and Lauren busied herself wrapping newspaper around the set of wineglasses one of the patients had given Midge.

She was about to use a page from the classified section when the ad leapt out at her.

Wanted. Young, aspiring actress for special assignment. Must be reasonably attractive, intelligent and mature, with a spirit of adventure. Good character and morals. Free to travel and commit 100% of time for thirty days or longer. All expenses paid. Excellent pay for the right person.

It was the answer to her prayers.

All she had to do was tell Dr. Brockworth that she was burned-out and needed a leave of absence. If he said no, then she would just quit. After all, she could always find another job as a dental hygienist.

It was also the answer to the situation with Robin. The lease was up in a few months. She would leave her things in the condo till after the assignment, then find another place. So what if it wasn't as nice?

Change was good.

"I can do this," she whispered, heart pounding and hands shaking with excitement.

"Do what?" Midge asked.

"Er…" Lauren floundered, then, with a feeble grin, said, "I can—" she held up a goblet "—wrap it so it won't break. I should work for a moving company. I'm really a good packer."

"Oh, that's nice," Midge said, giving her a strange look.

I'm also a good actress, Lauren thought happily, *or at least, I intend to make somebody think so…for a couple of months, anyway.*

Over two weeks had passed since Lauren had called the phone number listed in the ad. The recording of a man's voice had instructed that a résumé and recent photograph should be sent to a post office box, along with an address where she could be contacted.

Lauren did not have a formal résumé, so she just listed the jobs she'd had thus far. As for the aspiring actress part, she had ultimately decided it best to be completely honest and admitted she had never even thought about acting but was willing to try. She had gone on to explain how she was eager for a change in her life, and that the job sounded intriguing.

She gave the clinic as her address, not about to divulge her home location to a stranger. After all, she was taking a chance answering such a mysterious ad.

She had called the classified department at the newspaper in an attempt to find out more about the ad. When that had proved futile, she had dialed the number again to listen to the voice once more, trying to decide whether it sounded honest. Then she told herself she was being silly. Jeffrey Dahmer had probably sounded real nice over the phone.

The man, she opined, did not sound very old. She guessed him to be somewhere in her own age group—close to thirty. He also sounded self-assured, confident. And his voice was pleasant. If he was in telemarketing, he probably did very well.

Enclosing a photo taken at the office Christmas party,

she mailed her letter, but when days passed without response, she decided her candor had probably eliminated her from consideration.

So her life continued drearily on.

Midge returned from her honeymoon, but Lauren seldom heard from her because she was too busy being a happy newlywed.

Robin was still pressuring her to let her share the apartment, and Lauren was still managing to hold her at bay.

She had also given in and apologized to Mr. Pollard but had stood her ground against sending flowers. Dr. Brockworth had Robin send them, anyway, and Mr. Pollard was so impressed that he called in to make the appointment for his next cleaning.

Lauren could only hope Dr. Brockworth would keep his promise and assign Mr. Pollard to someone else, but maybe by the time another six months rolled around she would have managed to make a career change and be working somewhere else.

But, so far, she had no ideas and was just taking one day at the time, and, beginning another, asked Robin who was on the schedule for that morning.

Robin began reading the patient names from the appointment book.

Lauren was flipping through her mail as she listened. There was the usual advertising from toothpaste and mouthwash manufacturers, along with samples. A new style toothbrush got her attention, but her head snapped up as she heard an unfamiliar name. "Who's Sam Rutledge?"

Robin shrugged. "I have no idea. He called last week. I remember, because I wouldn't have been able to work him in if Mr. Smith hadn't canceled."

Lauren was putting instruments in the autoclave when Robin came to tell her that Sam Rutledge had arrived. "I know he's early, but I went ahead and put him in your chair."

Lauren noticed she seemed flustered and asked, "So what's wrong with you?"

Robin grinned. "I guess it's not every day I get to meet Kevin Costner's twin."

Just then Greta appeared at the door to whisper, "Hey, Lauren, don't look now, but Kevin Costner is sitting in your chair."

Lauren quickly closed the autoclave and declared, "*This* I've got to see."

Sam Rutledge was not a total Kevin Costner clone, but he definitely brought the star's image to Lauren's mind. With his straw blond hair, caressing blue eyes and winsome smile, he was ruggedly handsome. But he also had a little-boy appeal about him that tugged at the heartstrings.

"So you're Lauren," he said, looking at her name tag.

"Yes. And you're Mr. Rutledge. It's nice to meet you."

"Call me Sam."

"Sorry. Dr. Brockworth says we're not to call patients by their first names."

"Then I should call you Miss Gentry?"

"No, that's okay. Lauren is fine."

She fastened the white bib around his neck, then pressed her foot on the hydraulic pedal to tilt the chair back. "Open, please."

With mirror and pick, she began to probe in his mouth, wondering why her hands were shaking. Good heavens, she'd been around handsome men before, but the way he was watching her so intensely was unnerving.

"You have wonderful teeth," she said when she had finished her examination. "Looks like you just had them cleaned."

"Uh, no, I haven't," he said, glancing away for the first time. "It's been a year, at least."

"And who was your dentist? It would help if we had your last X rays."

"That would take too long." He wriggled uncomfortably in the chair. "He's in another state."

"Well, we can send for them and just do the cleaning today and then reschedule another appointment for an examination after we get them."

"I'd rather just start all over."

She thought that odd but didn't push the issue. Maybe he didn't mind spending money needlessly. Besides, after the incident with Mr. Pollard, she was supercautious with her patients, avoiding any kind of confrontation. So if Sam Rutledge didn't want his records transferred, it made no difference to her.

"How do you like being a hygienist?" he asked as she assembled her instruments.

Her reply was curt. "It's a living."

"Is that all? I should think you would have to enjoy this kind of work to do it. Where are you from?"

"The country." She began picking between his teeth. They were spotless.

"You like the city?"

"Uh-huh." She wished he would hush.

"You got a boyfriend?" he spoke around the pick.

Good grief, was he going to hit on her? Firing a glance at his ring finger, she did not see a telltale gold band but knew that didn't mean anything. Usually the first thing a married man did when he was trying to score was take off his ring.

"Married?" he pressed on.

"No."

He continued to ask questions, making it extremely difficult for her to work on him. And not all of his queries were about her, personally. He wanted her opinions on a myriad of subjects—books, TV shows, films, even politics.

Turning at one point to make the usual notations on his chart, she noticed the time and realized she had to get moving. She was taking much longer with him than usual for routine hygiene.

She began to work more diligently, putting more of her hand in his mouth than necessary so he couldn't talk.

When she had to allow him to rinse, he began again. "I get the impression you don't like it here. What other kind of work would you like to do?"

She decided maybe he was merely trying to be friendly, and there was no harm in taking a brief moment to chat. Besides, he did seem nice, and she liked his eyes...a lot. "I guess if I'd had the opportunity for a college education, I'd have wanted to be a teacher."

He smiled. "Really? What level?"

She wondered why he seemed so pleased but answered, "Elementary. Maybe even kindergarten. I like little kids."

His smile grew wider. "You must have come from a large family."

"Actually, no."

"Not many sisters and brothers?"

She shook her head. "I was an only child."

"So was I," he confided with a nod of bonding. "Gets lonely sometimes, doesn't it? Of course, it's probably worse for me than it is for you—my parents are dead, so I don't have anybody."

She decided it was fair play for her to be equally nosy. "Aren't you married?"

"Nope. Came close a couple of times, but it didn't work out."

Her short laugh was bitter. "I know the feeling." An image of Stewart came to mind.

"And your folks? Do they live in Atlanta?"

"Don't have any." She held her instruments poised. "I really need to finish, Mr. Rutledge."

"Sure, sure." He opened his mouth.

As she leaned over him, she chided herself for feeling so unnerved by the closeness. What was wrong with her? She had worked on attractive men before but none of them had ever affected her this way.

The tangy scent of his cologne conjured images of those bare-chested hunks on the covers of the steamy romance novels that she devoured as time permitted.

She darted a glance at his shoulders. Broad. Strong.

Then his arms. Muscular. Brawny. She could imagine herself wrapped against his chest, and—

Stop it, Lauren! She commanded herself. Damn it, what was happening? Not even Stewart had affected her so intensely on first meeting. But Stewart had not shown interest in her as a person, with caressing eyes and tender voice. In fact, now that she looked back, with Stewart she had merely been an object—a doll, for partying...for sex.

Sam Rutledge, on the other hand, seemed bent on knowing who and what she really was about.

You're being silly, she chided herself. He probably acted the same with everybody. Besides, sitting in a dental chair made lots of people nervous, and that could be what inspired his chattiness. He had given no indication that he wanted to ask her out. Probably she would never see him again.

So calm down and stop acting like a silly schoolgirl, Lauren.

"Psst. Lauren."

She whipped her head about to see Robin standing in the doorway. She looked upset.

"Excuse me." Lauren patted Sam's shoulder, then drew her hand back as though she'd touched a hot coal. What if he mistook the gesture for flirting? Oh, if she didn't hurry and get him out of there, she was going to make a complete fool of herself.

Robin drew her down the hall to whisper frantically, "Oh, Lauren, I don't know what to do. Mr. Smith is here."

Lauren gasped. "You said he canceled."

"He did. I mean, I thought he did." She began to wring her hands.

"Do you suppose you got him mixed up with somebody else?"

She swung her head wildly in denial. "No, because he even asked me to verify his appointment before he canceled. He wasn't sure of the right day and didn't want to be a no-show.''

"Did you remind him of that?''

"Yes, of course.'' Robin glanced nervously in the direction of the waiting room, then turned miserable eyes on Lauren once more. "I don't know what to do. You know how he gets.''

Robin was bouncing up and down on the balls of her feet and wringing her hands. "He's going to make a scene, and Dr. Brockworth will hear and get mad at me and say I screwed up, but I didn't, Lauren. I swear I didn't.''

Lauren gave her an awkward pat. Probably she *had* made a mistake, but wasn't about to tell her that. Smith was a common name. "Look, find him a magazine that's not three years old and tell him to have a seat, and I'll work him in. Has my next appointment arrived?''

Robin looked sick. "Yes. Mrs. Jensen. And I hate to tell you, but you're ten minutes over into her time. What's taking so long in there?'' She nodded toward the room where Sam Rutledge waited.

"Uh, he talks a lot.'' Lauren saw no reason to say what about...or how it—*he*—had affected her. "But don't worry. I'll get rid of him quick. I'll talk him out of having X rays.''

Returning to his side, she swallowed against her frustration and said, "I really think we should send for those X rays, Mr. Rutledge. There's no need for you to spend money when you don't have to.''

"It's okay,'' he said quietly, watching her intently. "I'd rather take care of it today if you don't mind.''

"Well, actually, there's a problem. It seems the receptionist accidentally canceled someone's appointment and put you in his time slot. Now that person is here, and he's quite upset.''

"I'm sorry,'' he murmured.

It struck her that he didn't sound as though he really was. Hearing his next words, she was sure of it.

"Well, a couple of X rays shouldn't take long."

With a ragged sigh, she turned to get the plates.

"So what do you do in your spare time?" he asked, settling back.

Once more, she found herself drawn into conversation, enjoying the feeling that someone actually wanted to know another side of her. She told him she liked watersports. Swimming. Diving. Boating. She also liked bicycle riding, and once she had dared try in-line skating but fell and skinned her knee real bad and had retired from that sport.

He chuckled. "Wow. You're really active, aren't you? Don't you have a *quiet* side?"

"Sure. I love to read, and I like to watch old movies, preferably in black and white. Color just seems to take something away."

"Ah, a romantic," he said, obviously pleased. "But tell me something—" He adjusted himself in the chair, as though readying to focus completely on her response to his next question. "You said you liked children, but what about babies?"

She smiled as she manipulated the little cardboard bite wing in place in his mouth. "Everybody loves babies. I'm no exception. Now hold still, and don't breathe."

She stepped behind the protective screen and pushed a button. The machine clicked. "Breathe," she called.

When she removed the cardboard, he immediately asked, "How are you with them?"

"Who?" Focused on the X rays, she had already forgotten what they had been discussing.

"Babies. Are you good with them? I mean, you aren't nervous around them, are you?"

Startled, she was unsure as to how to respond and stammered, "Well, I don't know. I mean, I can't remember ever being around a baby. I guess I'd be okay. I've never really thought about it." She froze, another bite wing poised in her hand, ready to be inserted. Suddenly he seemed too

curious. "Why are you asking me all this?" Her tone rang
with the annoyance she could no longer deny.

"I just—"

Before he could speak, Robin rushed in to plead, "Lauren, can you hurry it up? Mr. Smith is demanding to talk
to Dr. Brockworth to tell him what happened and how long
he's been waiting, and now Mrs. Jensen is starting to get
mad. I can't handle both of them."

Abruptly Sam yanked the bib from around his neck and
got out of the chair. "This is my fault. I took up too much
of your time. I'm very sorry."

"Wonderful." Robin exploded with relief and turned to
dash down the hall.

"Robin will make another appointment for you." Lauren
concentrated on making notes in his chart.

"I'll do that. And, again, Miss Gentry, I'm really sorry
about any inconvenience I've caused, and actually I was
wondering if—"

She whirled around, jolted to remember how he had
called her by her surname when he'd first arrived. She
hadn't noticed then. Now, however, it dawned, and she instinctively began to step back from him as she warily asked,
"How did you know my last name? I didn't give it to you,
and Robin wouldn't have. It's against clinic policy."

She felt a quiver of fear to see the look that flashed upon
his face—like that of a criminal caught in the act.

He held up his hands as though to show he meant her
no harm. "I'm the one who's sorry. This was a bad idea.
I should've been honest with you from the beginning and
told you who I am."

"So who...who are you?" she asked, choking, aware
that she had backed herself against the counter, and he
stood between her and the door.

"Sam Rutledge is my real name, but I'm not a patient.
I mean, I didn't come here to get my teeth cleaned. I just
thought if I pretended that was the reason, I could find out
more about you."

She had no idea what he was getting at and didn't care. She only knew she wanted him out of there. What kind of kook was he?

He rushed on. "I can see now it was dumb, and that I've not only caused a lot of people inconvenience but frightened you, as well."

Slowly she moved her hands behind her, fingers creeping along the counter in search of a weapon in case he got really nutty. She could always scream and bring everyone running, but preferred to handle the situation quietly if possible.

"You see, Miss Gentry," he said finally, "I'm here about your response to my ad."

Chapter Two

Lauren felt herself sway with shock, ever so slightly, and she pressed back against the counter for support.

He took a step toward her but froze when he saw the scared look on her face. "You've no need to be frightened. I'm not going to hurt you."

She glared at him. "Why didn't you tell me who you are? Why all the secrecy?"

"I know I went about it all wrong," he said lamely, "but the fact is, your letter just sounded too good to be true, and I wanted to check you out before I went any farther."

"Well, it's not *going* any farther," she snapped, "because I don't like your method of interviewing. First, you lie to get an appointment—"

"I had to," he was quick to defend. "When I first called, they said you were booked up for the next three months. I couldn't wait that long."

"So you canceled poor Mr. Smith's appointment?"

He couldn't help smiling over his cunning. "It's a common name. I figured you'd have to have one on your schedule sooner or later, so I called and said I was Mr. Smith and couldn't remember when I was due to come in but knew it was sometime soon and needed to cancel. The receptionist flipped through her book to the next Smith on the schedule and bingo! She canceled. I called back a few minutes later and grabbed the vacancy.''

He looked so smug, which only made her all the madder. ''You're proud of yourself, aren't you? Well, did you stop to think of the chaos your little scheme would cause?''

''I'm sorry. I guess I wasn't thinking beyond finding a way to get to you.''

She was no longer afraid and positioned herself in front of him, hands on her hips. Neither was she mesmerized by the gentle gleam in his eyes, or the soft line of his mouth, or the strong set of his jaw.

Stop it, Lauren! Get real here. Fantasy time is over. You're dealing with a shrewd customer.

Her words were like the crack of a whip. ''Well, you can just find a way out of here, mister, and fast, because you've messed up my day all you're going to. I've got two patients out there ready to have both me and the receptionist fired. And you've also gotten me so far behind, I'll be lucky to get out of here at all tonight.''

''Miss Gentry, if you'll only hear me out—''

She pointed at the door. ''Out. Or I'll call the cops, so help me.''

''I know I did a terrible thing,'' he admitted once again, ''but when I explain everything to you, I'm sure you'll understand.''

She shook her head firmly. ''I never should have answered that ad. I should have known it was something totally wacko.''

His mouth twisted in a mocking smile. ''I suppose ten thousand dollars *is* a bit wacko.''

Lauren's mouth fell open. It would take her six months of standing on her feet five days a week to make that kind of money. "Did you say *ten thousand dollars?*" she asked when she could find her voice.

"That's right. Net, too. I'll pay the taxes."

"Ten thousand dollars for doing what?"

His smile faded, and his eyes narrowed. "I'm afraid I can't tell you anything else until I get to know you better. And, like I said, when I finally do explain everything, you'll understand the reason for my having to be so cautious."

Lauren was dizzily reminded of that Jamie Lee Curtis film, *True Lies,* when a guy pretended to be a CIA agent to put the make on her. She glanced around to make sure Sam Rutledge was not leaving a briefcase behind, like the guy in the movie, so he'd have an excuse to call later.

"I don't like this," she said finally...but thoughtfully.

"I must have received fifty letters, but yours was the one that caught my eye, because you were so candid. And I did interview a few and discovered they had really stretched the truth about themselves."

She challenged, "So you think you know everything there is to know about me because I cleaned your teeth?"

"No. But I found out enough to know that you're the top candidate for the job. I also liked your photograph. You have a natural beauty. Clean. Wholesome. That's important."

She did not get the sense his flattery had an ulterior motive. He appeared, she realized with startling clarity, quite businesslike.

"Could we have dinner, Miss Gentry—Lauren? Tonight, if you're free. I've spent longer than I'd planned going through other applicants, and it's important that I see whether you'll work out."

"And if I don't? Not that I'm still interested," she was quick to add, remembering her anger.

"There are a couple that might work out, but I'm still not a hundred percent sure."

Lauren closed her eyes and thought of what she could

do with ten thousand dollars. First she would pay off her credit cards, then think about studying for another career.

"Tonight?" he pressed.

Just then Robin returned, and this time she appeared to be just on the edge of hysteria as she exploded, "If you don't clear the room for Mr. Smith, he says he's going to break down the door to get to Dr. Brockworth and tell him what a bunch of incompetents we are. And Dr. Brockworth just happens to be doing a root canal. So will you please do something, Lauren? Now?"

The look she gave Sam indicated she blamed him.

"Bring Mr. Smith back," Lauren told her.

She turned on her heel and broke into a run down the hall.

Sam was studying Lauren's face, hoping to find some sign she would relent. He decided to dangle the carrot one last time. "Ten thousand net. All I need is your time. There's nothing immoral about any of it. In fact, I think you'll ultimately find it rewarding."

It was tempting. But she'd have to be crazy...

"There's no harm in our having dinner."

"You'd tell me everything?" she asked.

He shook his head. "Not tonight. I have to get to know you better. In fact, before I tell you the whole story, I have to be completely sure that you're the one I want for the job, and that you'll be willing to do it."

That was the most ridiculous thing Lauren had ever heard, and she bluntly said as much.

They could hear the sounds of someone coming down the hall, heels clicking in haste. It would be Mr. Smith, and they both knew time was up.

"Give me a chance," Sam pleaded, reaching out to touch her arm.

Lauren almost pulled away but didn't. There was something comforting in his touch—a gesture of friendship, perhaps. Whatever the message, it had the effect right then of melting her reserves. She decided to give him the benefit of the doubt—to a point.

"All right. I'll have dinner with you."

He grinned. "What time and where?"

"There's a coffee bar down the street."

Disappointment crossed his face. "I'd really like to buy you dinner. Not just coffee."

"Oh, they serve food at night."

He sounded dubious. "Well, okay. What—"

Mr. Smith burst through the open doorway, face red and breathing coming in such violent gasps, Lauren wondered whether he might have a heart attack. He was not young and was grossly overweight.

"It's about time, damn it." His words were raspy. "Let's get to it." He practically threw himself in the chair.

"What time?" Sam prodded as Lauren pushed him into the hall.

"Six...maybe. Six-fifteen." She was starting to have second thoughts. "Actually, I'm not sure I can make it. I'll probably have to work late."

She closed the door before he could argue.

Mr. Smith was pacified when she told him he would not be charged for the cleaning because he had been so inconvenienced. He settled back and grumbled no more.

Her thoughts flew as she worked, and they all fluttered around Sam Rutledge.

Just what would she be expected to do for that kind of money? All kinds of horrible things came to mind, but then she rationalized that if he had something sexual in mind, he'd have asked for a swimsuit photo, not merely a head shot. Besides, the requirements for good morals and character didn't fit that kind of scenario, anyway.

Drug smuggling? Maybe he wanted her to pose as a nun and hide cocaine in the folds of her habit.

Her imagination began to run away with her as she envisioned all kinds of partner-in-crime situations.

Whoa, Lauren, you're getting carried away here.

But why not? she answered herself. Hadn't she heard an inner voice shouting "Sterrrikkke three, you're out!" when she'd walked in on Stewart and Sherry? She was oh for three where men were concerned, and therefore she felt she had a right to be suspicious of them.

She finished with Mr. Smith in record time, then ushered in Mrs. Jensen who, by then, had been tapping her toes impatiently for almost an hour. To placate her, Lauren had to repeat her offer for a free cleaning—which, like Mr. Smith's, would come out of her salary.

But money would not be a problem for a long time if Sam Rutledge offered the job—*if* she decided to accept it if he did.

It was nearly six-thirty when she finished with Mrs. Jensen. Everyone else had already left, and she knew if she were going to keep the dinner date, she needed to be on her way.

It was possible, however, that he had already left. After all, she hadn't asked him to wait.

She sat behind the receptionist counter and tried to make up her mind whether or not to call the coffee shop and ask whether he was still there. Then the thought struck her that he might have been lying about his name, after all.

Opening the drawer, she took out Robin's receipt book and flipped through to find one recorded to Sam Rutledge. He had paid cash, so there was no way of tracing him through an address or phone number.

So Lauren knew no more about him now than she had before—except that he was attractive and, despite the mystery, had an air of charm about him. He was sort of a Pierce Brosnan-James Bond, which, she opined with a little shiver, was not a bad thing.

Six forty-five.

He would be gone.

Forget it. She would survive without the money.

Forget *him.* She didn't want to get involved with anyone for a long time.

At least not until she turned sixty.

It had been a dumb idea in the first place. What could she have been thinking, anyway, answering a mysterious blind ad in the paper. She told herself she was lucky he hadn't turned out to be a psycho, or a stalker, or even a serial killer.

Pushing down a little feeling of disappointment, she decided to hang around the clinic a while longer. She didn't want to chance running in to him outside.

By eight o'clock, Lauren had cleaned her treatment room from top to bottom, rearranged all the posters of Smiley Good Tooth and Harry Happy Brush and could find no further reason to dawdle any longer.

Surprisingly, however, her mood had begun to swing the other way. Maybe she should have kept the appointment just to satisfy her curiosity. What would have been the harm? The coffee shop was a public place. He still wouldn't know where she lived. All she would've had to do was hear him out and then say no if she didn't want it to go any further. If he came around later at the office, or started stalking or scared her in any way, well, she could call the police.

And to think she had been so brazen as to respond to an ad calling for someone daring, when she had even wimped out on the interview! How could she have ever thought she could qualify for anything exciting?

"I deserve a boring life," she said out loud as she set the security alarm on the wall beside the back door. "This is as good as it gets, and it's all my fault."

Outside, the last leaves of autumn danced around her feet in the rhythm of the night wind. The air was chilly. She wished now she had driven her car to work instead of walking, but the morning had been nice with a bright, warm sun, and she had enjoyed the stroll. Now, however, she was cold and hadn't brought a sweater, forgetting how unpredictable Atlanta weather could be in November.

Shivering, she quickened her pace. There was still a lot

of traffic, and it was a nice area, so she had no reason not to feel safe.

Ahead, she could see the lights of the coffee shop. It was actually a mom-and-pop operation. Once it had been just a café, frequented by everyone in the mostly residential neighborhood. Then the business complexes began squeezing in around it, along with the demand from office workers for coffee and bagels during the day. The owners, Sarah and Clyde Cavanaugh, had adapted but still offered homey type food in the evenings.

A delicious smell reached her nostrils, and she breathed deeply. Chicken and dumplings. Sarah made the absolute best in the whole word.

Lauren's stomach growled loudly to remind her that it had been one of those days when she hadn't had time for lunch. She had nibbled on a few of Robin's ever-plentiful supply of chocolate-chip cookies and sipped on a cola, and that was it.

An image of the inside of her refrigerator came to mind, and she slowed. Leftover pizza, some sandwich meat that she couldn't remember when she had bought—she didn't want to think about what it would look like now.

The contents of the cabinets wouldn't be much better.

Lauren had to admit that since Midge had moved out, she had lost all interest in cooking. Together they'd had a lot of fun taking turns experimenting with recipes. Scott would come over and bring wine, and sometimes Lauren would invite a date…but not often. Men were like rich desserts—too often they didn't turn out to be as good as they looked.

Between hunger and thinking of what awaited at home, dinner at the café seemed logical—unless Sam Rutledge was still waiting there after two hours.

But surely he wouldn't be, she argued with herself. He'd said he was considering other applicants. Besides, he seemed like an intelligent man. He would have figured out that after getting off to such a bad start, things could only go downhill. It just wouldn't work.

And if he *was* still there? The thought provoked a little chill, for it would mean that he was determined to keep after her, and that was scary to contemplate.

Okay. The café was small. Booths on one wall, stools at the counter. She could see the whole place from the front window. All she had to do was peek in, and if she saw him, she would just keep on going.

She was almost there when a couple came out and started down the sidewalk toward her. The man was pushing a stroller, and she recognized him and his wife. Kaye and Paul Waters lived a few blocks on down and had only recently had their first baby.

When they met, they stopped to exchange pleasantries. Lauren bent over the stroller but could not see the baby for all the blankets. "May I?" she asked, her hand poised.

"Of course." Kaye beamed proudly. "If it weren't so windy, I'd let you hold him."

Lauren drew the blanket back gently, her heart warming at the sight of the sleeping cherub. "He's precious," she whispered. "How old is he now?"

"Nearly a month," said Paul, adding, "and he eats like a horse and grows like a weed. You should've heard him crying for some of Sarah's meat loaf."

"Well, who can blame him? I'm about to have some myself." Then, seizing the opportunity, Lauren asked, "Did you by any chance see a man in there who looked like he was waiting for somebody? Tall. Probably as tall as Clint Eastwood. Looks a little like Kevin Costner?"

Kaye laughed and asked incredulously, "You mean you'd keep a hunk like that waiting?"

Lauren felt her cheeks redden and chided herself for sounding like a silly schoolgirl. "Oh, it's nobody special," she said with a shrug. "I'm just not very good at describing people."

"Sorry," Kaye said. "I'm afraid I was so busy keeping an eye on the baby, I didn't notice anybody else."

Paul scratched his head, then said, "Well, there was a guy sitting in the back booth. I didn't get a good look at him, but I remembered thinking he was sure sitting there a long time without ordering anything."

"Is he still there?"

"Come to think of it, I don't remember seeing him when we left. But, like Kaye said, we were busy with the baby and not paying any attention to who came and went. He probably left, though."

Lauren pushed aside the disappointment that tried to mingle with a wave of relief. She would always wonder what it was all about—*what Sam Rutledge was all about*—but it was probably best this way.

"We'd better be getting the baby out of this night air," Kaye said.

Lauren stepped back. "Sure. Just remember when you need a sitter to give me a call."

Kaye gave her a friendly pat on her shoulder. "Honey, you need to be spending your time with a man and thinking about marriage and having your own babies. Not baby-sitting someone else's."

Paul chimed in to agree, "She's right. You're not getting any younger, and—"

Kaye gave him a playful shove. "Stop it. She's younger than I am." She turned to Lauren once more and made her voice compassionate as she said, "Honey, we heard what happened with your engagement, but don't give up. The right guy will come along, believe me. And then you'll have the daddy for all those babies you want. I've never forgotten your telling me you didn't care how many you had."

Lauren gave a reckless shrug and grinned. "Oh, I don't have to get married to have a baby. I can just hire a sur-rogate father. You know, pay somebody to father a baby. Then I wouldn't have to put up with a man, and—"

That was it!

That was the job Sam Rutledge had to offer.

He wanted a woman to have a baby for him. He either wanted to be a single parent or was scouting for both him and his wife. Whichever it was, she wished she had figured it out sooner so she could have told him he was out of his mind. Never, ever, would she sell her own child. The nerve of him!

Oh, it all made sense—wanting someone with good morals and character, needing a photograph to make sure she was reasonably attractive. And, yes, the questions about children, babies. It all fell into place.

Kaye and Paul were exchanging glances again, this time nervously, because Lauren's face had turned red, and she was clenching her fists and looking mad enough to chew glass.

"Uh, we'll see you," Paul said uneasily as he maneuvered the stroller around her.

Kaye hurried along with him. "Yeah, Lauren. You take care and come see us."

They rushed away, not looking back.

Lauren, lost in revelation, did not notice as she continued on to the café. Now she hoped he would call, so she could tell him straight-out what a first-class creep he was for stringing her along. He should have come right out in the ad and made it clear what he had in mind. Then she'd have never wasted her time and wound up having another stressful afternoon with her patients, not to mention having to pay for two cleanings herself.

Damn you, Sam Rutledge, she whispered under her breath, yanking the door of the café open with a vengeance. *If I ever see you again...*

She froze.

He was still there, sitting in the back booth, grinning like a Cheshire cat and waving at her as if she were a long-lost friend.

She was half in, half out of the doorway, and people were beginning to stare.

Then she bolted forward, walking rapidly toward him, eyes narrowed to furious slits.

Sam's grin faded as she drew closer, and he automatically drew back against his seat in readiness for her wrath...whatever the reason for it.

Reaching the booth, she leaned across the table, right in his face, not wanting anyone else to hear. "First of all, you sneaky, conniving creep, I'd never sell my baby. And second, I would never sleep with a man to make one so he could buy it from me."

He was stunned. "Lauren, you've got it all wrong. Believe me. That's not—"

"You think money will buy anything, don't you? Well, you're wrong, mister, where I'm concerned, anyway. You and your wife can pay somebody else to have your baby."

He looked stricken as he attempted to reason, "I told you—I'm not married, Lauren. And this isn't about your having a baby."

Clyde Cavanaugh seemed to appear out of nowhere. A big, brawny man, he wiped his hands on his greasy apron as he looked warily at Sam, then Lauren, and asked, "This guy making trouble?"

"Not anymore," she snapped.

Sam tried again. "If you'll only listen..."

Clyde cut in, "Maybe you'd better leave, buddy. You've been sittin' in this booth long enough to hatch eggs. Two hours and you haven't bought nothing but iced tea."

Sam stiffened, his own ire rising. Folding his arms across his chest, he fixed Lauren with a defiant stare as he said to Clyde, "I paid for the tea. When I finish it, I'll go. Not before."

"Let him stay," Lauren said. "*I'll* leave."

Sam bolted from the booth to go after her, but Clyde tried to hold him back. There was a brief scuffle, with Sam managing to get away without blows being exchanged.

He raced after Lauren, who had already disappeared outside, as Clyde yelled after him, "Hey, I'm calling the cops."

Sam caught up with her a short distance away. She struggled against him as he held her arms pinned at her sides, but she managed to plant a sharp kick on his shin before he maneuvered out of range of her viciously swinging foot.

He gave her a gentle shake as he pleaded, "Hear me out. I don't know where you got that kind of notion, but it's absolutely crazy. I don't want to pay you or any other woman to have a baby."

"Then why all the questions about babies?"

"I wish I could tell you now, but I can't." He let her go and stepped back. Then, running his fingers through his hair in agitation, he declared, exasperated, "Look. Maybe we'd better forget the whole thing. You're leery and suspicious, and I guess if I were in your place I'd feel the same way. But I can't tell you any more than I already have—not till I get to know you better and trust you.

"Hell," he said as he turned away, "I was a fool to think I could find anybody to do it, anyway."

He was over a block away when Clyde came running out of the café, a meat cleaver in his hand. "Cops will be here in a minute," he said when he reached her. "Where'd he go?"

She pointed in the opposite direction. "That way. Just forget it, Clyde. It's over. Call the police back and tell them they don't need to bother. Please."

"Are you sure? What was that all about, anyhow?"

"Just a misunderstanding with an old boyfriend," she lied. "Now go call the police back, okay? There's no need to make a big deal out of this."

"Well, okay."

"And thanks, Clyde," she called after him.

Turning to look in the direction Sam had actually gone, she saw him getting into what looked like a sports car. He would be coming toward her but something told her he would pass right on by. It was over.

Or was it?

With a thundering in her chest, she stepped off the curb and into the street like a seasoned New Yorker hailing a cab.

Her curiosity had been aroused, and she knew she would never know a moment's peace until Sam's secret was unveiled...and the mystery solved.

She held up her arm.

Chapter Three

Lauren stared at her reflection in the mirror and announced, "You are crazy, Lauren Gentry. Absolutely crazy. Bonkers. Basket case."

She had to be, she reasoned, to be going out with Sam Rutledge.

Hadn't she promised herself not to get into any kind of relationship with a man for a long, long time?

Hadn't she sworn to make a career change her number one priority?

She wrinkled her nose at that. No need to be so hard on herself. After all, answering the ad *had* been an attempt to find a new job, and there was no telling what it might lead to.

She frowned.

So exactly where did she *want* it to lead?

She did not know and was not sure of anything, except that Sam Rutledge was affecting her in a way she neither wanted or needed in her life right now. But, for some strange reason she felt compelled to stick it out...for the time being, anyway.

He had pulled over to the curb last night when she flagged him down—just as she had anticipated.

"Maybe we should try again," she'd said. "If you feel the same, you can call me at the office tomorrow."

She had walked away, and first thing this morning, he had phoned. There hadn't been time to discuss anything then, which was fine with her, because she wanted to talk face-to-face. So they had made an appointment—she wouldn't let herself call it a date—for dinner at seven.

She had changed clothes a half-dozen times, finally deciding on a navy blue suit, with shorts that looked like a skirt. Accented by a polka dot blouse, the outfit presented her as businesslike, yet with a casual, feminine side.

She was almost out the door when she paused. Even though Sam Rutledge seemed like a trustworthy sort, there was no denying a lot of nuts were running around loose these days.

She would take no chances.

Returning to the kitchen and the drawer where everything that wouldn't fit in her purse seemed to wind up, she found her can of pepper spray and stuck it in her coat pocket. She wasn't sure how old it was. It might even be outdated. Still, just the sight of it in her hand would make him back off should it develop that he had ulterior motives after all.

As added precaution to ensure that justice would prevail if she were actually walking into danger, she took pen and paper and scribbled a note saying where she had gone and whom she was meeting.

For reference, she placed a copy of the ad next to the note.

That done, with crossed fingers that everything would turn out well, she was on her way.

* * *

She had chosen Antonio's for their meeting, a quaint little Italian restaurant.

The tables were covered with red-and-white-checkered cloths and, in the center of each, a softly burning candle dripped wax down the sides of a basket-wrapped wine bottle.

Hanging baskets trailed lush vines and, punctuating the charm, a violinist strolled from table to table in serenade.

Ambiance, however, was not Lauren's sole reason for selecting Antonio's. It was also quiet, secluded...the perfect place to meet and talk without a lot of hubbub.

She wondered whether Sam Rutledge would be late, or even show at all, but chided herself for the silly schoolgirl fears. He was a businessman. This was an interview. Not a date. He would be there, all right. He...

She swallowed hard.

...was waiting just inside the door.

"Hello," he cheerily greeted. "I'm glad you came."

She was merry right back. "Did you think I wouldn't? I'm not very late, am I?"

"Actually, you're right on time. I was just anxious, that's all."

The host confirmed their reservations and led the way to the table Lauren had requested in a far corner.

"This is nice," Sam commented as he leapt in front of the waiter to pull her chair out for her. "You've got good taste, and—" he gave an exaggerated sniff "—I love Italian food."

"Me, too." She primly unfolded the napkin that matched the tablecloth and spread it across her lap. "They make wonderful garlic bread with lots of butter and Parmesan."

He took his own seat. "And naturally they have a secret process whereby all fat and calories are removed, right?"

"Right." She was delighted to find that he had a good sense of humor.

The waiter handed Sam the wine list, assuming that was their beverage of choice in an Italian restaurant.

Sam peered over the top of it and asked, "Do you drink?"

She countered with her own query. "Will it count against me if I do?" Because if social drinking made the difference in whether or not she got the job, then, like the song said, he could take his job and... Not that she was a heavy drinker by any means, but if he were the type to protest a single glass of wine, who knew what other restrictions he might insist on?

He allayed her concern. "Of course not. And I happen to love wine. What's your preference?"

"I'm going to have the lasagna, so I think red."

"That's fine with me." He gave the list back to the waiter. "Bring us a bottle of your best Chianti."

While waiting, they chatted nonsensically...a bit uneasily. They were, after all, strangers who had gotten off to a very bad start, and both seemed anxious to begin anew but were uncertain as to how.

As they sipped the wine, they began to mellow. Conversation became easier and, finally, Lauren broached the subject. "So when does the interview officially begin?"

He smiled, a dimple flashed, and Lauren felt a little tingle inside and told herself to grow up.

"I think we both know it already has," he said.

"And I passed so far?" She rolled her eyes. "Gee. That's hard to believe."

"Well, I'm the one who goofed." He shook his head at his own antics. "That was pretty dumb of me. I mean, I knew the real Mr. Smith would show for his appointment. That's why I went early, hoping by some miracle you'd be finished by the time he arrived."

"The way you were jabbering? Impossible."

He looked sheepish. "Yeah, I guess I did ask a lot of questions."

"That's for sure."

They fell silent, each wondering where to go next.

Finally Lauren said drily, "I think it's my turn."

"To ask questions?" He lifted a brow. "Okay. But I can't promise to answer all of them. Not now, anyway."

She was aware of that but determined to find out as much as she could. "First of all, why all the secrecy? I feel like this is some kind of game."

"And I can understand why you feel that way," he conceded. "But believe me, if we get to the point that I offer you the job, it will all come together, and you'll understand."

"And what makes you think I'll take it if you do?"

"Ten thousand net." He lifted his finger to draw the figure in the air.

She felt an indignant bristle building along her spine and fought against it. She'd promised herself she would be cool, calm and collected, no matter how difficult. Still, she felt the need to emphasize once more, "Money won't buy me, Mr. Rutledge, if what you have in mind is against my principles."

"I don't think it will be. And please," he added, "call me Sam."

She made little circles on the tablecloth with her wineglass. "Okay, then—*Sam*—if you won't tell me about the job, then tell me about you." She looked him straight in the eye. "If everything is on the up and up, you shouldn't mind answering a few personal questions."

"Well, you're the subject of the interview," he reminded. "I'm the one who's supposed to ask questions."

"True. But I think I have a right to know a little something about the person asking them."

"We'll see. Try me."

"How old are you?"

"I'll be thirty-one in March."

"And you said you were never married?"

"Like I said, I came close. It didn't work out."

"Why not?"

He, too, began circling on the table with his glass. "My

job involved a lot of traveling. We were both immature. She met somebody who was always around."

Changing tack, she asked, "What do you do for a living?"

He described how, for the past ten years, he had worked as a troubleshooter for a large oil company.

"I guess that did require traveling," she commented.

"Yeah, including a lot of overseas trips. But I enjoyed it—for a while. The last few years it got old."

"You don't do that kind of work anymore?"

He hesitated a moment before saying, "Actually, I'm on a leave of absence to take care of a personal matter."

She seized on that and ventured a guess. "And that has to do with this job you have to offer, right?"

He nodded curtly.

Her suspicion that he suddenly seemed uncomfortable was confirmed when he raised his hand to signify he would field no more questions, and declared, "Enough about me. I'd like to hear more about you. Yesterday we only brushed the surface. I want to hear everything."

She obliged by explaining she was an orphan and had managed to work her way through night school to get where she was. "But I'm wondering now if I want to continue this line of work," she went on to explain. "I haven't been really satisfied, and I happen to feel that a person has to genuinely like what they do if they're going to be good at it.

"Maybe that's why my patients bite me," she added with a sardonic chuckle.

The waiter came to take their order for lasagna, Caesar salads and lots of garlic bread.

With their glasses refilled, Sam attempted to delve deeper into the real Lauren Gentry.

"You didn't say anything about romance."

She blinked as though she were unfamiliar with the word.

"You know—romance? Love?" he prodded genially. "Are you divorced? Widowed?"

"Neither. And I don't see why—"

"Engaged? Steady boyfriend?"

She looked at him sharply, annoyance creeping. "What does this have to do with anything?"

He shrugged. "Maybe nothing. Maybe everything. The bottom line, Lauren, is that you are a very attractive young woman. You are also nearing thirty, by what you said in your letter, and I find it difficult to believe that you have never been married or had a serious relationship."

The indignant bristle became a porcupine, prickling along her spine. "I didn't say there hadn't been a serious relationship, but I don't think that's any of your business."

"Yes, it is," he contradicted. "Because if you've never gone anywhere near an altar, I have no choice except to believe that there's something about you that doesn't lend itself to romance. In short, you scare men away."

"That...that," she sputtered, overwhelmed by his impertinence, "is the most ridiculous thing I've ever heard. And I won't be goaded into telling you about my private life."

He spread his hands on the table in a helpless gesture. "I have to know, Lauren."

"No, you don't."

She pushed back in her chair, as though to rise, but his arm shot out to block her.

Casting anxious glances about to make sure no one was witnessing the hastily developing scene, Sam sought to stop it before it went any farther. "Listen, I'm sorry if you're offended, but the fact of the matter is I do have to know about any past serious relationships you've had. But if you don't care to tell me, I guess we're back to square one."

She eyed him suspiciously. "Are you sure this isn't what this is all about anyway—your getting some kind of sick thrill out of making women talk about themselves and describe their personal lives?"

She was cute when her dander was up, he thought as he suppressed a smile. Her eyes flashed like summer lightning, and the tip of her upturned nose actually turned pink.

He found her positively delightful and knew that could present problems *if* he let it. But he vowed not to. Everything had to be kept strictly business.

It was the only way his scheme could succeed.

Finally, framing his words carefully, he quietly reminded her once again that, in time, *if*—he emphasized—things progressed to the point that he offered her the job, all the pieces of the puzzle would come together. Till then, she would have to bear with him and cooperate, or there was no point in continuing.

Lauren's face grew stormy as she listened, and for a moment she actually thought about walking out on him—again. But their order arrived, and she took one look at the layered cheese and pasta and sauce and decided she might as well have a meal for all her trouble.

They ate in silence for a few moments before he felt compelled to say, "This is truly the best Italian food I've had around here, Lauren. If nothing else comes from this evening, I'll be grateful for your having introduced me to this place."

She took a sip of wine before quipping, "That's great. You'll have somewhere to take the rest of your applicants."

His eyes were somber as he met her mocking gaze. "Actually, I'd like to focus on only one of them."

"Which, I take it, is me."

"Correct."

"But you want to hear about the romantic side of me, right?"

"That's right. But actually all I want to know is whether you've ever really been serious about a man. You don't have to tell me all the spicy stuff...unless you want to," he teased.

She was not amused.

Pushing her plate away, she leaned toward him and said

in a cold, clipped tone, "Okay, I've had a few serious relationships. They were good while they lasted. I was even engaged and almost made it to the altar, only it didn't work out, and now I see it was for the best.

"All of them," she went on to declare, "turned out to be two-timing liars. So I plan to stay single for a long, long time. Maybe for the rest of my life, because, quite frankly, I peg all men as being emotionally undependable."

His eyes went wide, and he pressed back in his chair in a subconscious effort to escape the anger and resentment spewing from her.

She knocked on the table three times and whispered, "One. Two. Three. I'm out."

He still found her adorable when she was mad, even though he was moved by the obvious pain he had awakened.

"You ask me how I feel about children?" she continued. "Babies? Well, I happen to adore them. And I want them. But I don't have to be married to have them. I can adopt, because I know, firsthand, what it's like to want desperately to be a part of a family. I know what it's like to cry at night because there's nobody to read you a bedtime story, or tuck you in, or hear your prayers, or any of those mommy and daddy things that millions of kids take for granted.

"I know this because—" she paused to draw a ragged breath "—I've been there, done that, as the saying goes. I grew up in foster care, and I can't think of a more rewarding life than to keep some other kid from going through what I did. And who knows? Down the road I might even have a baby by artificial insemination. That's not uncommon for a single woman anymore.

"But for the moment," she continued, "I've got to concentrate on finding a job that I like, so I can be successful and support all the kids I plan to have one day. And quite frankly, ten thousand dollars would be a big push in that direction, provided it's not for doing something illegal or kinky. But I'm starting to have my doubts. After all, *you're* a man," she said with cold finality.

Leaning back in her chair, she folded her arms across her chest and gave him a curt nod. "So what's your next question?"

"Whew" was all he could say with a shake of his head. He studied her for a moment, the play of a smile on his lips, then murmured, "I figured you for the candid type. I was right."

Lauren sipped her wine slowly in an attempt to soothe her jangled nerves. She was known for her frankness, but feared this time she'd gone too far. She'd blown it. He was probably sitting there hoping she'd hurry up and finish her dinner so the miserable encounter would end.

"I'll pay half the check if you want," she mumbled.

"You'll do no such thing." He chuckled, taking up his fork to attack the lasagna again. "We'll enjoy our food. I'll ask you some more questions. And tomorrow night we'll spend more time getting to know each other. All right?"

"I...I suppose." She was stunned.

"I will tell you one thing," he said between mouthfuls. "If the position ultimately goes to you, it's extremely important we get along well."

"I suppose that's where the part about the aspiring actress comes in," she said.

"If you have to pretend to like me, then I guess so."

When they had finished eating, she dared hope aloud, "Is the interrogation over for the evening?"

He studied her anxious face. It bothered him that she was so reluctant to disclose the personal side of her. Most women—at least ones he had known in the past, and especially the ones he had interviewed thus far—enjoyed talking about themselves. In fact, some of them had been real bores.

He wondered what she was hiding. Perhaps not anything. It could be that Lauren Gentry was just a private kind of person.

And, of course, she'd had romances, as pretty as she was in a pixie sort of way. He liked her fiery red hair, and her sea-green eyes that, when not sparkling with anger, shone with a tenderness that was almost a caress.

Her figure was also knockout, and—

He gave himself a mental shake.

He wasn't supposed to be thinking about the swell of her breasts or the curve of her hips.

Not for what he had in mind.

He had to keep everything in perspective.

Romance was out of the question.

Not with her.

Not with anybody.

Not for a long, long time.

Maybe never.

Finally he pulled himself from his musings. "I'm afraid not. There are other things I need to know. You don't smoke, do you?"

"No."

"Can you cook?"

She smiled to remember all those crazy nights when she and Midge had attacked the kitchen like gladiators, determined to win the battle of gourmet cooking. Sometimes they won. Sometimes they lost. But always they had fun.

"I get by," she said. "But, again, what does that have to do with anything? If you plan to ask me to be your private chef, forget it."

He waved that idea away. "What about housekeeping? Do you like cleaning house?"

At that, she laughed so loud that people at a nearby table turned to stare. "Are you kidding? Only a masochist would admit to such a thing."

He couldn't help but be amused by her reaction, yet asked, "You aren't messy, are you?"

"Oh, really, Sam. What is this?" She slapped her palms down on the table and gave her hair a wild toss. "First, you want to know if I like kids. Then you ask about my personal life. Now you're interested in whether I'm a good housekeeper and if I can cook. If I didn't know better, I'd think you're planning on asking me to marry you.''

"You never can tell," he said, a mysterious twinkle in his eye. "You never can tell."

Feeling suddenly ill at ease and wanting a moment to compose herself, Lauren excused herself to go to the ladies' room.

Too late, she realized her foot had gone to sleep, causing her to stumble and bump against the table.

Alarmed, Sam bolted to his feet. "Are you okay?"

"Fine, fine." She laughed nervously.

And then she sneezed.

"Bless you," a woman called from the next table.

"Thank you," Lauren responded—and sneezed again.

Sam held out his hand. "Are you sure you're—"

"I'm fine—" another sneeze "—really." And another. "I'll be right back."

Lauren sneezed all the way to the ladies' lounge, embarrassed as people stared.

The woman attendant gave her several tissues and asked if she could do anything for her, but Lauren shook her head wildly between sneezes and managed to convey the message that she must have suddenly developed an allergy to something.

She repeated that explanation when she returned to the table, where Sam had heard her coming and was on his feet, ready to leave and signaling to the waiter to bring the check.

"I'll wait outside," she said, unable to bear the curious, sympathetic looks of the other patrons any longer.

Outside in the cool night air, she took deep breaths and began to feel a little better. By the time Sam joined her, the sneezes were coming farther apart.

"I don't guess you'll let me see you home," he said.

"No. I'll call a cab."

"There's one at the curb. I'll get it for you. But Lauren…" His voice trailed as his gaze lowered.

"What?" She sneezed again.

"I hate to add to your problems, but you must have spilled something on your jacket."

She glanced down and saw the stain spreading from the pocket.

At the same time, he leaned down for closer inspection—and sneezed himself. "What the—?"

Taking her by surprise, he reached inside her pocket and drew out the can of pepper spray that must have begun to leak when it hit the table when Lauren had stumbled.

"You really don't take any chances, do you?" he said incredulously.

They looked at each other and burst into laughter, at the same time being seized once again by a round of sneezing.

Finally, with the spray can trashed and her coat rolled up in a ball, Lauren got into a cab.

His coat was wrapped around her shoulders, and he plucked at it and said, "Now you've got to keep our date tomorrow night. You have to return my coat."

He gave a little salute and closed the door.

Lauren leaned back against the seat, gathering the coat around her to breathe deeply of the scent of him.

He'd said *date,* she mused dreamily. Not *appointment.*

But no matter, the bruised, cynical side of her sharply reminded.

Sterrrikkke three, Lauren, you're out!

Chapter Four

Midge leaned against the door frame, watching as Lauren finished with the little freckle-faced girl in her chair.

"Now remember," Lauren instructed as she handed her a new toothbrush, "if you want to make every tooth a Smiley Good Tooth, you have to use Harry Happy Brush after every meal or snack."

The little girl took the toothbrush, brow furrowed. "But I can't brush at school. There's never enough time, and—"

"Brush as soon as you get home," Lauren said, helping her out of the chair. The child was cute but a difficult patient. Having to deal with her fidgeting and whining had taken a lot of time. She was now running behind and, seeing Midge, apologized, "Sorry. I don't have a minute to spare. It's great seeing you, though," she was quick to add.

She brushed by her to usher the little girl out to the reception area, then returned with her next appointment— a chubby little boy who looked like the kind who stayed awake all night, thinking of ways to be obnoxious.

Midge had settled on her stool and appeared to be in no hurry to leave.

"Midge, I'm sorry. Maybe we can do lunch one day."

Midge inspected a sculptured nail. "From what I hear, you probably couldn't fit me into your schedule till sometime next year."

"Don't be silly."

"Well, from what Robin tells me, you've got quite a social life going. Secretive, too. You disappear during lunch. You get calls every day from a mysterious man who won't give his name. And I know I've called the apartment every night but always get the machine."

The little boy glared at Midge. "Is she gonna stand there and watch? I don't want her watchin'. She'll make fun of me." He yanked at the bib Lauren had just fastened around his neck. "If she don't leave, I'm outta here."

Lauren caught his hand and fought the impulse to squeeze, patting it firmly instead. He was the same little brat that had bitten her during his cleaning six months before. "Stay right where you are, Chad. I'll speak to the lady outside, and then she'll be leaving."

Handing him a comic book with the latest episode of Smiley Good Tooth battling the Decay Demon, she motioned to Midge.

In the lounge, Lauren got them both a soda from the refrigerator. A minute's break wouldn't make any difference when she was already running late.

Lauren plopped down on the sofa, noting how good it felt to get off her feet. "So tell me about the honeymoon."

Midge stared at her incredulously. "I've been home nearly a month, remember?"

"Yes, well. I don't see you much." Had it really been that long? Lauren marveled. With her hectic schedule, she seemed to have lost all track of time.

Midge plunked down next to her. "So tell me," she said, eyes glowing with anticipation. "I want to hear all about him."

Lauren hedged. She had considered telling Midge about Sam Rutledge but wasn't sure how she would react. After all, it was a bizarre situation to say the least.

With a forced smile, she countered, "Who says there *is* a him?"

Midge gave her a playful nudge with her elbow. "Oh, come on, Lauren. You think Robin and the other girls haven't noticed there's something funny going on? You can tell me. We've always shared everything."

"You never wanted to share Scott," Lauren teased in an attempt to turn the focus from her. "Remember when the Braves won the World Series? The two of you got so loopy celebrating, I don't know how you made it back to the apartment. He dumped you on the bed and then crawled in himself, and the next morning when you woke up and saw him lying between us, you went bananas because you thought the three of us had..."

Her voice trailed as she saw the way Midge was staring at her and shaking her head slowly from side to side.

"It won't work," Midge said quietly. "You're not going to change the subject. And besides, I never thought anything about that night. I was acting—just like you're acting now by pretending there isn't a man in your life. So fess up, gal. We've never kept secrets between us."

That was true. From the day they'd met, Lauren had looked upon Midge as the sister she'd never had. She could not count the nights they'd sat up till dawn sharing hopes and dreams, and, yes, sometimes heartaches, as well.

"Oh, all right," Lauren said with a deep sigh. "There is somebody, but it's not what you think, and I don't have time to tell you about it now. I have a patient waiting, in case you forgot."

Midge grinned and gave her hair a flip. "Nope. I didn't forget, but what do you mean—it's not what I think? Explain, or I'll never let you out of here." She clutched her arms as though to hold her captive.

"It's not a romance."

Midge let her go and stared, aghast. "You don't call meeting a man for lunch every day and going out with him every night a romance? What then—" Her eyes narrowed with suspicion as she cried, "Lauren Gentry, I'm ashamed of you."

Lauren blinked, not understanding.

"No wonder he won't give his name to Robin. Married men like to be discreet. They don't toss their names around."

"Married men?" Lauren echoed. Then it dawned. "You mean you think…?" She threw her head back and laughed. "Oh, you've got it all wrong, Midge. He's not married. And the reason he doesn't give his name to Robin is because he thinks she's just being nosy. Like some other people I could name," she added with a wink.

Midge ignored the barb. "But you said there was no romance. It's natural to assume it'd be that way with a married man who couldn't commit, and—"

"I don't want a commitment," Lauren cried, frustrated.

"So why are you seeing him? I mean, if he's single, and you're dating him, and there's no romance, is it just for sex? I never took you for the type to engage in casual sex, Lauren," she added scornfully.

"I'm not," Lauren confirmed, feeling pressure in her temples and hoping a headache wasn't revving up.

"*What* then?"

Lauren knew she had to tell her something, or she'd never get rid of her. "It's business. He may offer me a job."

Midge's brows crawled into her bangs. "*May* offer you a job? Did I hear that right? You're seeing him all the time in hopes he'll put you to work? What *kind* of work?" Her expression turned grim along with her tone. "This doesn't sound good, Lauren. I'm worried about you."

"There's no need to be. I was leery at first, too, but we've gotten to know each other, and I trust him when he says he has to make sure I'm the right one for the position before he tells me about it."

"How did you meet him?"

"He put an ad in the paper."

Midge slapped her hand against her forehead and screeched, "You answered an ad? Oh, God, Lauren, it's a wonder you weren't raped, or murdered, or both. I can't believe you did that."

"Well, I did." Lauren stood. "And now I've got to get back to work."

Midge bolted to her feet to block her way. "I want to hear more about this guy. What's his name? Where does he live? Where does he work? How old is he? And what does he look like?"

"Sam Rutledge. I don't know. He's on a leave of absence. Thirty. He's gorgeous." Lauren stepped around her.

Midge was right after her. "You have to bring him over so I can meet him. Scott's good at judging character. He can give us some feedback. How about dinner tomorrow night?"

At the door, Lauren paused. "I'll ask him tonight." *If I see him tonight.*

"I'll let you know tomorrow," Lauren went on to say, "Meanwhile, stop worrying. I've been around him enough to be confident that he's not a rapist or a serial killer. I believe he really does have a job to offer, and when he gets around to trusting me enough to tell me about it, it will all make sense.

"And I promise you'll be the first to know," she added with a quick hug.

"How long will that be?" Midge anxiously called after her.

"Soon. Very soon."

Lauren could only hope it would be. The suspense was becoming maddening every time she and Sam were together.

When she reached her room, Chad was not there. She

found him in Dr. Brockworth's private office, where he had wandered. Bent over Dr. Brockworth's aquarium, he was trying to catch the expensive tropical fish with his hands.

With a gentle scolding, she led him back for his cleaning.

As she worked, he whined and whimpered, and she wondered why she was the one to always wind up with the problem children. Maybe Greta was bribing Robin not to book them with her.

Oh, if only Sam would hurry and make up his mind. If he didn't, she was afraid she was going to lose hers. Something had to give. And *soon*.

They'd shared a good laugh over the incident with the pepper spray outside Antonio's, and it had sort of set the stage from that point on for even more candor and honesty between them.

That had been over three weeks ago, and they had been together almost constantly since.

They'd hit just about every notable restaurant in Atlanta, trying out all kinds of foods.

For lunch, Sam would bring takeout, and they would drive to a nearby park and eat in his car.

They had been to the zoo, to the malls, to craft fairs and even to Christmas parades, for the holiday season was upon them.

He had managed to get tickets to an Atlanta Falcons game, where Lauren had listened avidly as Sam explained what football was all about. She found she enjoyed it immensely and began to read the sports section of the paper. Soon, their conversation was spiced with scores and statistics and comments about what player did what right...or wrong.

They rode the cable car at Stone Mountain.

He took her fishing in a cold mountain stream and burst into laughter to see the look on her face when he asked if she knew how to clean the big trout he'd landed.

Finally, when she felt confident enough, Lauren had invited him to her apartment for home-cooked spaghetti, her only specialty. He had brought wine, and the evening went well...although she did notice him scrutinizing her bookshelves and taking note of pictures on the wall—anything that might be significant of her taste and personality.

It turned out they liked the same kinds of movies—action and excitement on the big screen, black-and-white classics on cable. .

Curling up with a bowl of popcorn at home was as much fun as the formality of a concert.

Religion entered the picture. Lauren sometimes visited a small nondenominational church in her neighborhood, and Sam insisted on going with her. Afterward, he admitted to having enjoyed it.

They were friends, buddies, companions, bonding for a reason that continued to elude Lauren's wildest imagination.

But now, like a roller coaster, other emotions were taking over—the man-woman kind of emotions.

All because of last night.

He had taken her dancing. And she had the distinct impression he had waited to do so till they had tried everything else, as though he'd known all along how it would turn out when he finally took her in his arms, and—

"Arb yew frew yhet?"

Chad was tugging at her smock, his mouth full of toothpaste.

With a start, she realized she'd been polishing his teeth way too long. It's a wonder they weren't worn off at the gum.

Removing the instrument, she quickly rinsed his mouth and declared, "All done."

"About time!"

Lauren whirled at the sound of the high-pitched and very annoyed voice from the doorway.

"I've been waiting over a half hour," said Mrs. Pendell, another of Lauren's least favorite patients.

"Sorry," Lauren mumbled. She handed Chad his free toothbrush and sent him on his way.

Mrs. Pendell plopped into the chair, and the routine began all over again.

Lauren allowed her mind to drift away, back to the music, back to the dance, and how wonderful it had felt to have Sam's arms around her.

At first, they had shared the cheery banter that had become second nature between them. It was like they were role-playing. He, so charming and affable; she, ever so lighthearted and witty. They were the picture-perfect couple.

Someone had even told them so one night. They were in a grocery store, shopping for ingredients for the Reuben sandwiches Sam boasted was his only claim to fame in the kitchen. An older woman pushing a shopping cart paused to say, "You two are so cute together."

"How much did you pay her to say that?" Sam had asked with a mock grimace after the woman had walked away.

To which Lauren had innocently responded, "Why would I even want to?"

And he had smiled and murmured once more how she would understand later.

That night, however, the night they danced, the banter had melted into a new kind of awareness. Without either of them realizing it, their embrace had become closer.

Lauren's head had dropped to press against his shoulder. He dropped her hand to move his to the small of her back, and her fingertips began to brush along his neck.

She leaned yet closer against him, weakness spreading from the heated flames soaring through her.

She heard his breath quicken and knew the same, sensuous wave was coursing over him, as well.

When the music finally ended, they both sprung back, jolted by how they had gotten so carried away.

"You're a great dancer," he'd said, tugging at his collar as though it were the room that was sweltering.

The spell had broken quickly as the music changed to a livelier beat. Sam had said he was too tired for a fast dance. Lauren agreed it was the same for her.

Then, as though wanting to escape the intimate mode, Sam suggested breakfast at a noisy, crowded waffle house. When he had taken her home, for the first time he hadn't said anything about seeing her for lunch the next day.

In fact, he'd not said anything about seeing her again at all.

Maybe it was over.

Maybe the surge of passion between them last night had frightened him away. Once, during one of their many deep conversations, he'd told her he was not looking for romance with any woman, mysteriously adding that a personal commitment of another kind had to take precedence over anything else in his life. She had asked what he meant, but, of course, he had declined to answer.

That was it. As the afternoon wore on, with no call, she was sure of it. It had all been part of the plan. For whatever weird reason, desire and passion between them had no place in Sam's job offering.

She had blown it.

They had blown it.

Perhaps it was just as well. She had no business getting involved. And she had wasted enough time on Sam Rutledge and his mystery job.

Midge was right. It was crazy.

So now it was time to put it all out of her mind and get back to the problems she'd been neglecting—like what she was going to do with the rest of her life...

"Lauren, that man's back."

She was putting instruments in the autoclave and jumped, startled, when Robin rushed up behind her. "What man?"

"You know. The Kevin Costner lookalike. He asked for

you, and I told him he didn't have an appointment, and the office was closing, anyway, but he insisted on seeing you."

"It's okay," Lauren said, heart pounding like a jackhammer. "Send him back."

A moment later, she was staring into Sam's blue eyes and wondering why they looked so troubled.

"I realized I didn't make a date for tonight and was worried you wouldn't be free."

"You didn't call, either," she pointed out, miffed that he had kept her dangling, miffed because there seemed to be no end in sight to the waiting to learn what it was all about.

"Sorry. I had some paperwork to do at the office. I'm going to put in for the next position that comes open locally so I can stay around here and not have to travel."

Because of me? Because of the job? Oh, Sam, what is it about you that draws me so? Why can't I just walk away from you and to hell with you and your puzzle?

"So, can we have dinner?" he prodded.

"Sure." She shrugged as though it made no difference, then remembered Midge and said, "A friend of mine has invited us for dinner at her place tomorrow night. Is that okay? She wants to meet you. I think you'll like her and her husband. They're real nice, and—"

She fell silent to see the almost frightened look on his face. "Is something wrong?" she ventured.

"I...we can't," he stammered. "We can't go out with other people. I'm sorry."

She did not try to keep the edge from her voice. "Why not?"

He ran his fingers through his hair in that way of agitation that she knew so well. Regret mirrored in his eyes. "I'm sorry, Lauren. I can't tell you just now, but I will—"

"When?"

He stared at her mutely.

"I asked when," she repeated, then the dam finally burst and impatience erupted. "I'm afraid I've had it, Sam. Either you tell me whatever the heck this job is all about and whether or not I'm the one you want for it, or I'm not going to see you again.''

She was uncomfortable beneath his contemplative gaze. It was as though he were trying to see into the very soul of her.

Finally he drew a deep, almost shuddering breath, let it out slowly and declared, ''You're the one I want, all right. I'm sure of it. But this isn't the time or place to explain things, Lauren. Tonight—''

''No.'' She swung her head briskly from side to side. ''Not tonight. It's now or never, Sam. I mean it.''

He stared at her for long, tense moments, then shrugged and said, ''Okay. I guess I don't have any choice.''

He reached in his pocket. His hand closed about something and then he held it out to her.

Rippling with nervousness, she irritably prodded, ''Well? If this is show-and-tell time, let's have it.''

He opened his hand.

Lauren gasped and reeled in shock.

He was holding a gold wedding band.

Sam had asked for a table in direct line with the front door so he could spot Lauren the second she appeared...*if* she appeared. Worrying that she wouldn't was why his heart was pounding like a bongo drum.

She was nearly a half hour late, but he attempted to soothe his fears by remembering she was seldom able to leave the office on time, anyway.

But he had blown it.

He was sure of it.

Her shock when she saw the ring had said it all.

She thought he was a nut.

He hadn't meant it to turn out that way, hadn't even planned to show her the ring then, but he had feared she meant it when she had issued her ultimatum—tell all or else.

So he had kind of panicked.

Kind of?

He snorted softly and shook his head. It hadn't been a *kind of* panic. It had been *major* panic, and for him, of all people, to even remotely lose his composure was ridiculous. In his line of work, he'd faced life-threatening situations many times but always with a cool head. Battling a fire on an offshore oil rig was not a job for wimps. And never once had he gone beyond a state of normal apprehension. Always he had been in complete control.

But maybe he was being too hard on himself. After all, once he'd pulled the ring out of his pocket, his plan had been to show it to her and then quickly explain that what he wanted was for her to *pretend* to be his wife. He had then intended to give a quick, capsule explanation. After that, if she were still interested—and he had been confident she would be or else he'd have never let things go this far—they would have made plans to meet later so he could fill her in all the details, past and present.

Only, it hadn't worked out that way, because, at the precise moment he had showed Lauren the ring, the receptionist—Robin, her name was—had burst into the room to remind Lauren that she had a patient waiting.

Thank goodness he was trained to react quickly under stress, because his hand had snapped shut so fast Robin hadn't seen what he was holding.

But Lauren had reacted just as swiftly herself. In the moment it took him to hide the ring, Lauren had bolted from the lounge like a frightened deer.

She had never said a word.

She had not looked back.

Still, he was not ready to give up, not when he had come to the ultimate conclusion that Lauren Gentry was the perfect woman to play the role of wife—and mother.

He'd had plenty of responses to the ad, most of which he had eliminated at once. There had been a few possibilities among those remaining, but, after meeting Lauren, he hadn't pursued anyone else. He had liked her from the start and liked her even more as they got to know each other.

She was, he conceded, the kind of woman he should have met long ago.

Before Gaynelle.

Before...

Again, he shook his head, this time with a vengeance, for it took great effort to cast away the misery that overwhelmed whenever memories of the wasted years came flooding back.

Lauren was the kind of woman he should have met, all right, but it made no difference now. He wasn't interested in falling in love, because he had a commitment to someone else now, someone who held a special place in his heart...and to whom he intended to dedicate his life.

However, in order to do that, he needed Lauren's help.

After leaving the clinic, he had driven about aimlessly for over an hour before mustering the nerve to try one more time.

He called the clinic on his cellular phone. Robin, the receptionist from hell, had smugly informed him that Lauren did not wish to speak with him.

In desperation, he had then asked her to convey the message that he would like Lauren to meet him at Antonio's for dinner at seven o'clock. He was hoping that Lauren would sense and appreciate the significance of the restaurant—the place where their friendship had begun.

Robin had promised to pass the message along, but he was not taking any chances.

It was now or never.

He had to do whatever it took to persuade Lauren to let him tell her the whole story.

He found a florist and had two dozen roses sent with a hastily written note of pleading that she meet him for dinner:

One more chance. Please.

Because if it didn't work with Lauren, there wasn't time

to find anybody else. It was just too late to start all over again, even though there had been moments the last few times they'd been together when he found himself wishing it weren't.

Not, however, because Lauren wasn't perfect for his needs.

She was.

The problem stemmed from how, for some unknown reason, she was triggering both physical and emotional reactions in him that he'd vowed to put into cold storage.

Like the night they'd danced; he felt a heated rush even now to think about it. They had fit so good together. Eventually he'd had to draw back from her a little, because he had become helplessly aroused and feared she might feel him pressed against her.

And it wasn't merely because it had been a long time since he'd had a woman. It was more than thoughts of how nice it would be to make love to her wholly and completely. It had been—he groped for an apt description, then seized upon it—*sensuous.*

Sensuous longing beyond the desire for mere physical gratification.

Holding Lauren close had inspired thoughts of wholeness, completeness, with a woman. Hand holding, sharing beliefs and values and dreams as well as disappointments and sadness and the bad things that inevitably happen in life. Sharing and being a part of her life…a part of her.

He tossed down the last of his beer.

Maybe it was for the best that she didn't show up. Having to struggle within himself against the emotions she evoked was a battle he did not need to have to deal with.

He had enough stress going on his life for the moment, thank you.

The waiter asked if he'd care to order.

Sam knew what he really meant was that it was becoming obvious that whoever he was waiting for wasn't going to show, and if all he was going to do was nurse a beer, management would prefer that he relinquish the table and sit at the bar.

But Sam was not quite ready to throw in the towel. Instead, he dealt with the waiter's unspoken message by placing a twenty-dollar bill on the table and quietly saying, "One more beer, and then I'll get out of here."

The waiter's eyes lit up, and he quickly palmed the bill and said, "Of course, sir. Enjoy yourself as long as you like."

Sam knew he shouldn't be throwing his money around. That was why he was in his present financial jam, anyway. Fast cars. Fast women. Live it up. Party animal. That had been his life-style. But no more, and if twenty bucks would buy him some time without dirty looks from the restaurant staff, well, it was worth it.

Just like paying Lauren ten grand was money well spent if he could accomplish his goal.

Maybe, he brooded, he shouldn't have waited so long to level with her. Still, there had been the all-important need to feel confident that the time was right. Otherwise she might have refused and then told the wrong person about his scheme.

Word could spread.

All the way to California.

And that would never do.

So he continued to wait, hoping that by some miracle she would come.

This time, he wouldn't blow it.

Outside, Lauren paced restlessly up and down the sidewalk, oblivious to the curious stares of those entering or leaving Antonio's.

Her mind was spinning like a top, and she actually felt dizzy from the myriad of emotions whirling within.

The sight of that wedding band in Sam Rutledge's outstretched hand had felt like a jolt of electric current shooting from head to toe.

Unfortunately, because of Robin, there'd been no time to react, to ask questions—like whether he really was crazy enough to be willing to pay ten thousand dollars for a wife.

Not that she would have accepted, of course.

After hurrying from the lounge and having time to calm down and think about it, she had decided that no matter how charming and good-looking he was, it was best not to see him again. She had no interest in marrying him or any other man, no matter how much money was involved.

But part of her was burning with curiosity. Why would anyone offer that much money to get a wife?

If only Robin hadn't walked in when she had, surely he'd have offered some explanation.

Perhaps she should have talked to him when he called. But she hadn't, so now there was no other way to find out the truth except to confront him directly.

She'd gotten as far as the restaurant. So far, however, she'd not been able to muster the courage to go inside, which was why she had been walking around in the chilly, windy night for over an hour.

It was silly. *She* was silly. And whatever he had in mind had nothing to do with love, and wasn't that what she wanted, anyway—to have nothing to do with love, that elusive butterfly that had fluttered about her heart in the past but never landed and merely teased and taunted before flying away?

Of course, it was.

Sam Rutledge did not love her, and if she sold herself to him, she was no better than a hooker...*albeit a high-priced hooker,* she thought with a touch of jaded humor. She didn't come cheap, by golly.

Still, despite all the arguing within herself, there was one, indisputable given—she wanted to hear him out. Because, she reasoned, after all the mystery, she deserved to know, once and for all, what the heck it was all about.

"Psst. Hey, baby."

Lost in thought, Lauren had wandered a few blocks from

the restaurant and was startled to realize she had crossed into a district that was rather undesirable. Cheap bars, greasy cafés, kids lounging around on the sidewalk looking for trouble.

And hookers, too, which was obviously what the man calling to her from his car at the curb took her to be.

Eyes raking her up and down in a way that made her flesh crawl, he licked his smirking lips as he made his pitch.

She began walking briskly, glancing over her shoulder just long enough to feel relieved that it appeared he would take the hint that she wasn't interested.

Suddenly he was coming after her. "Fifty bucks isn't enough? All right, damn it. A hundred bucks."

Her heels clicked rapidly on the sidewalk.

He was obviously drunk. He let out a string of curses before screaming, "Okay, okay. A hundred and fifty." Then, anticipating a turndown, he scornfully shouted, "Hey, you ain't all that great-lookin', sister. You ought to jump at that kind of money."

At that, Lauren was suddenly struck by the humor of it all and whirled about to laugh and say, "I've already got an offer of ten thousand, mister. You willing to top that?"

She broke into a run for the restaurant, his curses fading farther behind with each step she took.

Sam got up from the table and pulled on his suede jacket. There was no need to wait any longer, and he wasn't the sort to drink himself blotto when he was disappointed.

He didn't know where he was going. Home was a room with kitchenette at a budget business motel where he stayed when he had to be at the home office for a while. It wasn't much and never had been, but with Christmas in the air, it was even more depressing, a reminder that he really didn't belong anywhere, to anybody.

He was transient.

Just passing through life, thank you.

Glancing at the restaurant's Christmas tree, decorated

with miniature toys, he got a lump in his throat the size of a tennis ball to think how he had dared hope this time next year he would also have a tree.

Only the toys would be underneath.

Toys supposedly left by Santa...*for his son.*

"Come back to see us," the cashier chortled when he'd paid for the three beers he'd had. "And have a merry Christmas."

"Thanks," he murmured. "Same to you."

When was Christmas, anyway? Soon. A few days. He hadn't paid any attention, too busy concentrating on Lauren. He had even skipped the office gathering, which had raised a few eyebrows, for he had always been the life of the party in the past.

Now, however, he just didn't feel like he had much of a life anymore.

Sure, he could go ahead and make his move without Lauren. After all, the law was on his side. He would win the war...*but not the battle.*

The doorman flashed Sam an obligatory smile as he reached to open the door for him, but at that precise instant, it flew open as a blast of wind came roaring in...along with Lauren.

Her smile was genuine as she breathed with relief and cried, "You're still here."

The tennis ball rolled from his throat to start bouncing around in his heart.

He smiled back at her. "Yeah. I was about to give up, though. I figured it was over."

"It may be," she said with candor. Then, cocking her head to one side, she wrinkled her nose and said, "But you know what? I figure I've got a right to know why you feel you've got to buy a—"

He pressed a finger against her lips before she could finish the sentence.

Taking her arm, he steered her back into the cold night

before saying, "Lauren, we really need to talk, but I'm afraid I've worn-out my welcome here."

She thought a minute, then drew a ragged breath. "Okay. We can go to my place. I guess if you're really Jack the Ripper I would've found out by now," she added with an easy smile.

"I sure fooled you, didn't I?" He grabbed her by the shoulders and gave her a gentle shake as she squealed with laughter.

Then, hand in hand, they ran into the night, leaving the doorman staring after them, shaking his head.

Chapter Five

Lauren made a pot of coffee. She wished she could offer sandwiches, but, as usual, the refrigerator was empty. Her stomach was growling, and she suspected Sam hadn't had anything to eat, either.

She did manage to scrounge around and find a box of cookies that weren't stale. Arranging them prettily on a plate, she set them on the tray next to the mugs of coffee and carried everything into the living room.

Sam was glancing around appreciatively at the turquoise painted walls adorned with Peter Max posters. The furniture was sparse—a futon sofa in a bold red-and-white print, two basket chairs and a bookcase made of varnished boards supported by concrete blocks, painted black.

She set the tray down on the coffee table she and Midge had found at a garage sale. "All this stuff is early Salvation Army, I'm afraid. I blame Midge for picking most of it out," she added with a grin.

"That's your friend who just got married and moved out."

"Yes, and she left everything with me since she was redecorating her husband's condo with new furniture and didn't want any of this old stuff. I'm not sure how much of it I'll be able to use if I move, though. I'll probably have a smaller place."

Alarm flashed in his eyes. "You're moving? But you never said—"

"Yes, I did. I told you I'd probably have to find a smaller place when my lease expires in a couple of months. Either that, or take in a roommate, and I'm not sure I'd ever find anyone as congenial as Midge, so I've about made up my mind to move."

He poured milk in his coffee and declined sugar. "Well, if you accepted my offer, the timing would be right, because it would be finished along about the time your lease expires. You could leave your things here till then."

She looked at him over the rim of her mug as she took a long sip, then said, "Well, I'm not so sure I'll want to work for you after today. To be perfectly honest, I was willing to see you again only because my curiosity is killing me, but I don't think it's anything I'd be interested in."

"Don't be so sure. It's not at all what you think. Believe me, the last thing I've got on my mind is marriage."

"That makes two of us," she said firmly.

"Then we'll get along just fine."

His throaty chuckle and the way he was looking at her sent warm ripples up and down her spine as she felt her cheeks grow hot.

"Your face is red," he said, leaning closer, his brow furrowed with concern. "You aren't getting sick, are you?"

She had admitted during the ride from Antonio's how she had been walking around for over an hour trying to decide whether or not to see him, and he had chided her and said she had no business being out in the night air like that.

He pressed his fingertips to her face, and she shivered uncontrollably at his touch.

"You *are* warm," he murmured, his own heat coiling in his loins just to feel her.

Lauren was the one to break the spell as she drew back. "I'm fine. Really. Now let's cut to the chase. Tell me what you want from me, for heaven's sake."

"No. Not for *heaven's* sake," he said quietly. "For *Jamie's* sake."

Lauren was truly bewildered, as well as exasperated. "Who is Jamie?" she demanded.

"Jamie—" he hesitated "—is my son."

She was even more baffled. "But you said you'd never been married."

"I haven't."

"But—"

"Hear me out," he pleaded. "Let me tell you the whole story, and then if you decide you don't want to be a part of it, I'll walk out of here and never bother you again."

With a nod, she urged, "Go on, please. I've been waiting a long time for this."

"I know you have." He leaned his head back on the sofa and stared at the ceiling.

Lauren's heart was racing in anticipation to at last have the mystery unraveled, but she bit her tongue to keep from screaming at him to please hurry but knew he had to take his time and tell it in his own way, because somehow she knew the story she was about to hear was going to be more involved than anything she could have imagined.

Finally he twisted sideways so that he faced her as he spoke. "I don't have any family, Lauren," he began. "I've had to pull myself up by my boot straps, as the saying goes, and work for everything I've ever had. But I had some baggage with me that was left over from my childhood."

He described how, when he was eleven, his parents had been killed in a boating accident. His only relative, an elderly great-aunt, had taken him in. Strict, austere, old-fashioned and lacking patience, she had no business raising a child.

Consequently, Sam had been raised in a very undesirable atmosphere. His aunt made him study or read quietly in his room in her gloomy, musty-smelling old house. He was not allowed to have friends in to play, nor participate in after-school activities or sports.

And when she was annoyed with him, she had beat him mercilessly with an old leather shaving strap.

It had been a sad time, and Sam had run away at sixteen. For the next few years, he'd rambled about, working odd jobs, doing anything necessary to survive. He took one day at the time, never worrying about the future.

When word that his aunt had died reached him, he was also informed that, because he had run away, she had disinherited him, leaving her entire estate to charity.

With a laugh of irony, he shook his head and said, "As it turned out, she was loaded. A millionaire. Who would've thought? She lived like a pauper. I can remember wearing clothes given to me by the church and going to bed sick to my stomach with hunger because a bowl of cold cereal wasn't enough to fill me up."

"So you wished you'd stuck it out?" Lauren asked sympathetically.

"I don't see how I could have, but, looking back, I can see it would have been the smart thing to do, I guess. After all, I was family. I was entitled to it. She didn't see it that way, though. She wanted me to dance to the piper, and I wasn't the type—then."

Lauren crooked a brow. She had a feeling all of it was going to tie in together somehow.

He went on to tell how he had eventually joined the navy where he had the grit necessary to become a navy SEAL. In addition, he had received training that eventually led to his work with the oil rigs after he was discharged in his mid-twenties.

"The baggage I carried with me from my youth," he

explained, "was my need to live it up, because, after escaping from my aunt, I felt like I'd been let out of prison. But, unfortunately, I didn't know how to handle all that freedom for the first time in my life. Suddenly I could go where I wanted, do what I liked. But I was wild. I was crazy. I raised hell everywhere I went.

"That's why I fit right in with the SEALs," he added with a wink. "You have to be a little mad to do what those guys do."

Lauren gave a perfunctory nod. She'd never known anyone in the elite group but had heard they were extremely daring. It was easy, however, to see how Sam was able to make their ranks, for there was an air about him that exuded not only strength, but courage, as well.

And, with a delicious wave, she knew the reason for his terrific build. No doubt he had continued to work out in order to maintain the glorious physique he'd developed during his SEAL days.

Sam Rutledge was quite a man.

Stop it, Lauren, the familiar nagging voice inside her warned. *This is business. Strictly business. The man is being very serious, and you're getting all mushy inside, because he's sitting so close, and for weeks he's mesmerized you like a cobra charming a bird. Cut out the schoolgirl fantasy. Didn't he just make it clear that he's not thinking marriage? So what do you want? An affair with the boss?*

"Then I had an accident," he went on, oblivious to Lauren's disquietude. "I took a bad fall off a rig that laid me up for a while. But it could have been worse. I could've wound up a quadriplegic, but I was lucky. Still, I was out of commission and found myself with a lot of time on my hands—time to think about my life and where I was headed. So that was when I decided I needed to slow down. You know—wife, house in the suburbs, kids."

What was he leading up to, she wondered dizzily. "But you said marriage is the last thing on your mind."

"It is—now. This was before..." He hesitated, his eyes

searching hers as though to confirm once more that he could trust her. Finally, with a curt nod of self-affirmation, he continued, "before Gaynelle."

Lauren was jolted by a sudden wave of jealousy and reminded herself she had to keep everything in perspective and remember this was all business, by golly.

But, oh, did she wish he'd hurry up and get to the point.

"The company I work for has its home office in Atlanta, and they gave me a desk job so I could recuperate from my injury. But I didn't know anybody there and eventually got bored and started making the bar scene and partying again. That's where I met Gaynelle—in a bar near the airport. She was a flight attendant.

"And," he added grimly, scornfully, "she was as wild as I used to be. But we hit it off, and soon we were spending all our time together when she wasn't flying. After a while, I proposed, but she turned me down."

Lauren made no comment. Instead, she focused on her empty coffee cup, wanting to go to the kitchen for a refill but not daring to interrupt him when he was on a roll at last.

"Gaynelle didn't want to be married. Not to me. Not to anybody. She wanted to taste everything life had to offer. She wanted to travel, see things, do things. That's why she was a stewardess—for the fun of it—because she sure as hell didn't have to work for a living. Thanks to her parents leaving her a very generous inheritance, she was financially independent."

He shook his head in sad reverie. "I tried to change her mind, but I couldn't. Then she accidentally got pregnant."

Lauren drew a sharp breath. "And she still wouldn't agree to marriage?"

"She wanted to have an abortion."

Tears sprang to Lauren's eyes. She was such a softie when it came to babies. It would never occur to her to have an abortion, unless it was a matter of dire circumstances—thus her stance of being pro-choice.

"But she didn't, did she?" Lauren asked fearfully. "I mean, you said you have a son."

"No, she didn't, and, yes, I do, but that's not the way she intended it to be. You see, I was so damn mad when she said she was going to abort and nothing would stop her that I just left town to get away from her. I couldn't stop thinking what a fool I'd been to ever think I was in love with her. Gaynelle was selfish and spoiled and didn't care about me or the baby. All she wanted was a good time."

"But she had him," Lauren said, relieved.

"Yes, she did. But not because she wanted to. You see, a few months after I left town, I received a letter from her that had been forwarded from my old address in Atlanta. She wrote how, when she was in California visiting her grandmother, her grandmother overheard her on the phone making plans for the abortion. Her grandmother then went into a rage and that was when Gaynelle found out about the clause in her parents' will that she'd not bothered to notice before.

"You see," he went on, "her parents evidently were afraid Gaynelle would squander her inheritance, so they gave her grandmother the legal right to terminate the trust anytime she felt Gaynelle was unworthy of having it."

"So…" he said, his eyes shining with some unnamed emotion, "Sophie lowered the boom and warned Gaynelle that if she had the abortion, she wouldn't get another dime—ever."

"Sophie?"

"Her grandmother—Sophie Rogers. She's a sly old bird with all the charm of a rattlesnake. At least, that's my opinion after our conversations on the phone."

"Well, she can't be all bad," Lauren pointed out. "She saved your son."

"True. But nothing could save Gaynelle."

Something in his tone made Lauren raise her head sharply to look at him, and that was when she saw the pity, the sadness, mirrored on his face.

"She went on in that letter to ask if I would want to adopt the baby since I'd always acted like I thought fatherhood was the greatest thing since sliced bread."

"Isn't it?" Lauren laughed softly, despite his stern expression.

Lost in the past, he continued without comment. "I was in Alaska when the letter reached me. I wrote her back right away at the return address she'd given—her grandmother's in California—and told her I sure as hell did want the baby. When I didn't hear from her again, I figured she'd gone on and had the abortion, anyway. She could be so damn stubborn. But I had to know for sure, so when I finished up my assignment, I tried to find her. That's when I learned she was dead."

Stricken, Lauren's hand flew to her throat. "She died giving birth?"

He scowled. "She died two weeks after Jamie was born, after smashing into a tree while riding on the back of a motorcycle after leaving a bar with a man she'd just met."

"I'm sorry," Lauren whispered. It was such a tragedy for everyone concerned. Then, despite the sadness, she remembered the reason he was telling her about it and gently prodded, "So, where is your son now, and what does all of this have to do with the job you want to hire me for?"

"Bear with me," he pleaded. "I'm getting to all that. Sophie, you see, has him now. Gaynelle's former roommate gave me her phone number, and I called her, and that's how I found all this out, but she's not willing to give him up to a man she considers unfit. Her theory is that any man hanging out with her granddaughter, as wild as she was, has to be a roustabout himself, and, therefore, unworthy."

"She can't refuse though, can she? I mean, he *is* your son. Sure, it's understandable she'd want to keep him and raise him herself, since he's her great-grandson, but a judge would certainly make her give him up to you."

"You're right. But—" he lifted a finger to make a point "—it would be history repeating itself."

"I don't understand."

"I walked away from my inheritance. I don't want the same thing to happen to my son. I don't want him to miss out on what's rightfully his."

She shook her head. "I'm afraid I don't follow you."

"Sophie says that she'll fight me and admits she'll probably lose, but she'll put me in debt for years with legal fees, and she'll also see to it Jamie never gets a dime of his mother's inheritance."

Lauren found it hard to believe anyone could be so cruel and said as much.

"Well, I know it sounds that way," he conceded, "but as Sophie explains it, the money is the only weapon she has. She says if I'm serious about being a good father to Jamie, I'll be willing to prove it. And if I can't, then she'll use my failure against me in court."

"She wants you to pass some kind of test?" Lauren asked in disbelief.

"That's right."

Lauren tapped a finger against her chin as she thought a moment, then said, "Okay. Let me see if I've got this right. Jamie's great-grandmother is willing to put you to some kind of fatherhood test, and if you pass it, she'll hand him over to you without a fight, along with his inheritance."

Sam nodded.

"But if you refuse to take her test," Lauren went on, "she'll fight you in court and, if you win custody, she'll deny him the money."

"Exactly."

"But can she do that legally? Keep his money, I mean?"

"Yes, she can, because there's also a clause in the will that stated that if Gaynelle died while Sophie was still alive, the money would revert back to Sophie. She can do what she wants to with it."

Lauren was now perched on the edge of the sofa, totally caught up in his dilemma as though it were her own. "So what are you going to do?"

He explained that when he had first contacted Sophie to say he wanted his son, she had bluntly refused. "She said between my being single and traveling so much I couldn't provide a stable home for a baby. Naturally, I was furious and went running to a lawyer."

"And?"

"He came right out and told me it was going to cost a lot of money and could drag on in court for a long time and that it would be a lot simpler if I just got married, found a job that didn't require traveling and let Sophie see that I could, indeed, provide a good, stable environment for my son. In other words, take her little test."

"Especially," he emphasized, "when we're talking about a million dollars or more trust fund."

"And what is this test she wants to give you?"

He spread his hands in a helpless gesture, his expression sheepish. "To be perfectly honest, Lauren, after I hung up talking to her that first time, I was so mad I couldn't think straight. I called her back a week later and told her I'd just gotten married, to a girl I met in Alaska."

"You lied?" Lauren asked incredulously.

He met her accusing stare. "Yes, I did. I'll stop at nothing to get my son."

Lauren, in her trademark candor, could not resist saying, "Well, it sounds to me like you'll stop at nothing to get his trust fund."

"Hold it," he flared, eyes blazing. "Get something straight. I don't want a dime of that money for myself. It will be handled through an administrator who will see to it Jamie doesn't get any of it till it's time for him to go to college. And then it will be in increments. He won't get the bulk of it till he's twenty-one. Maybe older.

"I'm not doing this for me," he went on in an indignant rush. "I only want to make sure I'm not responsible for screwing it up for him."

"Sorry." Lauren was ashamed to have thought the worst.

"No need to be," he said, smiling to let her know he was no longer mad. "I really can't blame you for thinking that way, but trust me. It's simply not true."

"So where does the test come into all this?"

"Sophie wants to make sure my marriage is stable. She says young folks these days—" he wrinkled his nose to mimic "—don't take their wedding vows seriously. And she also wants to make sure I haven't married some bimbo in a rush just to try to gain her approval."

He reached in his pocket and groped for, and found, the wedding band. Holding it out to her, he said, "This is where you come in, Lauren. I need your help."

She stared at the ring uncertainly. The pieces of the puzzle were finally coming together, but it all seemed so preposterous.

"I want you to be my wife. I mean, my *pretend* wife," he was quick to amend. "I want you to go to California with me and make Sophie think we're happy, stable—whatever it takes."

Lauren gave a nervous little laugh as she stared from the shiny gold ring to his anxious, worried eyes. "But it won't work, Sam. She's not going to hand your son over to you just because I walk in her house wearing a wedding band. She'll want to see a marriage certificate."

"That's no problem. I've got a friend who can take care of that, and I can trust him not to say a word. But Sophie will want more than that. She's already said so."

"Like what?" she asked warily.

"She wants us to live with her for a little while."

"Live with—?" Lauren nearly choked on her own breath.

"Yes. In California." He went on to explain that perhaps now she could understand why he had not wanted to have dinner with Midge or meet any of her friends, because he could not chance anyone finding out about the ruse. They had to just disappear for a few weeks. No one could know where they were going.

"I hated having to be so mysterious," he added, "and I apologize for putting you through all this without being able to level with you, but surely you can appreciate the need for secrecy. Just say you'll do it, please."

Lauren's head was spinning. She felt dizzy. "I don't know...."

"See why my ad said 'aspiring actress'? It'll be putting on an act, but you can do it, Lauren. I know you can. That's why I've grilled you so much these past weeks. I was feeling you out as to your likes and dislikes, making sure we're compatible so we can get along for however long it takes. That's also why I asked all the questions about babies, to make sure you can act like you adore Jamie...act like you really want to be his mother and raise him like he's your own.

"You can do that, can't you?" he rushed on. "He's six months old now and bound to be a little sweetheart. I haven't seen him, not even a picture...." His voice cracked as his hand snaked out to wrap about hers. "Say you'll do it, please. You're my only hope. I don't have time to find anybody else, and if I keep stalling about going out there, she's going to get suspicious and make matters worse. I've already arranged for a leave of absence from my job, and you can do the same. You said you weren't happy there, anyway."

Lauren quivered at his touch. "I don't know...." she repeated, even more uncertain. To masquerade as his wife, knowing it was all a sham and when it was over they'd go their separate ways and never see each other again, was a role she was not sure she could play...especially since she was undeniably drawn to him.

He leaned closer, his face mere inches from hers as he pleaded desperately, "You've got to do it, Lauren, because without you, I don't stand a chance."

"Sam, I—" Oh, what could she say? She wanted to help him but was afraid of—what? That she would goof somehow and expose it all for what it was? Or that she'd embarrass and humiliate herself in some way, perhaps by being thrown so close to a man she found dangerously desirable?

"Say you'll do it, Lauren. It's only for a month or so. However long it takes for her to make her up her mind we're okay together. Then you get the ten thousand, and we go our separate ways."

Lauren had a suspicion that the ten thousand dollars Sam offered represented all the money he had in the world. The road would be hard for him as a single parent, for she knew he would give up his high-paying job of danger and travel and settle down to be a doting father to his son.

But the money also represented to her a jump start on a new life. She could throw herself into studying for a new career and not look back.

She could also program herself not to get emotionally involved in any of this. Sam would not expect otherwise. He certainly regarded her as merely an actress in a play. He felt nothing for her personally.

So be it.

She could do the same.

"Well?" Beads of perspiration were dotting his forehead. "Don't keep me waiting any longer, Lauren, for heaven's sake."

"No. Not for *heaven's* sake," she corrected him. "Like you said, remember? For *Jamie's* sake."

She forced a smile, wondering why she felt like crying as she whispered tremulously, "I'll take the job."

Chapter Six

The worst part, Lauren decided, was having to make arrangements to practically drop off the face of the earth.

The easy part was making arrangements to take a leave of absence from work. Actually, Dr. Brockworth seemed relieved. "It's what you need," he'd told her. "And if you ultimately decide you don't want to return, well, I'll understand and assure you I'll give you a good reference."

All he asked was that she wait till after the holidays. Sam was disappointed. He'd wanted to be with Jamie on his first Christmas but understood Lauren could not leave on such short notice. Appointments had to be kept. Arrangements for her replacement had to be made.

She had planned to tell Midge first but couldn't reach her, so she'd gone to Dr. Brockworth, thinking there'd be time to talk to her before word spread.

But no such luck.

She decided Robin must have gone on the Internet to tell everybody, because by the end of the day, everyone she knew in Atlanta, it seemed, was calling to ask what was going on.

Lauren offered the explanation that she just felt the need to get away for a while—to *find herself,* she'd said, feeling silly to use the antiquated expression. She planned to travel to places she'd never been, she explained, see the country, and meditate and muse.

When Midge heard, she rushed right over to the apartment, using the key that she'd forgotten to turn over to Lauren.

Lauren was in the bedroom, sorting through her clothes. January and February could be cold in Southern California, too, Sam had said, especially on the ocean.

"What is this?" Midge cried, bursting into the room. "Where do you think you're going? This is the craziest thing I've ever heard of. You can't just go off by yourself. Are you out of your mind?"

Lauren was folding a sweater against her chest and laughed. "I guess this means you've heard."

"You're darn tootin' I have." Midge plunked down on the bed. She was wearing sweats and floppy slippers.

Lauren swept her with an astonished gaze. "I can't believe you just charged over here without a coat or shoes. Why didn't you just phone?" She put the sweater aside and calmly reached for another.

Midge eyed her coldly. "I figured if you didn't think enough of our friendship to tell me first, you'd have the machine on and not pick up and talk to me."

"The machine is always on, Midge. You know that. And, yes, I would have talked to you. In fact, I had planned to tell you first but couldn't get hold of you."

"Then why didn't you leave a message on *my* machine?"

"It didn't seem right to tell you that way."

Midge threw up her hands. "Well, it sure isn't right for you to just run off without telling anybody where you're going, either." Her eyes narrowed. "But you're going to tell *me,* aren't you?"

"Nope."

"You don't mean that. We're best friends. We tell each other everything."

Lauren tossed her an apologetic glance. "Sorry. Not this time. I wish I could, but I can't."

Midge covered her face with her hands and spoke through her fingers. "I can't believe I'm hearing this. We've shared so much."

Lauren sat down next to her. "I'm sorry. I truly am." She slipped her arms around her.

The phone rang, and they listened as the machine clicked on to answer, then Lauren groaned to hear Sam's cheery voice saying, "Hi, it's me. I guess you're out tying up loose ends. Well, I'll call you later and see how things are going. I'm anxious to leave, as you well know." He laughed and hung up.

Lauren braced for Midge's explosion.

Bounding to her feet, Midge pointed an accusing finger and cried, "So that's it. It's *him.* Your mystery man. I might've known. You're running away with him, aren't you?"

Lauren was speechless. What could she say without giving herself away?

"Something funny is going on." Midge thought a second, then snapped her fingers. "I know. He's married. That's it, isn't he? He's married, and you're running away together. And you aren't coming back, but you don't want people to know that, and that's the reason for going through the motions of pretending it's just for a short time."

Lauren bolted from the bed. "That's not how it is. I'm coming back."

"But you're going away with him, aren't you?" Midge challenged. "He's behind all this, isn't he? And the secrecy is because he's married."

Lauren felt trapped. She could not confide the truth but

neither could she allow her to think something so awful. "Listen," she began, "for reasons I can't explain...reasons I can *never* explain, I do have to go away with him. But it's not what you think. He isn't married, and this is strictly business. He's paying me to do a job and paying me well, I might add, but I can't tell you what it is."

Midge was horrified. "I thought I knew you, and here you're telling me you're a—"

Lauren had to laugh despite everything. "No, I am *not* a prostitute. He doesn't want me that way. We aren't romantically involved at all."

"Are you sure?" Midge's expression said she did not believe her.

"Yes, I'm sure."

"But you've been seeing him for a while."

"That's right. We needed the time to decide whether we could—" She struggled for explanation, then lamely offered, "work well together."

"But why the secrecy?"

"That's the part I can't tell you about."

"Is it illegal?"

"I promise you it isn't." Well, maybe a little, she thought guiltily. There had to be something illicit about pretending to be married, but when the intentions were good, maybe it wasn't really a bad thing.

Midge began pacing around the room as she fretted. "I can't let you do this. I just can't. You have no family. You could drop off the face of the earth, and no one would notice."

"That's not going to happen. I'll be back in a month or so."

Midge shook her head fiercely. "Nope. You can't do it. Not unless you tell me where you're going so if you don't come back I can tell the police where to start looking for you."

"I am truly sorry, but there is absolutely no way I can do that. And believe me when I say I appreciate your concern, but I gave my word that I wouldn't tell, and if you understood the situation, you'd know why it has to be this way."

"I still don't like it," Midge said grudgingly.

Lauren was touched to see tears in her eyes. Clasping both her hands, she said, "I have an idea. I can call you once in a while. Will that make you worry less?"

"I don't know." She still looked upset.

Lauren gave her a good-natured punch on her shoulder. "Will you please stop worrying? I know this man. I trust him."

Midge slapped her palms against the side of her head and swung it from side to side like a pendulum as she wailed, "I can't believe you're doing this. I absolutely can't believe it."

"Well, I am. So wish me luck," Lauren said cheerily.

"You know I do. But tell me one thing. Are you really getting paid well?"

"Absolutely. And I really need the money, Midge, because I'm about almost convinced now that being a dental hygienist is not for me. What I'm getting paid will help me start over."

In an obvious attempt to accept that which she could do nothing about, Midge finally conceded, "Okay. I wish you luck.

"And while I'm chewing my nails, hoping you're all right," she hastened to add with an impish grin, "I'll be thinking about new careers for you."

Lauren hoped she could, because for the time being, she couldn't think past playing the role of Sam's wife—and helplessly wondering what it would be like if she really were.

Sam glanced around the motel room to make sure he hadn't forgot anything.

But what was there to forget? he morosely wondered.

He sure didn't have very much.

Clothes. Shaving kit. Some tapes and a portable player. That was it.

All his possessions could be crammed into a suitcase and duffle bag.

It was depressing to contemplate, especially since he'd made a heck of a lot of money in the past ten years.

And he had spent a lot, too.

Women, he had found, could be very expensive.

So could living like there was no tomorrow.

But he had managed to save a little, which was how he was able to offer a tidy sum to Lauren.

Lauren.

Lord, he hoped he wasn't getting in over his head. There was no denying he was attracted to her. She had, however, made it very clear that, after striking out three times, she had no intentions of battering up at the romance plate again. He would be wasting his time, not to mention making a fool of himself, if he tried to change her mind.

She wasn't interested...even if he did dare to think that maybe they'd had a moment there when they were dancing.

But that was only natural.

Man and woman. Together. In each other's arms. Swaying to the music. Romantic ambience surrounding like a misty fog. It was only normal that for a few moments there they were pulled together.

He could not, however, let it happen again...could not allow them to be caught in the proverbial tender trap.

But, oh, he moaned to think, that was going to be tough.

Especially since they were going to find themselves caught in intimate circumstances for a month—or however long it took to convince Sophie their marriage was stable enough to provide a good home for Jamie.

Maybe with another woman, one who didn't set his pulse to racing with just a dimpled smile, it would not be a problem. After all, he had always taken pride in self-control. It was part of his SEAL training. Emotions could not be allowed to get in the way of a mission.

The fact was, he should have torn up her letter and concentrated on an applicant whose photograph did not captivate him at first glance.

But he hadn't been able to do that.

What he had done was sit there for maybe ten minutes studying Lauren Gentry's pretty face, all aglow with the lights from the Christmas tree, and think how she seemed just perfect for the image he wanted to present to Sophie—mature, intelligent, honest, wholesome.

The perfect wife.

The perfect mother.

It was going to work.

He was going to convince Sophie to give up his son peacefully.

Sure, he would endure some cash flow problems for a while, because once he got back to work, his salary would be nowhere near as much as when he was working in the field. There would be a lot of expenses, that would go along with renting and furnishing an apartment. Then there was the cost of day care and everything else that went with parenthood.

But still, he was looking forward to being a daddy.

Big time!

And however tricky it might be to pull off this mock marriage in the meantime, it would all be worth it. How difficult could it really be?

"Are you sure you've thought of everything?" Sam asked as he glanced about the apartment as he held a suitcase in each hand.

Lauren was checking to make sure the answering machine was on and called over her shoulder, "Yes. I talked to the maintenance man, and he told me what to do."

"And you explained you'd be away a month or longer?"

"Yes, but I don't see it taking that long."

He was amused by her optimism. "Sorry, but I have a

feeling Sophie is going to try to put us through every kind of test imaginable, no matter how long it takes.''

"Well, she'll just have to understand we both have to get back to work. We can't take off indefinitely. And remember,'' she hastened to remind him, "you don't really know her. You've only spoken with her on the phone. Maybe it won't be as bad as you think.''

"That's wishful thinking. I've talked to her enough to know she's cunning and mean. But I'll play her game and win, and I won't stay around her one hour longer than necessary. I just want to get this over with.''

Lauren slid a glance at him, noting the determined set to his jaw, the tight line of his mouth. He seemed angry, and she was puzzled, because during the past weeks of planning, he'd been so upbeat. But she chalked up his demeanor to apprehension. After all, she was also anxious to get the job done so she could get on with her life...lonely though it was.

"Cab's waiting,'' he said, a touch impatient.

Lauren took one last look around. "Well, I guess this is it. Seems kind of sad, though, to know I've left my one and only responsibility in life with my next-door neighbor.''

He lifted a quizzical brow.

She made a face. "My geranium.''

"All right, then.'' With a grin, he gave her a pat on the back and declared, "California, here we come!''

Lauren was not about to let on that she had never flown before. Sam, however, picked up on her nervousness and teased her into admitting it, then sought to comfort her. "You're going to enjoy it, and as soon as we're on board we'll have a glass of champagne to celebrate the beginning of our adventure. That will relax you.''

Lauren wasn't so sure.

"Welcome aboard,'' a perky stewardess greeted them.

She showed them to their seats at the front of the plane,

and Lauren whispered to Sam, "First-class? Isn't this terribly expensive?"

"It would be if I hadn't had a bunch of frequent-flyer points saved up. It's a long flight. Nearly five hours. I wanted you to be comfortable."

It was thoughtful, and she told him so.

The stewardess brought champagne, then noticed how ill at ease Lauren seemed and said, "You're nervous. I can tell. Is it your honeymoon or first flight?"

Lauren was too stunned to react, but Sam said easily, "Both...sort of. We haven't been married but a few months, and this is her first flight. Not mine."

She patted Lauren's shoulder. "My name is Tina, and I'm going to see to it you have a wonderful flight. If you need anything at all, just push that call button there."

After she walked away, Sam hesitantly said, "You've got to try to appear more at ease with all this, Lauren."

Lauren was seated next to the window and pressed her forehead against the cool glass and wondered, not for the first time, exactly what she had gotten herself into. "Is it too late to forget the whole thing?" she mumbled drearily.

He squeezed her hand. "Sorry. There's no turning back. For the next few weeks, you are Mrs. Sam Rutledge, like it or not."

Mrs. Sam Rutledge. A chill went through her, even as she reminded herself this was all pretend.

His touch, as always, ignited a heated rush, and suddenly she heard herself asking the question she'd been holding back for some time. "What about...sleeping together?"

"Sleeping together?" he echoed.

"Yes. Sophie is naturally going to put us in the same room, unless you can convince her we'd rather stay at a motel...which would be best. Separate rooms there, too, of course," she hastened to add.

He took a long sip of champagne, as though trying to postpone having to address the delicate subject. Finally he said, "Well, to be perfectly honest, I thought of that. If we had a suite with two bedrooms, she'd never know we weren't sleeping together, but when I mentioned going to a motel, she was adamant that we stay at her house. I said we didn't want to put her out, but she insisted. And when I kept arguing, she got huffy and said 'Look, how can I make a decision if I'm not around you all the time?''' He shrugged. "What could I say to that?"

Lauren gulped her champagne. The thought of the intimacy of sharing a bedroom was unnerving, to say the least.

As if by magic, Tina appeared to refill their glasses.

When she was gone, Sam told Lauren not to worry. "It'll work out. I'll sleep on the floor. Everything is going to be fine. You'll see. Because once the bedroom door is closed, the role-playing stops, okay?"

Lauren settled back, pretending to relax, all the while wondering why she felt so attracted to him. Unless she got a grip on her emotions, she was headed down a one-way street to heartache—again.

Tina and the other flight attendants came through the cabin with their pre-flight instructions. All the talk of oxygen masks and flotation devices made her a little anxious.

Sam continued to hold Lauren's hand, and even though she told herself not to be scared, she couldn't help squeezing his fingers as the plane finally lifted off the ground.

Taking off was an exhilarating experience, and she eventually did relax, enjoying the sight of the metropolis of Atlanta below, as it eventually became a Lilliputian village before finally disappearing beneath the clouds.

When the plane leveled off, Tina brought more champagne, along with a basket of all kinds of treats—chips, cookies, peanuts, candy. Lauren declined, but Sam helped himself, saying, "I've got all ideas Sophie is one of those little old ladies who has a bowl of bran at five in the afternoon and calls it supper."

"One of the elderly couples I lived with for a time used to eat like that," Lauren recalled. "They said people don't need a heavy meal at the end of the day."

He let his seat back. "We can buy some groceries, too, so we can have what we want to eat. Besides, we won't have her hovering over us every minute, anyway. I plan to take Jamie on outings with just the two of us. To the park, the beach, the mall. Everywhere families go. Because that's what we're going to be—a family."

Yeah, right, Lauren thought sarcastically. He and Jamie would be a family, and she would go home alone with her ten thousand dollars. Suddenly she realized she envied Sam's future more than her own.

Dinner was served on white linen-covered trays, with linen napkins and real china and crystal. There was a choice of wines, as well as entrées—steak or chicken cordon bleu. Dessert was a creamy chocolate mocha.

Sam was pleased she seemed to be enjoying her meal. "This is why I dislike flying coach. I sit crammed in with all the other passengers and think about the wonderful service I could be getting. But we may have to ride back there going home. I only had enough frequent-flyer points for two one-ways."

"Ah, but we'll have the baby," she said on a positive note. "We won't care. He'll be such a joy."

He smiled. "You really like kids, don't you?"

"Uh-huh." She daintily nibbled on an after-dinner mint. "Especially babies."

"Were you ever around any in the foster homes?"

"No. But I wish I had been. The homes I was sent to were for older kids. Babies were always in demand for adoption."

"Must have been tough." His voice was thick with compassion.

"No big deal." She didn't mean to sound so flip, but she never allowed herself to wallow in self-pity. Besides, it was all in the past.

Sam sensed she didn't want to touch on painful memories, and turned to the present and the all-important task at hand. "Okay. Reality check." They had spent countless hours going over what Sam referred to as their "background," but he was taking no chances. There could be no slip-ups.

Lauren giggled as Sam screwed up his face like he'd just bitten into a lemon, then mimed Sophie's voice. "Tell me about yourself, my dear. Exactly how and when did the two of you meet?"

Folding her hands in her lap, Lauren primly responded. "I'm a bookkeeper with Allied Oil, and I was sent to the field office in Alaska on temporary assignment to work on the books there. That's how I met Sam."

"And just how long had you known each other when you were married?"

"Six months."

"That's not a very long time for a courtship."

"Well, some people might not think so, but Sam and I knew the moment we met that it was meant to be, and—"

"Hold it." He held up a hand. "You sound like you're reading a script. Put some feeling into it, as if thinking about it makes you feel all dreamy inside."

Lauren teased, "I think you've been sneaking and reading my romance novels."

"Come on. Get serious now."

She sighed, then repeated herself, this time with feeling.

He had changed back to his own voice. "That's good. Now tell me about married life. What's it like for you two?"

She responded without hesitation, for she had memorized each and every detail. "We both work. Sam has a desk job now, you know. He no longer travels. We have a nice condo but we hope to get a little house in the suburbs later, so Jamie can have a yard to play in."

"What about your spare time—hobbies and so forth?"

"We go out once in a while, to visit friends or go to a movie. We lead a quiet life, really. We work hard and save our money."

"And do you want to have children of your own one day?"

Lauren did not have to pretend enthusiasm, answering from her heart. "Oh, yes. I want three at least. Maybe more. I love children, and—"

Sam interrupted. "Don't overdo it, Lauren. If you come across like Mother Hubbard, she'll figure it's a put on."

But it's not, Lauren thought defensively. She *did* want children, no matter what it took to get them. She had no intentions of going through life childless.

Sam noticed her pensive expression. "Is something wrong?"

"I don't know. Maybe nothing. Maybe everything."

"What's that supposed to mean?"

"I'm not sure. I just worry sometimes."

"About what?"

So far, Lauren had gone along with all his plans, because he seemed to have thought of all the angles. Still, there was something that bothered her.

"Go on. Please," he urged.

"Well, it's about Sophie."

He laughed shortly. "All of this is about Sophie. If she'd just hand over my son and not try to cheat him out of his trust fund, none of this would be necessary. We could all just get on with our lives."

"Maybe she won't be able to."

"What are you talking about?"

"She *is* his great-grandmother, Sam, and she's cared for him since he was born. Don't you think it's going to hurt her to give him up?"

"I'm not coldhearted, Lauren. She can visit him anytime she wants."

"And if she does, what will you say about my not being there?"

"Well, I guess it's something I'll deal with when the time comes," he said finally.

"Deal with *how?*"

"I'll just say we're divorced, that it didn't work out."

"That's not going to make her feel very good after she relinquished her great-grandson to our care, because she thought we'd give him a secure home."

"I can give him that," Sam defended.

"If she thought that, this charade of pretending to be married wouldn't be necessary, would it?"

"Not if she weren't being so difficult."

"She's being difficult, because she loves her great-grandson and wants only the best for him."

His eyes went wide. "Well, if that were the case, she wouldn't be threatening to take away his inheritance, would she?"

"It's the only weapon she has."

"And why does she need one? I'm his father."

"I'm not trying to upset you, Sam. I just feel all of this will go a lot smoother if you can have a little compassion for Sophie. After all, you've got to realize that as far as she's concerned, you're the irresponsible clod who got her granddaughter pregnant. To her, you're no different than the one who drove his motorcycle into a tree and killed Gaynelle.

"That is why she's putting you through this," Lauren said with finality. "She has to be convinced that you've settled down and will make a good father. After all, Jamie is all she's got left of her granddaughter, whom I'm sure she loved and grieves for, despite all the woes she might have caused her through the years."

Lauren settled back. The champagne and wine had made her sleepy. "That's all I had to say," she murmured, closing her eyes.

Sam stared beyond her and out the window. The plane was banked by thick, white clouds. Trying to see through them was like attempting to look into his future.

There was no way.

He could only take one day at the time and do everything in his power to secure his son's birthright.

But Lauren was right.

It would be easier if he could muster some compassion for Sophie, and he made up his mind then and there to put forth every effort to do so.

He jumped, startled, as Lauren's head slumped to his shoulder as she slept.

Having a woman cradled against him felt good.

And the scent of her was intoxicating.

But it wasn't just her warmth or smell that quickened his pulses. It was Lauren, herself.

Attractive, witty, smart…and sexy as hell.

Truly she was everything a man could want in a woman.

Yes, he'd made a wise choice for his wife, albeit make-believe. And, he sharply reminded himself, a make-believe wife was the only kind he wanted.

Chapter Seven

The announcement came over the speakers. "In preparation for landing in San Diego, the captain has turned on the seat belt sign. Please make sure all trays are securely fastened and that your seats are returned to the upright position."

Sam gave Lauren a gentle nudge, but she continued to sleep, her head still resting on his shoulder.

Tina, the stewardess, walked by and murmured, "She must have been exhausted. She slept through the movie."

"She doesn't drink much, and I'm afraid all the champagne and wine got to her."

Sam wriggled his shoulder. Lauren didn't move. He wished Tina would disappear, but she seemed intent on lingering, so he had no choice. He said, "Honey, wake up," and gave her a light kiss on her forehead.

Tina smiled approvingly and said, "Don't forget to straighten your seats," before moving on down the aisle.

At the touch of Sam's lips, Lauren had sat up quickly.

"Sorry to startle you," he said. "But I had to wake you. We're landing."

"You didn't have to kiss me," she admonished.

He held a finger to his lips. "Shhh. The stewardess was right over me, and I had to do what any loving husband would do to wake up his wife."

"You've been reading my books again," she grumbled, pressing the button to bring her seat upright. "And you didn't have to kiss me," she repeated, somewhat haughtily.

"What did you want me to do? Shake you like a rag doll? I'm afraid you're going to have to get used to the fact that there are going to be times when I have to touch you, Lauren."

"Like how?" She cut him a suspicious glance.

"Like holding hands. Putting my arm around you. Kissing you once in a while."

"You can leave off the kissing."

He thought again how cute she was when she was mad—the dancing sparkle in her Caribbean green eyes, the way little pink dots appeared on her cheeks, and especially how her lower lip trembled ever so slightly as if she was a petulant, but adorable, child.

He yielded to the temptation to goad her a bit and pretended innocence as he asked, "So what's wrong with kissing?"

"Nothing when it's not pretense. Otherwise it seems kind of—" she paused to think about it "—cheap, somehow."

"Well, we won't have to do it often. Just enough to make Sophie think it's real…that *we're* real. But are you sure you like kissing even when it isn't pretend?"

"Now what kind of question is that?" she bristled. Taking her bag from beneath the seat in front of her, she took out her brush and gave her hair a few angry strokes. "Of course, I like kissing. What woman wouldn't if she cares about a man?"

"Meaning you don't care about me?"

"Not that way," she lied.

"As a friend?"

She saw the gleam in his eye and knew then he was just teasing. "Yes, I like you as a friend, but I don't go around kissing my men friends intimately, okay? A peck on the cheek, and that's it."

"I kissed you on your forehead, and you jumped like a spider had landed."

Her shudder was reflex. "I don't like spiders, either."

"Well, try not to think of me as a spider so you won't cringe every time I touch you."

He covered her hand, and she jumped.

"See?" he frowned. "Lauren, you've got to relax." They had been whispering, but he leaned closer so he could lower his voice even more. "You've got to pretend you're used to me touching you in *every* way. I might even make some sexy little innuendoes from time to time. Be ready for them. Throw some back. We're newlyweds. It's expected."

"Dear heavens," she said, stunned. "You mean you expect me to fawn all over you in front of a total stranger?"

He didn't like the way she was looking at him, as if he was some kind of weirdo pervert. "Will you please stop staring at me like that?"

"Then don't say things to make me. Good grief." She swept him with incredulous eyes, "I hope you invite me over when you do get married. I want to see if your wife drools all over you in real life."

She twisted in the seat, pressing her face to the window to watch the landing.

Sam wanted to kick himself. He could have explained things differently. He didn't have to antagonize her. After all, they weren't going to have to drool all over each other, for Pete's sake, but he'd made it sound as though they did. All they had to do was get along, be pleasant and act happy.

Simple.

Easy.

So why was he trying to make things so complicated?

He also turned away. He'd planned to point out some interesting sights to her as they came in, but if she wanted to puff up like a bullfrog, so be it.

He felt a pain shoot through his jaw and realized he was grinding his teeth together in anger—but not at her. Oh, no. He was furious with himself for breaking his rule and allowing his emotions to get stirred up again.

But he couldn't help it, damn it.

After all, he was only human, and having her cuddled up next to him for almost the entire flight had been a sweet kind of torture.

So maybe it was good that they had a little tiff now and then to ease the sensual tension he was unable to resist. After all, as long as they fooled Sophie, what difference did it make whether or not they got along in private? Wasn't it better for them to spar once in a while than to have to face up to the potent chemistry between them?

Damn straight it was.

He leaned closer to her, his tone sharp, but quiet. "This has got to stop, Lauren."

She whipped her head about. "What do you mean?"

"You're pouting."

"No, I'm not."

"Yes, you are. You aren't talking to me."

Lauren started to speak, then bit her lip.

He nudged her. "Go ahead. You've got something on your mind. Let's hear it."

Leaning back in her seat, she was quietly thoughtful for a moment, then said, "Us having to kiss and touch each other just wasn't in the deal."

"You will recall I stated in my ad that I was looking for an aspiring actress."

"And I told you in my letter that I wasn't."

"True." He folded his arms across his chest and stared straight ahead. "But I never thought you'd refuse to co-operate by trying."

Lauren felt ire rising and stiffly said, "If you're so disappointed in me, maybe when we land I should just turn around and go home."

"That's the second time you've made some reference to quitting. You wouldn't do that to me, would you?" He turned soulful eyes upon her.

She knew she couldn't—for many reasons. "No. I just wish you wouldn't be so impatient with me, Sam. This isn't easy, you know."

"Tell me about it," he said with a little laugh, then, attempting to appease her, he said, "Look, we've come too far to mess it up now. I'll try to be more patient, okay?"

"Okay." She managed a smile. "And don't worry. Once I get into it, I'll give the performance of my life. Sophie will think our marriage was made in heaven and angels were my bridesmaids. But I want you to remember one thing."

He nodded. "What's that?"

"Don't touch me unless it's absolutely necessary."

"Understood."

She gave a low whistle and shook her head. "Boy, you think you know somebody and then—bam! You find out you don't know them at all."

Sam's glare was not altogether feigned. "Now it's my turn to beg *your* pardon."

"It's really quite simple. I thought you were an all-right guy, and now you get me all the way to the West Coast and show your true colors."

"Like how?"

"By being so...so bossy sometimes."

"I'm sorry. I'm just nervous. This is so important to me, Lauren. It means everything."

He hoped he was saying all the right things to smooth things over, but it was hard to tell because she was still looking at him with fire dancing in her eyes. This time he took no pleasure in the sight.

"I know," he pressed on, "that you'll do a good job, or

I wouldn't have hired you. Again, I'm sorry. I guess I'm just antsy, knowing it's all about to begin.''

Lauren pursed her lips thoughtfully, then nodded. "I can understand that.''

Good. He could breathe easier. And he would think positive, get the job done, get the hell out of California, go home...and do his damnedest to banish all thoughts of Lauren Gentry from his mind...and heart.

Lauren was washed with feelings of self-recrimination over what she felt had been her prudish behavior.

There had been nothing wrong with his brushing his lips against her forehead. Her reaction had been solely to cover up how much she had enjoyed it.

She had also felt guilty for only pretending to be asleep, for actually she had been awake a long time. But it felt so good to have her head on his shoulder and his arm around her.

That was why she'd pretended to be mad, to make what she was feeling dissipate as fast as possible. And if that's what it took to survive the next weeks, to be a little witch once in a while, so be it.

Still, she felt the need to smooth things between them for the moment and pleasantly said, "It must be quite a thrill to know you're about to meet your son.''

"Yes, it sure is. Did I tell you I haven't even seen a picture of him? I asked her to send me one, but she never did.''

Tina was coming up the aisle, making sure everyone was ready for the final approach and ultimate landing. She smiled at Lauren and Sam. They smiled back. Sam wrapped his arm protectively around Lauren. She did not pull away.

A few moments later, there was a loud grinding noise as the plane's wheels came down to lock into place.

Lauren tensed and instinctively reached out for something—someone—to cling to, which happened to be Sam. "So much for my scolding you about unnecessary touching,'' she mumbled self-consciously. "I'm sorry to be such a wuss.''

She attempted to withdraw her hand, but he held tight. "It's okay. I'm always a little froggy during takeoffs and landings. I think everybody is.''

He let her go as the plane came to a stop at the gate.

Lauren hated that he had. She loved holding hands with him. "Do you think Sophie will meet us?''

"I doubt it. When I called her last week to tell her we were finally coming, she didn't say anything when I told her what time we'd get in. I have her address. We can take a cab. I was stationed in Coronado when I was a SEAL. I know my way around. It's an island, and not a very big one, at that. We reach it by a bridge.''

They made their way through the tunnel-like exit ramp and into the crowded terminal. Lauren was lost in a maze of sights and sounds and rushing people as Sam looked around for directional signs to the baggage claim.

Walking and taking escalators, they finally found the luggage carousels.

Lauren stood back while Sam went to find their bags.

Spotting a stand selling fresh sourdough bread—a trademark of the West Coast—she felt a thrill to think that she was actually in California. It was a place she had always wanted to visit, and she vowed, then and there, that despite everything, she was going to enjoy herself.

She was glancing around, not wanting to miss anything, when suddenly she did a quick double-take.

There were several men standing near the door, apparently drivers for limousine services, as they were holding up signs with names scrawled on them.

And one of them spelled out Rutledge.

Only, it wasn't a man holding up the sign.

It was a woman.

Lauren eased closer.

The woman holding the sign looked to be in her sixties. Her hair was a shade of red much brighter than Lauren's.

She was wearing a lime green blouse, knee-length shorts and trendy walking shoes. She carried no bag, but a leather fanny pack was belted around her waist.

Lauren's nerves quickened to wonder if the woman could be Sophie Rogers.

She stepped closer.

The woman noticed her staring and lowered the sign a little.

"Would you happen to be looking for Sam Rutledge?" Lauren ventured to ask.

The sign came down altogether.

"Yes, I am." The woman responded crisply, eyes raking Lauren in scrutiny.

"Well, I'm Lauren. Lauren *Rutledge*." She remembered to use Sam's name.

The woman continued to look her up and down.

"Sam's wife," Lauren explained.

After another moment of awkward silence, the woman introduced herself. "I'm Sophie Rogers."

Lauren politely held out her hand. "I'm pleased to meet you."

Sophie declined to take it. "You'd better wait a while before deciding that, my dear. Now where's Sam?"

After greeting Sam as coldly as she had Lauren, Sophie led the way out of the terminal and to the parking deck.

With the suitcases stowed in the trunk of her car, she got behind the wheel. Lauren settled in the back seat, and Sam took it upon himself to sit up front next to Sophie.

Then he asked the burning question, "Where's Jamie?"

Sophie was focused on backing her luxury sedan out of the parking space and waited till she was straightened and in the flow of traffic before answering. "I left him at home."

"Well, I wish you had brought him," Sam said pleasantly. "I'm anxious to see him."

From the back seat, Lauren chimed in, "That's a fact. It's all Sam's talked about for weeks."

"As you will soon find out, it's a major operation to take a baby out," Sophie said crisply. "There's so much you have to carry."

Lauren quickly argued, "Oh, that's no problem. It will be fun. And I'll bet had you brought him, he would've enjoyed seeing the planes."

Sophie shot her a scathing glance in the rearview mirror. "I should remind you Jamie is not quite seven months old, much too young to care about planes."

Uh-oh, Lauren thought, seeing how Sam wriggled uncomfortably in his seat. She was getting off on the wrong foot and told herself to let him carry the conversation.

"Well, we'll see him soon enough." Sam tried again, sounding extra bright and genial. "How's he doing?"

"Fine. His pediatrician says he's doing everything a baby is supposed to at his age. He's had no problems."

"You must have a good nanny."

"He doesn't have a nanny, Mr. Rutledge. *I* take care of him myself."

"Then who has him now?" Sam's voice had an edge to it.

"My next-door neighbor. She baby-sits now and then."

"But—"

"Mr. Rutledge, I'd hoped this could wait until we were home, and I was not having to concentrate on my driving, but maybe we'd best get something understood between us here and now."

Double uh-oh, Lauren thought. Sam wasn't doing any better than she had. In fact, he had succeeded in punching the old gal's buttons before they were hardly out of the parking deck.

With a stiff nod, Sam said, "I'm listening."

"I have had the complete care of Jamie since the day he was born. As you know, Gaynelle was killed when he was only two weeks old. But what you don't know is that she left my house when he was only three days old, and I didn't see her again until I identified her body in the morgue."

"I'm sorry," Sam said quietly. "I know it hasn't been an easy time for you."

"Actually, it's been a *wonderful* time."

Sam said he didn't understand.

Lauren bit her tongue to keep from butting in to say she didn't, either, and suddenly found herself wishing she were in the trunk with the luggage and not a part of all the tension.

"Jamie," Sophie said with warmth in her tone for the first time, "has been my salvation. He's my breath of life. He means everything to me. Therefore, I make sure that he has the best of care. He does not lack for anything. I have enjoyed every moment with him, and I want you to understand I will not give him up without a fight."

"Then why am I here?" Sam asked between clenched teeth. "Why did I go to all the trouble and expense to come out here if your mind is made up that this will only be settled in court?"

"I didn't say that."

"You said—"

"I said," she corrected, "that I will not give him up without a fight, and I consider your having to prove yourself to me quite a battle, Mr. Rutledge. If you think otherwise, then you are sadly mistaken...and will probably fail," she added smugly.

Lauren was watching Sam and could see how the lines of his jaw were tightening, the cords in his neck standing out as he struggled to hold back his temper. But she sensed he would not explode. He was a gentleman, through and through, and no matter how mad Sophie Rogers made him, he would treat her with respect.

"No, I will not fail," he responded to her calmly. "And I am well aware that it will be a fight all the way. I just hadn't thought of it quite so harshly."

"Harsh?" She laughed. "Mr. Rutledge, I just finished

trying to make you see how much that baby means to me. So I warn you—be very careful, because if I do, ultimately, find reasons for disapproval, I will use those reasons in my defense against your claim for custody of Jamie."

"Well, would you like to know what I'm beginning to think?" Sam asked, then continued without waiting for her response. "That you only wanted me to come out here in hopes of finding ammunition against me."

"Could be," she admitted.

Sam charged, "So you're going to make things as unpleasant as possible to try to bring out the worst in me."

"Oh, please," she scoffed, lifting a hand from the steering wheel to wave airily. "Regardless of your opinion of me, I wouldn't stoop that low. But, of course, if the thought of assuming such a great responsibility as fatherhood ultimately causes stress that makes you react in a less than desirable way, well, what can I say?"

She turned her gaze from the traffic long enough to give him an infuriating smile.

Lauren decided it was time for her to intercede. "I think maybe we've gotten off on the wrong foot here. Could we just start over?"

Sophie glared at her again and challenged, "Young woman. How do I know that you two didn't just jump off in the last day or two and get married because of all this?"

"We have a marriage certificate to prove it." Sam reached into his pocket.

"Don't bother." Sophie sneered. "You could have had the date faked. For that matter, the whole thing might be faked. You might not even be married."

Lauren pressed her head against the window, moving from Sophie's line of vision in the mirror should she still be watching her. She was afraid the truth might show on her face, for suddenly she felt awful about the whole thing and wished, again, that she had never gotten involved. How embarrassing it would be if Sophie found out it was all a sham.

"Well, we are married," Sam was saying, his quiet rage making it easy for him to lie and sound convincing. "And we will make you see that the place for Jamie is with us. I'm his father. You can't deny that. And Lauren wants to be a mother to him. We have only the best intentions."

Lauren felt the need to show her support. "He's right, Mrs. Rogers. Now can we please start over and try to be friends? How about if we begin by calling each other by our first names? Would it be all right if I call you Sophie?"

Grudgingly, Sophie nodded.

"Great. There's no need in our being so formal if we're going to be living in the same house."

"And a small house at that," Sophie said, sounding pleased.

"Small?" Lauren felt her heart slam into her chest. She had hoped the house would be large enough they could have plenty of privacy.

"Yes, small," Sophie confirmed. Then she asked of Sam, "Didn't you tell me you were once stationed at the naval base here?"

He nodded.

"Then surely you remember that most homes here are small because real estate is very expensive...even for *very* small houses. Especially when they're near the water like mine. I live across the street from the beach, but my home is quite modest. Three bedrooms. Two baths. Living room, dining and kitchen. That's about it.

"So..." she concluded. "If you two were planning on hiding from me, I'm afraid you're going to be greatly disappointed. It's just not possible in my house."

Sam was clenching his fists in his lap. "We have nothing to hide."

"Then there's nothing to worry about, is there? We'll all be just one, big, happy family."

"For how long?" he asked sharply.

"I don't know yet."

He pushed on. "You were vague on the phone. You're being vague now. My company would like some idea—"

"I told you. A month. Maybe longer."

Sam was seething, Lauren could tell. She ached to sneak her hand across his seat to give him a comforting pat on his shoulder but was afraid of how he might react. She wasn't his wife. Actually, she was nothing to him except an employee, and it wasn't her place to touch him—not when it wasn't part of their performance. He might be so stunned, he'd jump straight up and hit his head on the roof of the car, and that would never do. No, it was better to sit quietly and let him do battle with Sophie, who was turning out to be quite a formidable foe.

In the ensuing silence that had dropped like an invisible curtain, Lauren drank in the beauty of the night as they crossed the arching Coronado Bridge. Below, the azure waters sparkled with lights from anchored boats and the bridge itself.

On land once more, Lauren could see in the late-evening light that flowers seemed to be blooming everywhere—bougainvillea, azaleas, jasmine and roses. Palm trees swayed in the gentle breeze.

And the houses, she observed, were as Sophie said. None of them was very large. "It's all very pretty here," she was moved to comment. "It must be a wonderful place to live."

"It is," Sophie assured her, actually sounding amiable for the first time. "The real estate is too expensive for tourists, so almost everyone is a local. The military rentals are away from the water, so everything near the Hotel Del Coronado is upscale.

"The Del, by the way," she went on to explain, "is quite a landmark here. You can see the red towers in the distance. A lot of movies have been filmed there. Presidents and royalty have stayed there. It's quite magnificent."

"I can't wait to see the inside of it," Lauren said.

"And we have no crime here," Sophie continued proudly. "Absolutely none whatsoever. And you'll notice how clean everything is. Traffic is minimal. I ride my bicycle everywhere I go. I hardly use my car at all.''

"That sounds like fun,'' Lauren murmured. "I haven't ridden a bike since I was a kid.'' Maybe, she thought, pleased that Sophie was suddenly being nice, things would mellow and wouldn't be as terrible as she had first thought.

Sophie turned the car into a flower-edged driveway and came to a stop before a closed garage door and announced, "This is it.''

All Lauren could tell amidst the thick shrubs and palm trees was that the house appeared to be of white stucco and had a red tile roof.

"Sam, you can get the bags,'' Sophie said as she got out of the car. "We'll eat now. You've probably got jet lag and don't feel like a heavy meal, so I just made a salad for dinner.''

"No,'' Sam said firmly, stubbornly, as he stepped out of the car.

Sophie had taken a few steps up the walkway toward the front porch, which was nearly obscured by the draping trumpet vines, but turned to stare at him quizzically. "What did you say?''

He snapped each word like a cracking whip. "I said no. I want to see my son before I do anything else.'' He stood with hands on his hips, feet slightly apart. "The luggage can wait. Dinner can wait.''

Lauren went to stand beside him.

She wasn't thinking how it was a good move on her part, to play the role of supportive wife.

It just seemed the natural thing to do when her heart went out to him in his frustration.

"I would prefer,'' Sophie said icily, eyes narrowed, "that you wait until morning.''

But Sam was not to be dissuaded. "I hate to just walk right into your house and start searching every room, but if you don't show me to him, that's exactly what I am going to do.''

Lauren covered his fist with her hand, and he wrapped his fingers about hers. Together they faced Sophie as one.

Sophie's lips worked nervously, silently, as she assessed the situation. "Very well," she said finally. "If you insist, I'll take you to him, but he's probably asleep, and if you wake him, he'll be up for hours."

Sam squeezed Lauren's hand as he smiled down at her and said to Sophie, "That's okay. We'll tend to him if he is. We won't be going to bed anytime soon."

"It's going on nine o'clock," Sophie grumbled, but then, with a ragged sigh, motioned them to follow her.

Lauren was sure that Sophie was unaccustomed to having anyone question her wishes, and it was not setting well with her at all. But so be it. It was understandable that Sam would want to see his son before doing anything else.

They stepped through the front door into a foyer. An archway to one side framed a living room furnished with plush sofas and chairs in earthy tones of blue, peach and sand. A potted twisted ficus tree gave the room an outdoorsy accent, and baskets of fragrant gardenias sweetened the air. Marble floors were mostly covered with expensive alpaca rugs.

A woman seemed to appear from out of nowhere, and Sophie, still disgruntled, asked her, "Is he asleep?"

"Yes," the woman replied. "He has been for over an hour now. He's down for the night."

"Well, not anymore," Sophie disputed irritably. "Thanks for staying, Gertrude. I'll call you tomorrow."

The woman left and Sophie led the way on down the hall.

Lauren could feel Sam's excitement and felt so happy for him. She knew if she were about to see her child for the first time, she'd probably be crying with joy.

There were three doors opening into the hallway, and Lauren was hoping against hope that the first one would be the bedroom where she and Sam would stay. It was opposite the two on the other side, one of which she noted as she glanced through the open door, had to be Sophie's. The bed was slightly rumpled, magazines scattered about, and a fat, white cat was curled up on the pillows.

Please let the nursery be the next one to it, she prayed. Thoughts of having to sleep on the other side of the wall from Sophie was something she did not want to think about. No doubt, she'd be nosy enough to have her ear to the wall to catch any sound.

Lauren's prayer, however, was quickly answered.

And the answer was no.

The guest room was, indeed, beside Sophie's, because Sophie motioned them to the other room, the one opposite hers, which looked more like a miniature version of a toy store than a bedroom.

In the gentle glow of a night-light, Lauren could see stuffed animals everywhere. The walls were covered in images of Winnie the Pooh and other childhood favorites. Colorful mobiles hung from the ceiling, and blue curtains adorned with puppy dogs framed the windows.

There was a yellow-painted dresser decorated with balloons, a changing table and, in the corner, a crib.

As Sam slowly crossed the room, Lauren was sure she could hear the thundering of his heart.

She did not want to intrude on the hallowed moment but caught a glimpse of Sophie watching her and knew it was expected that she would also be anxious to meet Jamie. After all, she was supposed to be looking forward to being his mother.

"Oh my God," Sam whispered hoarsely. "Would you look at that? He's magnificent."

Lauren stepped beside him and caught her breath in shared wonder.

Jamie was lying on his tummy, his fat, diapered bottom poking up in the air. His face was to the side, and he was making soft little smacking noises with his rosebud lips.

His hair was damp against his forehead, and Lauren could not resist touching a silky strand. She smiled to see how Sam had slipped his finger inside one of Jamie's tiny fists.

Then, miraculously, as though he knew somehow who Sam was, Jamie's hand opened to close about his daddy's finger.

"My son," Sam whispered brokenly. And, as though swept by the need to share the wonder and the joy, he wrapped an arm about Lauren to pull her against him.

She felt a quickening and was left to wonder whether it came from the moment...or from how he was holding her so close.

Chapter Eight

Lauren had slept little, as needles of worry kept her mind tossing and turning along with her body.

She lay on her side facing toward the window and could see the gray mist of morning through the partially opened blinds. Sam had told her the day usually began that way in this part of California—overcast and gloomy, but in a few hours the clouds would yield to dazzling sunshine and brilliant blue skies.

She could see the crimson hyacinths on the bushes lining the driveway and thought again how wonderful it was to have flowers blooming in the middle of winter.

The window was open to the near-balmy temperature, and she could smell the sweetness of jasmine and eucalyptus.

From somewhere in the distance she could hear the steady buzz of a lawn mower.

But there was no sound within the house. No one was

stirring about, and she could not hear a baby crying. All was quiet and still.

She grimaced to think how badly she needed to go to the bathroom but hated to get out of bed while Sam was still in the room. Personal needs were not something she'd had time to contemplate before they'd left.

Last night Sam had been unable to tear himself away from Jamie's crib. Lauren could tell he'd been aching to pick him up and hold him, but reluctant to do so because of Sophie standing there, practically daring him to wake him up. So he had continued to hover, marveling at the sight of his sleeping son.

Long moments had passed, and finally Sophie had said she'd like to show them around the house.

"Go with her," Sam had urged Lauren. "I want to stay a while longer."

So Lauren had dutifully followed after Sophie as she led her on a grand tour.

It was lavish and lovely, and Lauren could not help ooh-ing and aahing over the tasteful decor. She had expected thick drapes at the windows, lots of antiques and cluttering, dust-collecting bric-a-brac, pictures of long-dead relatives in ornate frames and many cats lazing about amidst the odor of litter boxes. To her surprise, everything was contemporary.

Lauren noted an expensive cockatoo on the glassed-in porch, and the only scent other than floral was the zesty, salty smell of the ocean just across the street.

There was a formal dining room, as well as a cozy breakfast nook with a bay window overlooking the rose garden and a small swimming pool.

"Just big enough to get you wet," Sophie had said of the pool. "Who needs anything larger with the ocean at your front door?"

Lauren had agreed, thinking all the while that any size pool was a treat for her.

Then Sophie had made the pointed comment as to how,

when Jamie got older, she would have the pool drained and filled in, for she intended to take no chances with his safety.

Lauren had kept silent, not about to start anything by remarking that would not be necessary, because Jamie was going to live in Atlanta. It was Sam's responsibility to spar with Sophie. Not hers. Still, it rankled, for she knew Sophie had said that only to goad.

Wondering what time it was, Lauren rolled over to check the clock on the nightstand. It was nearly seven. Back home it was almost ten o'clock. Though she still felt tired, she might as well get up. She was wearing an oversize cotton tee, which was anything but sexy, so even if Sam did wake up, nothing was revealed.

She would have preferred to just keep staring out the window, pretending to be asleep, until Sam woke up and left the room. She did not like seeing him curled up on the floor with nothing between him and the cold terrazzo except for the bedspread. But there was nowhere else. No sofa. No lounge chair. In fact, the only other furniture in the large room was a dresser and an old rocker.

"This was probably Gaynelle's room," Lauren had said when he had finally come in from the nursery. "I imagine after she died, Sophie just wanted to get rid of all the memories."

Sam had glanced about, then said, "Well, I'll be fine on the floor."

Now he lay on his side, facing her. His eyes were closed but his brow was furrowed, evidence of his discomfort. He had slept in his clothes, saying he was too tired to unpack.

Slowly she pushed back the sheet and sat up, again thinking how the room was large enough for more furniture. Then she noticed how, in the morning light, there was a slight color variance in different areas of the floor.

As she walked about for closer scrutiny, her suspicions were confirmed that there had, indeed, been other pieces of furniture in the room.

So why had they been moved out? If Sophie had wanted

to get rid of every reminder of Gaynelle, why leave the bed and dresser? Though nice, they were old. It just didn't make sense she would remove everything else, unless—

Lauren's eyes fell on Sam.

Unless, she was jolted to think, Sophie suspected chicanery and wanted to make things as difficult as possible by giving them no option except to share the same bed.

Suddenly Lauren gasped as she remembered something.

Last night, when she had prepared to undress, she had instinctively gone to the door to lock it. She did not want Sam to walk in on her naked. Only, there had been no lock. She hadn't found it odd at the time, but now she hurried to the door for closer scrutiny.

Seeing the marks on the door, her hand flew to her mouth.

There *had* been a lock at one time but it had been removed.

Sophie could enter any time she chose. But surely, Lauren frantically rationalized, she'd not be so bold.

Still, she would take no chances. First, she would get dressed, then awaken Sam. He'd have to go to a hardware store and buy a lock, and—

She was almost to the bathroom when the door opened and nightmare became reality.

Sophie was poking her head inside the room.

She saw Lauren and called softly, "Breakfast is almost ready." Then her eyes fell on Sam and she cried, "What on earth is he doing on the floor?"

Lauren groped for an answer, finally stammering, "He…he didn't want to wake me. I…was asleep when he came in, and—"

"What the—" Sam heard and sat up, groggily trying to figure out where he was and what was going on. Looking from Lauren's ashen face and then to Sophie's startled expression, he swore under his breath.

Sophie was the first to recover. "Breakfast will be ready in ten minutes."

She closed the door.

Sam bounded to his feet. "What was she doing in here?" he asked Lauren accusingly, as though she had invited her. "Oh, man, this is all we need."

"There was no lock on the door," Lauren explained. "I think it's been removed."

He hurried to check. "Yeah, it's been removed, all right. I noticed there wasn't one last night." He was speaking in hushed tones in case Sophie was eavesdropping. He wouldn't be surprised at anything she stooped to now.

"I was going to ask you to get one and put it on today."

"Believe me, I will. But that doesn't help the situation any now. No telling what she's thinking. Me on the floor, and you dressed like that." He gestured to her baggy tee.

Lauren felt a sweep of resentment. "What's wrong with me?"

"That's not exactly honeymoon stuff."

"I didn't bring any 'honeymoon stuff,' as you call it. And how was I to know she'd walk in and see what I sleep in, anyway?"

"No doubt she was counting on you thinking that. That's why she did it." He glanced about, as though expecting all the clothes she'd brought to be on display. "Don't you have any sexy stuff?"

She thought of what she had worn when she had been involved with Stewart. Stewart had loved to see her in scant lacy outfits, and she'd enjoyed wearing them. They had made her feel very feminine and incredibly sexy. Now they were packed away in the bottom drawer of her dresser at home, because the thought of bringing them along had never occurred to her. After all, she kept reminding herself, this was supposed to be strictly business.

"Well?" Sam prodded.

"Yes, I do," she said stiffly. "But not with me."

"All right. We can buy some."

"There's no need. I'm not sleeping in them."

"So okay. Don't. But if you have occasion to be around Sophie in the middle of the night, you can put one on."

Lauren, exasperated, said, "Whatever. Now, will you please get out of here so I can get my shower, unless you think she expects us to bathe together."

"She probably does. And if we were really married, I'd want to," he could not resist adding.

"Well, we aren't, so don't even think about it." She bit back a smile, aware he was just trying to tease her into a better mood.

Fleeing to the bathroom and locking the door, she leaned against it as dizzy waves swept over her. How was she ever going to get through the next weeks? It had been bad enough coping with her emotions as her desire for Sam grew each time they were together. Now she was also going to have to attempt to deal with the instant affection she had felt for his son.

Last night, as she had stood by and watched Sam's ecstatic face when Jamie squeezed his finger, she had been swept by an overwhelming longing to likewise reach for a precious little hand. More, her heart had ached to cuddle him and hold him close.

She looked at herself in the mirror over the vanity and shook her head in misery. Ten thousand dollars—or even a million, for that matter—would never compensate for all the anguish she had yet to face.

After all, how could she not help but fall in love with a motherless infant and long to care for him and raise him as her own?

Suddenly, the weeks ahead loomed long and weary...and miserable.

After showering, Lauren dressed in shorts, shirts and sandals—typical California style.

She finished unpacking, made the bed and finally decided she could not postpone facing Sophie any longer. She'd said it would be ten minutes till breakfast, and Lauren had taken a half hour. Sam would doubtless have been on time and soothed things over as to their weird sleeping arrangement last night.

It was safe, she decided, to join them.

But, to Lauren's horror, when she walked into the breakfast nook, Sam was nowhere around.

"He's taking a shower in the bathroom off the nursery," Sophie said in her usual chilling tone. "He said you were too slow."

Lauren's nervousness faded as she sat down next to Jamie in his high chair. Sophie was on the other side, methodically spooning oatmeal into his mouth.

He was wearing a blue shorts set, and Lauren could see he was plump and looked quite healthy.

"Hello there, cutie," she said, smiling and feeling warm all over. Babies had that effect on her, making her happy and glad to be alive. She gently tapped a finger to his rosy cheek, and he responded with a wide, dimpled grin and a gurgle that sent oatmeal drooling down his chin.

She grabbed a napkin and wiped it away before Sophie could make a move.

"You can finish feeding him," Sophie said, shoving the spoon across the table. "I'm trying to keep breakfast warm."

Eagerly, Lauren took over as Jamie clapped his chubby hands in delight to have a new playmate.

"I'm sorry we're late," she offered. "I guess it will take us a few days to get used to the time difference." She felt the need to say something about Sam sleeping on the floor, but what explanation could she give?

"You know anything about babies?"

Lauren's laugh was nervous. "Well, I think I bought every book ever published on the subject." And she had, only there had not been a lot of time for her to study them, so she had brought them with her.

Sophie placed a mug of coffee in front of her. "Cream and sugar is on the table," she said. Then she asked, haven't you had any experience with babies? Any little brothers or sisters that you helped take care of? Nieces? Nephews?''

"Actually, I'm an orphan and, no, I don't have any experience. I know practically nothing. But I'm certainly willing and eager to learn.''

"Well, you better learn fast," Sophie said curtly, "because he's all yours.''

Lauren looked from Jamie to Sophie in hopeful wonder. It sounded as though her mind was made up, as if she was handing over custody then and there.

"I mean," Sophie said, hands on her hips and a gleam in her eye, "that you can get your feet wet from the get-go, honey, like any new mother has to do. Use your books or whatever it takes, but I intend to find out whether or not you'll make a fit mother for my great-grandson.

"And don't forget, if I see that you won't," she added with a smirk and a punctuating wink, "I'll see you in court.''

Lauren's hand, holding a heaping spoonful of oatmeal, paused in midair. She was stunned, for she'd not anticipated confrontation...or an ultimatum.

Jamie, his hands impatiently waving, hit the spoon and sent the oatmeal flying across the table. Seeing the mess he'd made, he squealed with delight.

Momentarily, Lauren was able to forget about Sophie as she turned her full attention to the baby. "Little imp," she playfully scolded, wiping up the mess and cleaning his hand. "You don't fool around when you're eating, do you?''

She began to feed him again, and he rewarded her with coos and giggles and twinkling eyes as he wormed his way ever deeper into her heart.

"So you're mine," she whispered to him conspiratorially. "That means we can play together all day and have lots of fun. How would you like to go to the beach later and play in the sand? Meanwhile, I'll bet we can find a stroller around here someplace, and I'll take you for a nice long walk. You can show me around town, and—"

"Will you look at that."

Sam walked in, hair damp from the shower, and planted a kiss on top of Jamie's head before kneeling beside him to exclaim in wonder, "I can't believe you're real. Did you know that? You're like a dream come true. I've always wanted a little boy like you."

Jamie giggled. Whatever the man with the shining eyes was saying, it made him happy.

Sam asked Lauren, "How are you two getting along?"

Before she could respond, Sophie came out of the kitchen. She did not mince words but got right to the point as she addressed Sam. "I want to know why you were sleeping on the floor last night."

Sam straightened and met her steely gaze with one of his own. "Of course, you do, Sophie, and I can explain, but the fact remains that you wouldn't have known about it if you hadn't walked in without knocking."

She glanced away. "I knocked. Nobody heard me."

Lauren shook her head ever so slightly at Sam to let him know that Sophie was lying.

He was aware of that but did not want to come right out and say so. Instead, he said, "All right. Maybe you did. But I'll fix the lock today. Lauren and I like our privacy."

"You still haven't said why you were on the floor."

"I didn't want to wake her when I came in last night. She was tired and needed her sleep."

In a gesture meant to convey he considered the subject closed, he walked around to stand behind Lauren and caress her shoulders as he said, "Honey, I should've counted bags at the airport yesterday and realized the one with your lingerie was missing. I'll call and report it, and meanwhile we'll go shopping this afternoon and get you a few things. You can't keep sleeping in my tees."

Lauren's hand began to tremble. Afraid Sophie would notice, she put the spoon down and then began wiping off

Jamie's face, murmuring that he'd probably had enough. And all the while, her insides were churning at the thought of Sam buying her filmy, sexy nighties. Well, she wouldn't wear them, she decided then and there. Once another lock was put on the door, Sophie wouldn't know what she slept in. But if he wanted to do it for effect, so be it. It was his money.

"I think it's time we understood each other."

Sam and Lauren turned to Sophie.

"I don't know why you were sleeping on the floor last night, Sam, but if the two of you are trying to put something over on me, you can bet I'll find out about it.

"As for you," she addressed Lauren, "I don't give a tinker's damn what you sleep in. I only care about what kind of mother you'll make, and rest assured, you won't fool me if you're putting on an act. I'm a better judge of character than either of you realize, and I won't be easily fooled."

She disappeared into the kitchen, leaving Sam and Lauren staring after her in stunned silence.

Lauren was the first to speak, for Jamie had grown bored with sitting in the high chair and begun to fuss. She reached for him. "Let's get you out of there, little guy. I've got a sneaking suspicion I'm about to change my first messy diaper."

She lifted him in her arms. Cuddling him, she kissed each cheek in turn, then brushed her face against his hair and whispered, "There's no sweeter smell in the world than a baby. If anyone ever learns to bottle it, they'll make a fortune in the perfume industry."

Sam laughed but at the same time was moved by the sight of her holding his son. Yielding to impulse, he wrapped them both in his arms.

Lauren, startled, turned her face, only to find her lips mere inches from his.

Sam kissed her.

It seemed only natural.

And he kissed her deeply.

She yielded, returning the passion that quickly ignited.

Sam's tongue slipped inside her mouth, and she felt the heat rising from her loins as her pulse quickened.

A clattering made them spring apart.

Sophie was placing bowls of fruit on the table. She said nothing but her quick, jerky movements indicated she was annoyed to think the kiss, along with the cozy family embrace, had been staged for her benefit.

Shaken, Lauren hurried to the nursery, with Jamie held tight in her arms.

It had not been staged.

At least not on her part.

And it had been... *wonderful.*

Chapter Nine

Sam's heart was full to bursting as he watched Lauren and Jamie in the garden. Holding the baby in her arms, she moved about with all the grace of the delicate butterfly she pointed out to Jamie, who laughed with glee as he clapped his chubby little hands.

Sam was standing at the kitchen window, having obligingly washed the dishes after breakfast at Sophie's request...which hadn't been a request at all, but an order. She had a tennis date at the Hotel Del Coronado's courts, she'd said, and with him and Lauren around, she saw no need for the expense of having the housekeeper come in every day.

Sam didn't mind helping out. He was not the type to regard household chores as gender designated. What rankled, however, was realizing Sophie intended to make the coming weeks as difficult as possible.

She had, he knew, deliberately removed all the furniture from the bedroom so the bed would be the only place to sleep. Did she suspect they were pretending to be married? And, if so, did she think she could embarrass them by forcing them into the same bed?

It just didn't make sense, because he'd already latched on to the fact that Sophie was no blue-haired, cookie-baking grandma. She was sharp as a tack, and kept up with what was going on in the world, so she was well aware that men and women, whether married or not, were not embarrassed to sleep together and have sex.

The part about not having the maid he could understand. Sophie was trying to justify her opinion that he had no sense of responsibility. And he couldn't really blame her for feeling that way, since all she had to go on was the type of men Gaynelle had brought home in the past. Maybe he had actually been just like them…then.

But things had changed.

He was different.

Life was different.

And he intended to accept and fulfill each and every responsibility that life handed him.

Only, now it was Sophie dishing things out, and she was doing it with a *pitchfork*.

"My, my, aren't we the picture of motherhood?"

He whipped about at the sound of Sophie's voice.

She was standing in the doorway dressed entirely in white—blouse, short pleated skirt, shoes. Even the sweatband holding back her dyed red bangs was white, and she was carrying a tennis racket.

Sam turned his gaze back to the window and quietly remarked, "Yes, she is. Lauren will make a wonderful mother."

"Hmph," Sophie snorted. "It takes more than walking around and showing a baby butterflies to make someone a good mother. Yesterday she was a career woman, clean and neat and soaring in the business world. Today she's changing another woman's baby and having oatmeal spat in her face. Not very glamorous, I'd say."

"But decidedly more rewarding."

"We'll see. This is just her first day."

Sam turned on her then. Perhaps it was best to have it out then and there and stop playing games. "I know you're hoping I'll decide fatherhood isn't for me and forget about claiming Jamie, but believe me, it's not going to happen."

Sophie's chin jutted upward. "Need I remind you that I will fight for Jamie?"

"And how many times do *I* have to remind *you* that in the long run you can't win?"

"But you would lose Jamie's inheritance if you make me fight you."

He met her blazing glare with one of his own. "That's the key word here, isn't it, Sophie? *Jamie's* inheritance. Not mine. His. I wouldn't be able to touch it, and you know it. And besides, I'd never do that, anyway, even if I could."

"I'm not naive enough to believe an unscrupulous lawyer couldn't find a way around the contingencies of a trust. He could ask the court for stipends along the way for concocted reasons. You'd be able to dip your finger into the money pie if you were ever tempted, and you know it."

"And you think that's the only reason I want him, don't you?"

"That's right." She nodded towards the window and Lauren and Jamie beyond. "And her, too. But enough of this. I shouldn't have said what I did when I came in. That was wrong of me. I apologize."

Sam's brow furrowed with suspicion.

"But I must say," she continued, "that when and if I decide you won't make suitable parents for Jamie, that it isn't going to work out for me to peacefully relinquish him to you, I will ask you to leave and expect you to do so without argument."

"That won't happen," Sam assured. "About your deciding we aren't suitable, I mean. We're going to prove it to you. If I didn't think we'd be able to, believe me, I wouldn't have gone to the trouble of coming all the way out here and making arrangements to stay so long."

"Well, I don't mind telling you that I'm not impressed so far."

"Because you walked in and saw me sleeping on the floor?" He laughed. "That doesn't prove anything."

Again she lifted her chin, this time with a jeering chuckle. "Oh, really? I wasn't born yesterday, Sam. I know a little about a lot of things—one of them being that when a man and woman have a good relationship, one of them doesn't sleep on a terrazzo floor with a folded bedspread for a mattress. So something is wrong somewhere, and you can believe sooner or later I'll find out what it is."

"But—"

Sophie turned on her heel and walked out, leaving him staring after her.

He threw up his hands in frustration. Damn it, what could she be thinking? Surely not that he and Lauren weren't really married. Probably she suspected their marriage was in trouble already, and Lauren had kicked him out of bed.

He had to remedy that.

Had to make Sophie think different.

But how?

The sound of Jamie crying took his attention to the window once more. He saw that Sophie had stopped to say goodbye to him, and he was crying after her. It was obvious Lauren wasn't sure what to do, so he hurried outside to see if he could help.

Taking Jamie from Lauren, he tried to soothe him by patting him on the back and talking baby talk, only Jamie wasn't impressed. He stiffened his legs and screamed all the louder.

"She's walking to the hotel," Lauren fretted as she stared after Sophie. "She can hear him crying. Oh, what must she think?"

"That she left Jamie with people he isn't used to yet, and he's upset, but it's no big deal. What else could she think?'' he snapped, then, seeing Lauren's expression, instantly apologized. "Hey, I'm sorry. I didn't mean to be so short with you. How about if we get ready and go shopping? He'll like that.''

Lauren wasn't interested in the shopping part—only in finding a way to get Jamie to stop crying, which he kept doing until she had located the stroller and had him strapped in. Then he settled down, focusing his attention on the colorful beads across the front brace of the stroller.

"You know, she's really not so bad," Lauren remarked as they walked side by side, pushing the stroller. "She just loves him and wants the best for him, that's all."

"Maybe," Sam said. "But you don't know how tempted I am to tell her where she can stick his inheritance, and probably would if it weren't for having lost my own and knowing what it's like."

They each had a hand on the stroller's handle, and Lauren felt a delicious ripple when, as he got a better grip, they brushed against each other.

The sun had finally broken through the clouds, and a balmy breeze was blowing in off the ocean. It was a gorgeous day. People they met along the way smiled and said hello. A few paused to admire Jamie and say things that made him sweetly coo his own style of greeting.

It was, Lauren could not help thinking, a very easy way to make ten thousand dollars—but also a very miserable way, because no matter how hard she tried to keep things in perspective, there was no denying she was attracted to Sam.

And falling more in love with Jamie every second.

She protested when Sam spotted a lingerie boutique and insisted she go inside and buy several gowns and robes.

"I like my sleep shirts," she argued.

"We talked about this before," he patiently reminded her. "Sophie is making a big deal out of finding me on the floor. We've got to make her think that we're head over heels in love, and that you'll do everything possible to make yourself look attractive for me.''

Lauren pretended to be hurt. "You mean I'm not attractive in my big old sleep shirts?"

"Hell, yes," he said without thinking, then caught himself and tried to recover. "Not that it matters. I mean, not personally. But naturally, if I didn't find you attractive I wouldn't have chosen you for the job. *That's* what I meant to say."

Lauren's smile faded. What a fool she was. Of course, he was all business. She meant nothing to him and never would, and she was behaving like a silly schoolgirl by turning to mush every time he touched her.

Like the kiss in the breakfast nook.

It had been for show, intended solely to impress Sophie. It had not meant anything to him, and she could not let it mean anything to her, either.

He sensed what she was thinking and said, "Look. About this morning, I didn't—"

"I know." She cut him off before he could finish. "You didn't mean anything by that kiss. It was for Sophie." She gave a little laugh. "Don't you think I knew that? We talked about all this on the plane, remember? Relax, Sam. You don't have to apologize to me. I'm with you all the way on this."

"Good," he said, swallowing against the maelstrom of emotions churning within. He had enjoyed the kiss but had to remember it was all business with her. He couldn't let himself get carried away.

"So with that understanding," he managed to say breezily, "how about buying some nice lingerie? Sophie will see you wearing it when you tuck Jamie in or get up with him during the night. It's a nice effect."

Lauren gritted her teeth.

He was so into their role-playing, he probably wouldn't be turned on if she slept nude.

He didn't look upon her as a desirable woman he could ever feel romantic about.

Oh, no.

She was just some money-hungry bimbo out to make a buck any way she could, and he didn't give a damn about her and never would.

Play the role.

That's all he was interested in.

Help me get my baby without a court battle, take your money and then have a nice life, kiddo.

Furiously, silently, she was fuming.

Well, we'll just see about that, buster.

Sam waited with Jamie in a little park across the street from the boutique while Lauren went inside. She selected two beautiful peignoir sets, one in blue and one in pink. Then she moved to the more risqué section, where she bought a black see-through number that left little to the imagination.

As she paid for her purchases, she wondered whether she would really have the nerve to wear the black gown to deliberately try to entice Sam.

And, more important, what would she do if it worked?

Enjoy, she thought with a wicked smile.

Only, it would never happen.

Sam would see to it.

They stopped for lunch at an outdoor café.

Sophie had efficiently left information as to Jamie's food and schedule taped to a kitchen cabinet. Lauren was then able to pack a little bag with everything she would need during their outing. While she and Sam waited for their tuna salad plates to be prepared, she fed Jamie.

He was still taking his bottle when their order arrived. Sam offered to take over so she could eat, but she declined. "I'm really enjoying this. I never knew it was so much fun feeding a baby. He's so soft and warm and cuddly.'' Her heart squeezed with pleasure as she gazed down at him.

"But you don't have to put yourself out,'' he pointed out gingerly. "I mean, when we're alone, without Sophie breathing down our necks, I can take care of him. After all, it's something I've got to get used to doing on my own.''

Jamie was snuggled in her arms, his little head resting contentedly against her bosom. His fingers opened and closed against hers as she held his bottle. He was taking little pauses between sucking, his eyes closed. She knew he would soon be fast asleep. Smiling down at him, she said, "I don't mind at all. After all, you'll soon have him all to yourself, and I'll never see him again.''

Sam really hadn't thought of it that way, but she had made her feelings for children quite clear. It would probably be hard on her to say goodbye to Jamie. "But you'll have babies of your own one day.''

"That's right,'' Lauren was quick to agree, not about to let him see how she had so easily bonded with Jamie and ached to think of eventually having to walk away from him.

Sam held out his arms. "So let me have him. I've got to learn to take care of him myself.''

"Are you sure? You really don't know anything about babies, Sam. You haven't even looked at one of those books I brought along.''

He laughed. "How tough can it be? Women aren't the only ones who know how to care for babies. Now come on. Let me have him. He's mine, Lauren.''

As if Jamie were a toy being claimed by a selfish playmate, Lauren reluctantly handed him over.

Sam, however, was awkward with him and, as babies so often do, Jamie felt insecure and became frightened. His eyes flashed open and, seeing a strange face, he spit the nipple out and began to cry lustily.

Lauren bit back a smile as she picked up her fork and began to eat her tuna salad.

Sam jiggled him and bounced him as he attempted to

manipulate the nipple back into his mouth, but Jamie was working into a frenzy. He was also swallowing air, which made him gassy on top of the milk he'd just consumed, and a bellyache was fast developing, causing him to cry even harder.

He needs burping, smartie, Lauren thought. *And you're about to find out just how tough it can get, because I'm not going to tell you anything.*

And Sam was stubbornly not about to ask for help.

"Come on, little fellow," he coaxed. "Eat up. You'll feel better."

As Jamie screamed louder, a few of the other café patrons began to dart them annoyed glances.

Lauren felt sorry for Jamie, knowing he was in distress, and wondered how much longer she could refrain from snatching him from Sam's arms. And she was just about to do so when a grandmotherly sort sitting at the next table turned around and said to Sam, "For heaven's sake. The child needs burping."

Sam blinked helplessly. "Burping?" he echoed lamely.

"Yes, burping. Young people." The woman sighed with disgust, then got up out of her chair and walked over to Sam and Lauren's table.

Lauren was having a difficult time holding back giggles, and covered her mouth with her napkin, pretending to be wiping her mouth.

"Here. Let me." The woman held out her arms.

With a helpless shrug, Sam relinquished Jamie, then watched in fascination as the woman placed him on her shoulder and gave him several firm pats on his back.

In response, Jamie gave a loud, relieved burp.

There was laughter and applause, as Jamie's face lit up with a big smile of relief.

Giving Jamie back to Sam, the woman said, "A body would think you two just had this kid handed to you and don't know what to do with him. He's at least six months old. You ought to be able to tell when he needs burping."

She returned to her table to exchange critical murmurs with her companion.

Jamie, still unhappy to have unsure arms holding him, began to fret again.

"Want me to take him?" Lauren asked sweetly.

"You knew what was wrong with him," Sam accused. "You said you wanted to learn, and you did."

Sam could not really be mad with her, not when he found that mischievous little twinkle in her eyes so delightful. "Okay, wise guy." He grinned. "If you know so much, what's wrong with him now?"

She took a sip of iced tea, then nodded to the way he was holding Jamie a little away from him. "You're scared to death, and he senses it."

"But he's wiggling. I don't want to drop him, and I don't want to squeeze him to death."

"You can be firm without squeezing, Sam. Let me show you."

She took the baby and immediately he settled down.

"He feels your fright. Relax. And he will, too."

Sam grunted and began picking at his tuna. He was no longer hungry, felt like an idiot, knew he had a hell of a lot to learn and wished the charade could hurry up and be over with so he could get on with his life.

And also get busy trying to forget those mischievous, twinkling eyes.

Sophie was cooly pleasant during dinner, but it was obvious Sam and Lauren had far to go before winning her approval.

Sam tried small talk.

"We had a great day. Jamie was happy as a lark. We took him all over town. He was great, wasn't he, Lauren?"

Lauren's head bobbed up and down obediently. "Yes. Yes, he was. No problem at all."

Sam opined, "We aren't going to have any trouble at all once we get home. I can see that already."

Sophie had made a chocolate mousse for dessert that had turned out splendidly, and she was enjoying toying with the whipped cream dolloped on top. With a crisp smile aimed in Sam's direction, she said, "Perhaps Jamie isn't the only problem to be faced."

Exchanging an anxious glance with Lauren, Sam asked warily, "What do you mean?"

"To be perfectly blunt, from what I have seen so far, I have my doubts about your marriage."

Sam blanched. "Excuse me?"

Lauren stiffened in her chair. Dear Lord, had she done such a horrible job of acting that Sophie had decided in less than twenty-four hours that she was a terrible wife?

Sophie twirled her spoon in the whipped cream, then licked it. "I'm just not sure," she said finally.

"But—"

Sophie waved him to silence with her spoon. "Please. Let's not discuss it. I have weeks to see things in a different light. For now, let's enjoy our meal."

"So what was all that about?" Lauren cried the minute they had retired to their room, the door—with its new lock—closed behind them.

Sam began to pace about restlessly. "Damned if I know. Maybe we don't give off sparks or something."

"That's understandable. I mean, we *are* role-playing."

"And seemingly not doing a very good job of it."

Lauren felt an indignant surge. "And you're blaming me, I suppose."

"No, I'm not. It's just that I had it in the back of my mind all along that we might not give off the right kind of vibes. After all, Lauren, we are strangers. But I'd hoped if that happened, she'd chalk it up to our being so wrapped up in Jamie."

It bothered Lauren to see him so upset, for she knew how much it meant to him. "Tell you what," she said brightly. "I'll wear one of my honeymoonish robes when

I go into the kitchen in the morning, and I'll try to act sleepy, like we stayed up most of the night making mad, passionate love. You come in later and kind of mush over me, and maybe that'll do the trick.''

Suddenly he snapped his fingers. "I've got a better idea.''

Lauren was wary. "Such as?''

He threw himself across the bed, landing on his stomach. Grinning, he beckoned to her and whispered, "Come on. Let's do it.''

Instinctively she retreated a step. "Do what?''

"Put on a show for her. She's right in the next room, remember? We'll make a lot of noise, and she'll hear and think we've got one hell of a sex life and stop doubting our marriage.''

"Are you out of your mind, Sam?'' Lauren hissed, her eyes going wide. "You actually think I'm going to make love to you just for her benefit? That not only wasn't part of the deal—it's also twisted.''

"Oh, get real, Lauren. I didn't say I expected us to actually do it. I just want us to pretend. Now come here and let's moan and groan.''

"You're crazy. And it's a dumb idea. It won't work.''

"Yes, it will. And it will be fun. She deserves to be fooled, especially when she's probably got her ear pressed to the bottom of a glass stuck to the wall to hear any sound we make in here. Now come on.''

He bounded off the bed, grabbed her arm and pulled her back down with him and promptly began to bounce up and down on the bed as he made soft, moaning sounds.

Lauren started giggling. It was all so silly and ridiculous.

"If you can't moan, at least don't giggle,'' he growled with mock anger, covering her face with a pillow to stifle the sound.

Then, hearing him cry out, "Oh, Lauren, darling, you're wonderful, it's wonderful...'' she burst into gales of uncontrollable laughter.

Sam continued to bounce, the mattress squeaking rhythmically, and Lauren eventually joined in the fun and shoved away the pillow to say loudly, "Oh, Sam. Oh, darling, oh darling..."

Then they both began to laugh, and by the time Sam took the mattress to simulated climax, they were covering their own faces with pillows.

Afterward, they lay side by side, still rocked with amusement over what they'd done.

Then, suddenly, and without warning, the soft chuckles disappeared in the wake of awareness of each other...and how, in the midst of the humorous moment, arms and legs had become entangled, their bodies fused together.

They looked at each other for long, tense moments, then, as if on cue, sprang apart at the same instant.

Feeling very self-conscious, Lauren hurried to the bathroom to shower and change into her big, baggy tee, then crawled under the sheet and turned her face to the wall.

She heard Sam follow after her to the shower.

Moments later, she felt him gently draw away the spread to make his bed on the floor.

Chapter Ten

Between learning firsthand how to care for a seven-month-old baby and playing the role of loving wife, Lauren forgot about her promise to call Midge.

Ironically, it was Sam who unknowingly reminded her one morning at breakfast when he suggested, "How about taking Jamie on a picnic today at Point Loma? We could buy one of those ready-made baskets at the deli in town. It'd be fun. And I remember your telling me how you and Midge used to love to picnic sometimes in that park near your condo."

Lauren, about to spoon strained peaches into Jamie's waiting mouth, froze in horror to remember her promise.

Seeing her reaction, Sam asked, "Is something wrong?"

She was no longer hearing him as she thought about Midge and how frantic she must be.

"You *do* like picnics, don't you?" Sam continued worriedly as he tried to figure out what he'd said that had apparently upset her. "We've been here over two weeks and haven't done any sightseeing. It's a beautiful day, and—''

"Midge." Her voice came out a tiny croak. "I forgot to call Midge."

Jamie stirred impatiently and began to fret. He wanted his peaches, and the grown-ups were ignoring him.

Sophie was standing at the counter on the other side of the serving window to the dining nook. She was making fresh juice from oranges she had picked in the backyard that morning, and was listening to their conversation.

Sam darted an anxious glance in Sophie's direction as he said to Lauren, "She knows you've just been busy, honey."

"She'll be crazy with worry," Lauren murmured.

"Who's Midge?" Sophie demanded.

Without thinking, Lauren answered, "My roommate."

Sophie's head jerked up. "What did you say?"

"Uh, I mean she's my ex-roommate." Lauren did not miss the stricken look on Sam's face and hurried to smooth things over lest Sophie become suspicious. "She got married not long ago and moved out."

Sophie's eyes narrowed. "How long ago?" She paused, half an orange in each hand and oblivious to the juice dripping to the floor. As she looked at them in turn, her voice pricked like a needle. "You two claimed you'd been married three months when you got here."

Sam rushed to say, "We had been. Midge got married right before we did."

"And you moved into Lauren's apartment?"

"That's right. It was bigger than mine."

"Perhaps that's something we need to discuss."

Sam, sitting at the table and nursing a cup of coffee, edgily asked, "What do you mean?"

Lauren, her hand shaking, continued to methodically feed Jamie, who was kicking his fat little legs and clapping his hands happily. Peaches were his favorite, and he enjoyed them with relish.

She would let Sam face this confrontation with Sophie as she had with all the others. After all, it was his business, not hers, and she chided herself for secretly wishing it were. She cared about Jamie and his future.

And, though it seemed she was having to fight against it with every breath she drew these days—and nights—she also cared about Jamie's daddy.

A lot.

"Surely you aren't planning to raise my great-grandson in a tiny little apartment," Sophie said, frowning.

Sam was fencing. "It's not all that tiny."

"Jamie needs a yard to play in."

"Yes. When he's older. He'll have one by then."

"And meanwhile, where is he going to play?"

"He'll be in day care during the week."

Sophie snorted. "Seems to me your wife would want to stay home and tend to him the first years."

"She'd like to. We can't afford it."

He sounded miserable. Lauren looked at him and saw that he was. But she couldn't help him. It was a battle he had to fight alone.

Sophie turned back to her juice making. "I thought you made good money. Gaynelle said you did."

"That was when I worked the offshore rigs as a troubleshooter. I'm a pencil pusher now, and that doesn't pay as much."

"Well, it should be enough that your wife could be a full-time mother and not have to work, too."

Stiffly Sam pointed out, "My wife has a name, Sophie. You talk about her as though she weren't in the room."

"And why shouldn't I?" Sophie gave a sniff of disdain. "She might as well not be anywhere around, because she never says a word. She lets you do all the talking about Jamie's future. It's as if she doesn't care."

Lauren could keep still no longer and cried, "That's not fair for you to say that, Sophie. I do care. I love Jamie and want only the best for him, and the reason I don't jump in and take part in your conversations is because you and Sam have done all the negotiations about this, and I didn't feel it was my place to get involved in that part of it. But I do care. Never think that I don't.''

She saw the way Sam was looking at her with wonder. It was the first time she had been so outspoken. Did he think she was overreacting? Should she have continued to keep silent and let them hash it out between them? This was something they had not discussed—whether she should join in any sparring with Sophie.

Sam, in an effort to ease the tension, said, ''Look, Sophie. It goes without saying that I want the very best for my son, and I'll see to it he gets it, all right?''

''Well, I don't like the idea of your putting him in a nursery. Children are little germ bombs. He'll catch every bug around and stay sick.''

''Other kids do it and survive. Jamie will be fine.''

They continued their debate, while Lauren attempted to finish feeding Jamie without being obvious she was in a hurry.

Midge was probably frantic by now. She might have even called the police and reported her missing. Lauren knew she had to get to a pay phone—and fast.

''All done,'' she said finally, brightly, wiping Jamie's peach-smeared face with his bib. ''Now let's get you bathed and ready for your picnic.''

She removed the tray of his high chair and lifted him out.

Suddenly, abruptly, Sam asked Sophie, ''So how much longer have we got to spin our wheels here?''

Lauren paused. She wanted to hear Sophie's answer as much as he did. The sooner the charade was over, the better.

Sophie began pouring juice into glasses. ''I really can't say. I haven't made up my mind yet. Until I do, I would appreciate your concentrating on trying to impress me with the stability of your marriage—as per our agreement. These conversations only serve to upset everyone.''

"I believe you started it,'' he murmured with as much politeness in his tone as he could muster.

"Touché.'' She nodded with a capitulating smile.

Lauren started out with Jamie in her arms.

"What about your breakfast?'' Sophie called.

"I'll save my appetite for the picnic.'' She kept on going, anxious to escape before she said the wrong thing.

"She makes me so damn mad,'' Sam fumed once they were loaded and on their way in Sophie's car, which she had insisted they take. "I'm tempted every day to tell her to shove it and take off, but I've come this far. I'm going to see it through.''

"I agree,'' Lauren said absently, her eyes scanning the streets for a phone booth as they drove through the little town of Coronado. "But you have to remember she's hoping you'll ultimately give up and leave.''

He shot her an incredulous look. "You mean give up and leave Jamie with her? No way. When I leave, he leaves with me.''

"She wouldn't let you take him.''

"And how would she stop me?'' He sounded mad.

Lauren could see that he was, and hated having to point out, "All she'd have to do is call her lawyer, and he'd get an immediate injunction issued to prevent your leaving the state with Jamie, pending a custody hearing. She'd do it fast, too. The police would be waiting at the airport.

"The legal battle would begin, Sam,'' she continued, "and you'd have to fight it out here—in California. It could drag on forever, and the cost would be astronomical, and she knows it.

"And what about your job?'' she ventured further. "You have to go back to work sometime. They aren't going to hold a position for you indefinitely. And I need to get back, too.''

"Once the war begins, you can go," he said, his smoldering rage making him curt. "It won't matter then if she knows the truth."

Lauren's heart went out to him in his miserable dilemma. "Yes, it would, because it would make you look bad for concocting such a scheme. She would use it against you in court. Remember, she made it very clear that she'd use whatever reason she found to make her decide you're unworthy to raise Jamie."

"I don't care. And besides, I think you're wrong. I think a judge would understand a father willing to go to any lengths to gain custody of his child."

"Depends on the judge. Remember, too, that this is Sophie's home. She probably plays tennis with every judge in the county. And it goes without saying she's very well liked and respected around here. In fact, when you stop and think about it, if you take away all this sparring between you, she's really a very likable person. I'm sorry to say it won't be easy for you, Sam."

He was gripping the steering wheel so hard, his knuckles had turned white, and she reached across the seat to touch his shoulder in an attempt to comfort him. "Let's just keep going like we have been, okay? Maybe we'll ultimately win her over. It can't be but a few more weeks. I don't think she'll want this to drag on beyond then. It can't be much fun for her, either."

His eyes left the road long enough to give her an appreciative smile. "You're really trying to do your part, Lauren, and I want you to know I appreciate it. I made a good choice when I picked you for this job."

Her heart thrilled, especially when he reached to give her cheek a tender caress.

Behind them, securely strapped in his car seat, Jamie slept soundly.

Lauren leaned her head back, struck to think how right and normal it all seemed. They were a family having an outing. Mommy and Daddy and baby.

So good.

So right.

And so phony.

The sad part was, with each passing day, she wished it weren't all make-believe.

Turning her face toward the window, lest Sam notice the glimmer of the tears she was fighting to hold back, she suddenly spotted a phone booth and cried, "There. Stop, please. I've got to call Midge. She's probably out of her mind by now."

Obligingly, he pulled into a parking place, and Lauren hurried to place the call.

Midge wasn't home. At the sound of the beep, she left a message. "Midge, it's me. And I'm fine. Please don't worry. Everything is fine, really. I'll be in touch again soon. I'm sorry I haven't called before now. I've just been busy. Maybe next time I call I can tell you when I'll be home."

And I hope it's soon, she thought, hanging up and pausing to stare toward the car—and Sam. *Because the longer I stay, the harder it's going to be to say goodbye.*

Sam watched Lauren and thought how lucky he was to have found her. He was confident she would now see it through to the end, even if Sophie dragged it out just to try to wear them both down.

It was imperative, however, that he wrap things up as fast as possible, because he needed to get on with his life…as well as get Lauren out of it.

It would be so easy to fall in love with her.

If he let himself, he might admit he already had.

But he couldn't do it, couldn't let his guard down. To do so would be to invite heartache, something he did not want to risk again. After all, he still had scars from Gaynelle.

What a fool he had been to think it could ever work out between them, but he could see now that he had actually been in love with an idea and not Gaynelle herself.

At the time he had met her, there had just been too many wild, reckless nights resulting in sick hangovers and regrets the next morning.

He had wanted—needed—to settle down and have in actuality what he now had by deceit.

Love. Marriage. A baby.

Babies. He smiled to himself, having thought in the plural.

Yes, he wanted babies. Three, at least. Maybe more, if he could afford it, and his wife agreed.

He'd tried to share his dreams with Gaynelle, but, in all fairness, she'd been perfectly honest from the start about wanting her freedom and independence. She would agree to live with him and maybe even one day have children but did not want the commitment of marriage.

He had gone along with her, hoping she would eventually change her mind. Then she got pregnant. She was supposed to be on the Pill. She admitted later to having slipped up a few times due to hectic flight schedules overseas that got her all turned around.

He remembered how he had actually cried when he had begged her not to have the abortion. Then, when she later told him she was going to have the baby and offered to let him adopt it, he had been over the moon with happiness.

She took him down, lifted him up, then threw him down again when he feared she'd gone ahead with the abortion. And now, fate, which had been so cruel to Gaynelle, had smiled upon him—to a degree.

If he ultimately lost Jamie's inheritance, they would both survive.

But he'd had to try, if only to avoid a long, legal battle.

In the process, however, he had now opened up his heart to more anguish…because he had, despite all resolve, allowed Lauren to come in.

And once more he cursed himself for being a fool, because she had made it clear, from the beginning, that love and marriage were the last things on her mind. She wanted the money he offered to give her the independence she so desperately wanted to get a jump-start on life. She did not need him or anyone else.

But she sure as hell put on a good show of wanting to be a mother to Jamie.

And Sam felt she was performing well in the role of loving wife, as well.

Maybe she had missed her calling and should have been an actress, after all.

So, he thought with a deep, ragged sigh, he would enjoy what time they had left together...and try to keep from falling any deeper than he already had.

Lauren got back in the car, and to mask the tenderness he was feeling, he found himself snapping, "What took you so long? It's hot to have to sit here and wait."

Miffed, she fired back, "Well, you could have gotten Jamie out and sat in the shade. You know I promised Midge I'd check in with her.

"I do have another life," she added, then hated herself for sounding so waspish.

"Yeah, and I guess you'll be glad when you can get back to it."

He started the car and they rode in silence to the top of Point Loma.

They parked in the flower-bordered lot, and Jamie awoke in a good mood, delighting in the butterflies fluttering around him as his daddy settled him in his stroller.

They walked along the path, bordered by pansies and primroses in every color of the rainbow. A gentle breeze was blowing, and they drank of the crisp ocean air.

Finally, Sam, furious with himself, could not stand thinking any longer that he had hurt Lauren's feelings. "I'm sorry about snapping your head off back there. I guess I let Sophie get to me, and I took it out on you."

Even though she dutifully accepted his apology, she was still bewildered whenever he was irritable with her. She had come to know him well, and it just wasn't his nature to be anything except easygoing and pleasant.

So why did he sometimes appear to be deliberately trying to drive a wedge between them?

She knew her own motive—to hide her true feelings for him.

But his could not be the same.

Or could it?

She stole a glance at him out of the corner of her eye as she wondered if there was any kind of chance at all that he might care about her...if only a little.

But no.

He'd made it clear his son was all that mattered. There was no room in his life for a woman. Not now, anyway. So she was wasting her time to entertain any fantasies of him changing his mind.

They reached a lookout point and Lauren gasped at the splendor of the azure Pacific melting into a peacock sky.

Sam had lifted Jamie from his stroller and held him against his shoulder. With his other arm he instinctively drew Lauren to him to share the beautiful moment.

As always, when he held her close as part of their charade, Lauren's heart went into overdrive. Only, this time it was worse, because it was no charade. Sophie was nowhere around. There was no one to impress. He was holding her because he wanted to...and because it seemed the natural thing to do.

Daddy, Mommy and son.

Another sightseer, a woman, standing nearby, broke the reverie by cheerfully offering, "Would you like for me to take a picture of all of you together like that? You're such a nice-looking family, and the scenery around you is gorgeous." She gestured to Sam's camera, hanging from a strap around his neck.

"Of course," he said, freeing his hold on Lauren long enough to hand the camera to the woman. "That'd be nice." Then he pulled Lauren to him once more.

Lauren knew it would be a nice snapshot. Her smile came easily. All she had to do was pretend it was all for real.

Jamie, his big blue eyes shining, delighted everyone watching by laughing out loud and waving his little arms.

Afterward, the woman waved away their thank-yous. As she left, they heard her remark to her companion, "Wouldn't it be nice if all families looked so happy?"

Feeling suddenly awkward, Sam took his arm from around Lauren and said, "Well, if we can fool a stranger, I guess we can fool Sophie, huh?"

Lauren forced a brightness to her voice she did not feel. "Yeah, sure. Maybe we both missed our calling to Hollywood."

She took Jamie so Sam would be free to take pictures, but knew the one the stranger had taken would be the one she would always cherish.

Because, if only for an instant, the dream had become reality.

Chapter Eleven

*H*e touched her cheek as delicately as though she were made of finely spun sugar. His lips, warm and moist, grazed her temple.

Lifting her face to his, she could feel the honeyed heat of his breath and see the reflection of passionate longing in his eyes.

His hands held her waist tightly, imprisoning her in his embrace, but needlessly, for she had no wish to escape his luscious assault.

Lauren was still in her wedding dress. They had reached their honeymoon destination—a luxurious suite on a cruise ship. Beyond the floor-to-ceiling window, the ocean rippled like quicksilver in the glow of a full moon.

Sam dropped to his knees before her, lifting her filmy dress as he did so.

With deft, eager fingers, he gently drew down the frilly blue satin garter, then her white panty hose.

She swooned to feel his tongue encircling her navel, then continue downward, feathering little kisses over her thighs.

He stood and began to tug at her gown, and she laughed and warned, "You'll tear it. And it cost a fortune."

"And I'll buy you another," he murmured softly, "and another and another. Every anniversary, my darling, you'll have a wedding dress for me to rip away."

When the gown lay in tatters about her feet, and she stood before him naked, he raked her with steaming eyes and hoarsely proclaimed, "Oh, Lauren, my precious wife. I never knew I could love like this."

He lifted her in his strong arms and carried her to the bed, which seemed like an altar, for it was raised from the floor on a circular platform with miles and miles of lavender netting dripping like honey from above to fall upon them as he laid her upon the mattress.

Dizzy, Lauren moaned deep in her throat as she helped him remove his elegant tuxedo.

Finally, ultimately, he was naked beside her as raw flesh blended in a teeming fever of wanting…needing…loving.

This was no charade, her heart screamed. This was no playacting. He was real. She was real. Never had she known her body harbored such secret longings for any man…and never had she wanted a man more.

She had to have him.

She would die if she did not.

"Sam. Oh, Sam, please…." The words of pleading were savagely torn from her throat as she clung to him in desperation, nails digging into his rock-hard shoulders.

He was above her now, teasing between her thighs with the tip of his swollen member. Her legs wrapped about him, pulling him closer as she begged for him to take her…take her…please, please, take her.

Crying.

There was crying.

But who?

She was ecstatic with joy with no thought of tears.

And Sam was kissing her deeply as he continued his sweet torture.

But someone was crying.

Someone.

Somewhere.

Lauren awoke with a start to glance about the room wildly as awareness slowly swept over her.

It had only been a dream.

In the glow of moonlight filtering through the blinds, she could see Sam huddled miserably on the unyielding floor. He was sound asleep.

Realization it was Jamie crying brought Lauren to full alert. She pushed back the sheet, bounded to her feet, grabbed the filmy robe that matched the gown she was wearing and took off for the nursery.

She was surprised that Sophie was not already at the baby's side. The few times he had awakened during the night, she had gotten there before Lauren. She allowed Lauren to take over, of course, but always wanted to first check on things herself.

Lauren switched on a lamp, and the room was bathed in a soft, peach light. Jamie was on his back, flailing at the air with his fists, but his cries were more like wails, certainly not his usual lusty demands to be fed.

"There, there, it's all right, sweetie," she crooned, reaching for him, then wincing to feel how warm he was.

Touching her lips to his forehead, she was instantly alarmed.

He was burning up.

Her mind began to race frantically. What to do? What to do?

She tried to remember what she'd read in her baby books about sickness but knew this could be anything.

Her first impulse was to wake Sophie, but decided it best not to, fearing it would make her appear incompetent to care for Jamie when he was sick, and she certainly didn't want Sophie to have that impression.

Neither would Sam.

She then thought about waking him, but he didn't have better knowledge about babies than she did, and his fretting would only make her all the more nervous.

She patted Jamie's back. "Let's get you to the kitchen and see if we can figure this out between us, okay, little buddy?"

Glancing at the wall clock, Lauren saw it was nearly 6:00 a.m. If Jamie wasn't better soon, she would call his pediatrician. Sophie had posted the number next to the phone.

Jamie's cries became louder and even more pitiful as Lauren walked the floor with him while she heated his bottle in the microwave.

In her panic, she forgot what she had read about feverish babies, how milk was a no-no. Give water instead. Preferably a Ringer's solution. Sophie had shown her where she kept such emergency supplies, but Lauren was beside herself. She had never tended a sick baby before, and with no one to guide her or give moral support, she felt herself quickly becoming unglued and unable to think clearly.

Jamie's screams were like hot needles in her ears. She continued to cuddle him close as she tried to soothe him but to no avail.

The buzzer sounded on the microwave. Lauren took out the bottle, tested a few drops on her wrist, then sank into a chair and pressed the nipple to his mouth. "Okay, little fellow. Drink and see if you feel better. I'll bet you're just hungry, and it's given you a little tummy ache. Take a few ounces, and then I'll burp you and everything will be fine."

Jamie would suck a few times, then pause to utter a few sobs before continuing to take his milk.

When his eyes closed and he became quiet, Lauren dared to hope that her diagnosis had been correct—tummy ache caused by hunger. As soon as the pediatrician's office opened, she would call and ask about increasing Jamie's solid foods. His present diet was evidently not satisfying him.

Sam sleepily jerked on his robe. He hated wearing one, because he had never been cold-natured. It wasn't all that chilly, anyway, but he just felt it was necessary with Sophie around. Lauren, too, of course.

Just as the crying had finally dragged him from a sound sleep, everything had gotten quiet, but he wanted to see why Jamie had gotten wound up in the first place. He felt bad not to have roused sooner, but he'd been deep in a dream—a dream from which he had not wanted to awaken.

He'd dreamed it was Christmas Eve, and he and Lauren had put out toys from Santa under a tree that was so tall, it had burst right through the roof of their house.

And there were lots of toys, too, because there were three other children besides Jamie—two girls and another little boy.

It had seemed so real, and he and Lauren were both so happy. Then, just when the crying had started, he had begun to make love to Lauren, and she was responding, and things were really starting to get hot and heavy.

Now, as he padded down the hall toward the kitchen, he felt foolish to think about it. Sure, he could write the dream off as a natural result of being in close quarters with an attractive woman.

But it wasn't just his normal urges and needs that had inspired the dream.

Oh, no. It was more than that.

It was Lauren.

And the way he had grown to feel about her these past weeks.

He wanted her.

And not just for sex.

He wanted Lauren, wholly and completely.

When he reached the swinging door into the kitchen, all

was quiet. Opening the door just a crack, he peered in and was instantly warmed by the sight before him.

Jamie could not have looked more at home in his natural mother's arms.

And Lauren could not have gazed at her own infant with greater adoration mirrored on her face.

He wished he had his camera so he could preserve the moment for always.

Because soon, his memories would be all he had left of her.

He tiptoed on in, but Lauren heard him and turned her head. "I think he's finally sleeping," she whispered.

Sam knelt beside her, eyes worriedly on his son. "Sorry I didn't wake sooner. I was sleeping pretty sound. He was really raising a fuss, wasn't he?"

"Feel his forehead," she said, frowning. "I think he may have a little fever. There's a thermometer in the nursery. I'll take his temperature when I put him back to bed."

Sam pressed the back of his hand to Jamie's cheek and jerked it back, startled. "Hey, he is warm. Maybe we better call the doctor now."

"Let me burp him, and then I'll take his temp. If he does have a fever, I'll give him baby aspirin and a sponge bath, then check with the doctor."

Sam told himself to calm down. Babies got sick all the time. It wasn't serious. Just a little cold, maybe. Still, he'd feel better if he talked to the doctor. Better yet, they would take him in and let the doctor see him.

Lauren maneuvered to lift Jamie to her shoulder. Sam was hovering, eager to help.

Neither noticed that Sophie had silently the door open and was watching them.

Just as Lauren raised Jamie, he gave one loud, sharp burp—and threw up all over her, as well as Sam.

And he continued to do so in projectile gushes.

"Oh, dear," Lauren wailed, lowering him to her lap. Her hair, face and robe were spattered. "He's really sick."

Sam, also drenched, nervously agreed. "I'm calling the doctor. He can meet us at the emergency room."

With a feigned cry of dismay, Sophie rushed in, as if on cue. "What's wrong? What's the matter?"

"He's got a fever," Lauren explained. "At least, I think he does. He's burning up."

Sophie saw the bottle of milk on the table and exclaimed, "Do you mean to tell me you gave him milk when you knew he was running a fever? Why, of course, he's going to throw up. It soured on his stomach. What could you have been thinking? You should know better. What about all those baby care books you're always reading?"

Lauren's eyes were brimming with tears. "I'm sorry," she said, lips quivering. "I guess I was just so scared I didn't think."

Sophie took Jamie from her and said, more gently, "Well, these things happen. I suppose you thought you were doing the right thing."

Going to the sink, Sophie wet a paper towel and began to dab at Jamie's face. "I'll get him cleaned up while you two change, and then I'll call Dr. Faulkner and—"

Sam and Lauren both stared at her to see why she had suddenly fallen silent.

"What is it?" Sam asked anxiously, rushing to her side. "Did you find something?"

Lauren wondered if it were her imagination or if Sophie did, indeed, have the play of a smile on her lips.

"No. Nothing," Sophie said quietly, calmly. "Go take a bath. Both of you. You smell terrible. You can't go to the hospital the way you are."

Sam whirled around to Lauren. "She's right. You use the shower in our room. I'll use the one in the nursery."

Sophie sharply said, "No, you can't."

They looked at her, puzzled.

Sophie headed for the door, calling over her shoulder, "Something's wrong with the shower in the nursery. And you can't use mine. I never allow anyone to use my bathroom. You can just shower together to save time. Saves water, too," she added. "They're always fussing at us to save water around here."

"Together?" Sam and Lauren echoed in stunned unison.

"Oh, for heaven's sake," Sophie snapped. "You don't have to act embarrassed around me. You probably shower together all the time. So get to it. We need to hurry."

"So what do we do?" Lauren asked as soon as Sophie was out of hearing range. She could smell herself and wrinkled her nose at the sour odor.

"We take turns, anyway," he said firmly. "She'll never know, and we'll just set a record for bathing, that's all."

They rushed to their bedroom but were jolted to find Sophie there, sitting in the rocker and holding Jamie as she softly hummed to him.

"I washed his face," she said. "Now I'll try to keep him quiet by rocking him till you two are ready.

"He loves this chair," she continued sweetly, smiling down at him. "I rocked Gaynelle's father in it when he was a baby and then Gaynelle, when she was little."

When Sam and Lauren did not move but stood rooted, staring at her in wonder, Sophie glared up at them and snapped, "Well, are you going to just stand there? Get in there and get your showers, or I'll take him to the hospital by myself."

Not trusting herself to look at Sam, fearful her anxiety would show on her face for Sophie to see, Lauren quickly gathered her things and rushed into the bathroom.

Sam followed, swiftly closing the door as he pressed a finger to his lips for silence. Then he reached inside the shower stall and turned the water on full force before saying, "I saw in a spy movie once that it's impossible for someone to overhear a conversation when there's running water."

"So what do we do?" Lauren asked, frantic. "We're not bathing together, for God's sake."

He ran his hands through his hair as he always did when

he was worried. "Of course we aren't. You take your turn first, and I'll wait here, then go. Now hurry."

"Turn your back while I undress."

He obliged with a sigh.

"Sam?"

"Yeah?"

"Do you think she did this to embarrass us?"

"Huh?" He almost turned around but caught himself in time. "What do you mean?"

"Do you think she suspects we aren't married, and this is her way of embarrassing us? The bit about the shower in the nursery not working, not letting you use hers and her plopping down in that rocker to make sure we come in here together—it all looks suspicious to me."

"Well, yeah, but not when you think about it. I mean, bluntly speaking, most couples involved in a scheme like this would probably be sleeping together, so why would we be embarrassed? As for the shower in the nursery, the last time I used it, it wasn't working properly—the shower head was leaking like crazy.

"And I'm not surprised she didn't want to let me use her bathroom," he continued. "I've noticed she's funny about personal things."

"And the rocker?"

"She could be telling the truth. Jamie sure looked contented. We're just paranoid because *we* know the truth. Now hurry, please."

He heard her slide the shower door closed.

He stood rigid, staring at the wall, his hands clenched at his side, his teeth clamped so tight, his jaw ached. Damn it, he should be thinking only of his son and how he was sick, not of the image of Lauren in that shower stall, water raining down on her naked body.

But he was, after all, a man, and finally, helplessly, he yielded to temptation and whipped his head about for a quick glance—then swayed at the sight.

In the frosted glass of the shower door, the outline of her

body was framed against the early-morning light streaming through the window behind her. He watched, mesmerized, as she moved in the cascading water to soap her breasts.

She was every bit as glorious as he had known she would be, and he wanted her as he had never wanted a woman before.

"Done," she called finally.

He faced the wall again, breathing hard, perspiration beading his forehead.

He heard the door slide open, followed by her surprised cry, "You haven't even undressed, Sam. And you're telling *me* to hurry?"

"I...I didn't want to turn around," he stammered. Then he prompted, "Now it's your turn to close your eyes." He was not about to let her see the effect she'd had upon him.

His shower was quick, less than two minutes, and when he stepped out, Lauren was completely dressed. Her back was still to him, and he threw on his clothes and announced, "Okay. I'm ready."

When they opened the bedroom door, there was no sign of Sophie and Jamie in the rocker. Instead, they were waiting in the car.

Sophie announced, "I called Dr. Faulkner after I took Jamie's temperature. It was a little over a hundred. He said that wasn't so bad and to just bring him to his office, and he'd meet us there. It's not far."

Fifteen minutes later, Sam was washed with relief, while Lauren, likewise pleased, felt like a complete idiot.

"See?" Dr. Faulkner pressed his finger against Jamie's lower lip to open his mouth and display the tiny little tooth that had just broken through the gum. "He's teething. Babies sometimes run a fever when they do.

"He vomited," he continued, "because the milk soured on his stomach."

"Told you so," Sophie could not resist saying smugly to Lauren.

Lauren sank a little lower in her chair, although Sam's

comforting pat on her shoulder helped a little...as did Dr. Faulkner saying, "Don't blame her, Sophie. Mothers learn by experience. She'll know better next time."

Lauren was touched by sadness to think how it really didn't matter what she learned, at least not for Jamie's sake. She would not be caring for him much longer and could only hope Sam was soaking everything in.

But what also bothered her was recalling Sophie's strange little smirk earlier, while she was washing Jamie's face at the kitchen sink. Had she actually felt his new little tooth then but not said anything to make her feel foolish? If so, she had succeeded.

Lifting Jamie from the examining table, Lauren kissed the top of his head as she silently prayed it would all be over soon, for each day brought her even closer to the precious little fellow, which was going to make it all the more painful when the time came to say goodbye to him...and to his daddy.

Chapter Twelve

"I'm real sorry about this morning," Lauren said as she came out of the bathroom. "I should've known Jamie was cutting a tooth." She had wrapped her terry robe tightly around her. With the door safely locked, there was no need to wear one of the lush nighties for Sophie's benefit, and she certainly did not want Sam to think she was deliberately teasing him.

He was sitting in the rocker, waiting for his turn in the shower. "Don't be so hard on yourself. How were you to know? You've never been around babies."

"I read the books. I was just too upset to think, and that's not a good thing. You have to be on your toes around babies and not panic."

"It's okay, Lauren." He gave her a fond smile as he headed toward the bathroom. "Like the doctor said—you'll know next time."

Next time, she thought dismally, she probably wouldn't be anywhere around Jamie. When he cut another tooth, someone else would be taking care of him, and it made her very sad to know that. But Sam would take good care of him. She had no doubts about that. He was certainly doing everything he could to gain custody of him peacefully, because no matter what obstacle Sophie put in his way, he managed to sidestep and kept on going.

Staring down at his pitiful bed on the floor, she felt a rush of pity—and guilt. She was being well paid for doing something she enjoyed, while he was the one enduring miserable nights.

But thank goodness, she was relieved to think, he had remembered to pick up his bed this morning before leaving the room. Otherwise, it would have been there for Sophie to see when she came in to rock Jamie. Now he had spread it out once more in preparation for another comfortless night.

"Well, turnabout is fair play," she declared out loud as she settled herself on top of the folded bedspread.

It was hard. Terrazzo—a mosaic flooring combination of marble and cement—was also cold. And while Southern California days might be warm, the nights could be downright chilly, and Sam's bed was wretched and drafty. Still, he'd not complained, so neither would she.

When he returned, he saw her curled up on the floor and cried, "Whoa! What do you think you're doing?"

"I figure it's my turn," she said, the sheet she'd taken from the bed pulled tight about her. "It's only fair."

"No. Uh-uh." He was beside her in giant strides to kneel and pull her to a sitting position. "No way, Lauren. It's not part of our deal. It's nice of you to offer, and I appreciate it, but I can't let you do it."

She twisted against his firm grip on her arms. He was wearing only the bottom of his pajamas, and as his chest hair brushed against her skin, she felt a sensuous tremor stirring in her loins.

"Please, Sam, I want to," she argued. "I feel guilty about you sleeping down here night after night."

He was deeply impressed by her thoughtfulness but shook his head firmly. "Thanks...but no thanks. I've gotten used to it. Now come on. Back on your bed."

"But—"

"No buts, and I warn you—if you don't get up, I'm going to lay down next to you."

That did it.

She scurried to the bed. Then, seeing he was still standing there, his lips curved in a mischievous smile, she blinked and said, "What?"

"This."

He sat down on the side of bed and began to slowly bounce up and down on the mattress, making tiny, rhythmic, squeaking sounds. "Oh, Lauren, honey," he crooned, eyes locked with hers and grinning. "I want you so much."

Lauren did not want to play the game. Not this night when she was feeling so down about everything. To pretend they were making love—with sound effects and words—was more than she could bear.

Especially after last night's dream.

"I don't want to do this," she whispered, "So don't start, please."

"We have to," he insisted, also whispering and keeping the beat as he continued to bounce.

Lauren grabbed his shoulders to try to stop him, but he continued even as she pleaded, "Listen, I'm not so sure we're fooling her, anyway. I think she knew about Jamie's tooth and just wanted to make me look bad. I think she's only trying to justify doing what she planned to all along—decide we're unfit parents so she'll have an excuse to deny Jamie his trust fund."

"I don't think so," he whispered back, but at least he had stopped bouncing. "We've got to keep trying."

And all the while he was speaking, pleading, Sam could not erase the image of her in the shower from his mind. What he was doing was adding to his angst where she was concerned, but he had to do it—had to keep fighting to convince Sophie to give up.

But Lauren was in no mood to play. "Having sex doesn't prove you're in love," she muttered sullenly.

"But when you think you are, it's the greatest," Sam shot back.

"So now I'm supposed to pretend to be in love with you?" She gave her hair a reckless toss. "That wasn't part of the deal."

"Will you stop thinking about the deal?" he snapped. "That's all you ever say. We have to improvise sometimes, Lauren. We can't plan out every word and thing we do."

"Sam, I—"

"Just do it, Lauren. It won't kill you."

"But I don't feel like it."

"Do it or you're fired," he teased.

"You don't mean that."

"Sure I do. Now will you stop arguing?"

"Sam, please—"

Enough was enough. He silenced her with a kiss.

He hadn't planned to.

It just happened.

As spontaneous as thunder after lightning.

And then, just as naturally, he pressed her down on the bed, hands sweeping over her as emotions he could no longer hold back erupted.

When his mouth at last moved from hers, his tongue trailed hotly to her ear. "Tell me to stop, and I will," he said, praying all the while she would not.

And she didn't.

Lauren longed for the willpower to deny him—and herself—but he was gently drawing back the spread from her body.

Hesitantly he asked, "Are you, you know, protected? Or do I need to—"

She also hated breaking the spell to have to tell him, "Yes. You do." She had stopped taking the Pill after Stewart...after making up her mind there would not be a man in her life for a long, long time.

He moved about in the dark, and when he returned he had sheathed himself.

Quickly the fire was upon them again, and Lauren could only surrender as he opened her robe and slipped his hands under her nightshirt to finally cup her breasts in his waiting palms.

Then his tempest lips were there. He closed upon a tightening bud, sweeping it into his mouth with his tongue to lick and savor. She gasped and moved against him, fingers wildly dancing through his hair to ultimately settle upon his shoulders and dig into the rock-hard flesh as she clung to him.

She could no more have turned from him than held back the wind in a hurricane.

She was wearing the tee he feared Sophie would regard as evidence of a honeymoon that wasn't, but he drew it up and over her head, rendering her naked. And, as his mouth devoured her breasts, his strong hands slid to cup her bottom, then dive farther to spread her sinewy thighs.

Lauren caught her breath and held it in anticipation of what was to come.

His touch was gentle as he assaulted the pink petals of her womanhood, caressing, sweeping, exploring each and every mysterious part of her before plunging his fingers deep inside to feel the moisture of her own heated desire.

Lauren thrust herself against his hand, wanting more, her sighs of pleasure becoming deeper, louder, with each sweet-savage thrust he made.

His seduction began with his fingers but culminated with his tongue as he dove his face downward to taste her honeyed nectar.

She began to undulate her hips in rhythm with his tongue as she held him close against her. Great, grinding waves of ecstasy began to thunder through her, threatening to crest and burst as a wave upon the shore.

The peak was rising higher, like shooting stars in a velvet sky. She began to quiver deep within, shuddering, shivering, her legs beginning to twitch, finally lifting up and around to imprison him between.

Her nails sank into his shoulder as she clung to him shamelessly, wanting yet more of him...wanting to give him all she had to give, as well.

His fingers slid from her as he rose above her, and she lifted her head to rain kisses upon his chest.

"I want you, Lauren," he said huskily as his eyes, hot and moist with desire, locked with hers. "Say you want me, too. We have to both want this..."

She knew he was trying to convey to her that it was neither part of their arrangement nor promise of anything in the future. It was passion only, aroused by circumstances they had been forced to endure in order to achieve their goal. Sam would stop, she knew, if she asked him. But she wanted it as much as he did. Maybe more.

Because her passion was not born of mere desire.

Hers was born of the love she had come to feel for him.

"I want it, too," she murmured against his chest before raising her lips to meet the ardor of his mouth with a passion that was overwhelming and all consuming.

He entered her, hesitant, unsure, not wanting to hurt her with his hugeness. But brazenly, boldly, she reached to cup his buttocks and pull him hard against her. He drove into her then, filling her with himself, thrusting fiercely as waves of rapture washed over him like a storm-riddled sea.

Lauren held him tightly, her heels locked against his sides. She could feel him within, as though he had plunged into the very soul of her to rock and sway and tear away at every shred of resistance she might dare harbor.

But she held nothing back, matching his every thrust, rocking, undulating, swaying, bucking, whimpering softly with each shuddering ripple of ecstasy. Overwhelming rapture was carrying her to a pinnacle never before achieved.

Nothing...no one...had ever taken her so high.

Without losing his cadence, Sam straightened an arm on each side of her, lifting himself so that he could gaze down at her face, laced in the silvered moonlight that spilled from the window.

She marveled at the strength of him that plunged with such great hunger and force between her thighs.

Suddenly, it was as though they were no longer separate entities but one being, one force of light that ignited the darkness in a glittering explosion that rocked from head to toe in great spasms of rhapsody.

In unison, they soared to the heavens in climax, and then the shattering light quietly faded to darkness once more, their bodies racked by aftershudders as they gasped for breath.

Rolling to the side, Sam propped himself upon an elbow, devouring her with his eyes.

She trembled as he began to gently stroke her cheek with the back of his hand.

How she ached for him to pull her against him so her head could rest upon the greatness of his chest.

And then he did so, and she reveled within.

"There's nothing wrong with our enjoying each other these weeks," he said softly, thoughtfully. "That is, if you want to."

"Well, yes..." She felt a wave of disappointment, for she had dared to think lovemaking would change his feelings for her. To cover her sense of devastation, she forced a grin and said, "I mean, why not? You won't have to bounce up and down on the bed by yourself."

"And Sophie will have a real earful."

"And it means you don't have to sleep on the floor," she added with a nervous little giggle.

He matched her humor, grateful to have the tension broken. "Oh, I don't know. Maybe you steal covers...or kick...or snore. I still think it's a good idea to take turns."

She pretended to be indignant. "Well, I don't. Besides, if I snored, you'd have complained by now."

"Well, you offered to take turns tonight."

"I was just being nice, which isn't very often, so don't get used to it."

He longed to tell her how he could get used to *her*—in every way—but in an effort to quell the emotions swirling within, he instead kept up the easy camaraderie. "Yeah? Well, what if I insist? What if I just give you a push and make you sleep down there?"

He began to tickle her ribs, and she wrestled against him, laughing shrilly as she rolled from side to side, begging for mercy.

Snatching up the pillow, she began to pound at him, and he grabbed his own pillow and fought back, and soon their arms and legs were entangled and the playfulness came to an abrupt halt as their eyes met and held in a locked and searing gaze of awareness as desire kindled once more.

Lauren knew she was only making more memories that would haunt her forever, but could not help herself. If this was all she was to ever have of him, here and now, then so be it.

There was no turning back.

She kissed him, clung to him, and the rocket ride to the stars began again.

Afterward, she lay with her head on his shoulder, his arm about her, and she felt content and safe.

It was going to be difficult, she knew, to go on as they had been, for now she knew beyond all doubt that she loved him with every beat of her heart.

But she had to pretend it meant nothing.

Just casual sex because they were helplessly trapped in the most intimate of situations.

They were merely answering a need and enjoying each other, as well.

Nothing serious.

Nothing to worry about.

She would act as though it was not important.

For she would not, could not, let him know that for whatever time they had left to spend together, she would be living for the moment when he again took her in his arms...and all the way to heaven.

Perhaps, she mused as a tear slipped from her eye to trail down her cheek, her claim in her application letter for the job had been wrong.

Perhaps she was an actress, after all.

When Lauren awoke, her head was still nestled against Sam's shoulder, his arm yet holding her close.

It was one of those moments in a woman's life she wishes could last forever. Some, however, could take comfort in knowing they would be returning to their beloved's arms again and again. Lauren was not so fortunate, because time was running out.

Tilting her head so she could see Sam's face, she was moved once more to think how much she loved him. He was everything she could ever want—sensitive, kind, caring and, of course, a father made in heaven. It was comforting to know Jamie would always be adored and cared for, and she envied any future children Sam might have, though it was doubtful he ever would—not if it meant marriage.

He had made it clear so many times during the past weeks that never, ever again would he commit to anything or anyone other than his son. And, so he'd not think it mattered to her, she always countered that marriage was the farthest thing from her mind, as well.

Lauren squeezed her eyes shut against the sight of his precious face. Only God above knew how she longed to wake up in Sam's arms every morning for the rest of her life.

She was not sorry they'd made love, despite feeling a bit chagrined to think how all the pep talks she'd given herself had been for naught, because she had melted like chocolate in his arms.

But that was okay, she comforted herself. After all, she was only human—a woman with natural needs. Besides,

Sophie had forced them into every close situation imaginable. So Lauren supposed that it was understandable that it would have happened sooner or later.

Perhaps it was best it *was* later, for surely Sophie would make up her mind soon, and the bittersweet torture would end.

She turned so she could see the clock on the bedside table. It was nearly seven. Jamie would probably be awake and playing quietly in his crib, but she was not about to wait till he started crying to go to him.

Jamie, Lauren painfully acknowledged, was another heartbreak she would soon have to face, for she could not bear the thought of saying goodbye to him. Oh, sure, Sam would do the proper, kind thing and tell her she was always welcome to visit, but she knew she had to make a clean break with both of them. They would need to get on with their lives.

And, difficult as it would be, so would she.

Drawing the sheet back, Lauren quietly got out of bed and went into the bathroom to dress. When she returned a short while later, Sam was awake and sitting up, his arms folded across his knees, which were drawn to his chest.

"I...I didn't mean to wake you," Lauren said uneasily, for he was staring at her so intently.

"You didn't. I guess I've been awake for some time, just lying here thinking."

She wondered about what but didn't dare ask. "Oh? Well, I'd better get going. Jamie will be hungry. And *wet*," she added with a smile.

"And how old do they have to be before they're house-broken?"

"Housebroken," she echoed, laughing. "The first thing you've got to learn is that he isn't a puppy, Sam. You can't whack him across his nose with a rolled-up newspaper and point at the door."

He grinned. "I know that."

His face had lit up, and Lauren was reminded of how

she adored his laugh lines and dimples when he was happy. Come to think of it, she seldom saw him when he wasn't. Sam probably had the sunniest disposition of any man she'd ever known. True, he had his moments like anyone else, and perhaps more than his share of stress lately, but that was understandable. Still, he was wonderful company, and she liked being around him.

No.

She *loved* being around him.

"You can start potty training him when he's around two years old," she said.

She was almost to the door when he called to her, speaking her name like a caress.

Turning, she wondered if he would be able to see her heart pounding in her chest. "Yes?" she responded, tremulously adding, "I've really got to go, Sam. I don't want Jamie to start crying and wake Sophie. She'll think I'm too lazy to get up and tend to him in the mornings, and we don't want that."

"No. We don't. But I need to know what else we don't want."

"I don't know what you mean."

"I think you do. I'm asking—" he drew a ragged breath and let it out slowly "—whether you've got any regrets about last night, because if you do, it doesn't have to happen again. What I mean is, I won't expect it just because it happened once, and I won't try—"

She rushed to his side to press a finger against his lips. "Don't. Don't say it. Because it isn't necessary. It happened because we both wanted it. For my part, it was beautiful, and if it happens again, so be it. Let's don't worry about it. We've got a job to do, and if we enjoy ourselves while we're doing it, what's the harm?"

"Yeah. Right. What's the harm?" He settled back against the pillows, turning his gaze out the window as he murmured, "Looks like it's going to be another nice day."

Was it her imagination or did he actually seem annoyed?

She'd reacted in the way she felt he expected—casual, no commitment, just a seize-the-day, live-for-the-moment kind of outlook.

"See you in a few minutes," he said, dismissing her.

Shoving her personal quandary to a back burner, Lauren hurried to the nursery, only to find it empty.

Hurrying then to the kitchen, she pushed the door open to see Sophie seated before Jamie, feeding him oatmeal as he sat in his highchair.

At the sight of Lauren, his face lit up like a Christmas tree, his arms slinging and fat little legs kicking frantically as he squealed with delight.

"Well, I'll never be able to finish now," Sophie grumbled, standing and indicating Lauren should sit. "He wants you to feed him."

"And I'm happy to oblige." Lauren kissed him on each cheek and took Sophie's chair.

Sophie stood back and watched in silence for a moment. Jamie's eyes were shining and never left Lauren's face. Each time she spoke to him, he bounced and wiggled and giggled. It was quite obvious he adored her. "Where were you and Sam married?" she asked suddenly.

Lauren looked at her, bewildered. What had Sam said? She couldn't remember and frantically racked her brain. "Uh, A-Alaska," she finally stammered. That's where they had supposedly met. It seemed logical.

Sophie lifted a quizzical brow. "You mean you married right after you met? That's not what I understood."

Lauren cursed herself for the blunder. Of course, they wouldn't have married then. Quickly she bounced back to attempt to amend by saying, "Oh, you mean *where* we were married. I thought you asked where we *met*. Atlanta. We were married there. We have lots of friends." She offered a wan smile.

"But no family."

"No, no family." What was she digging for now? she wondered frantically. Sophie had never grilled her before;

it was always Sam whom she'd questioned. Lauren wished he would hurry and appear to take over, because she just wasn't good at this, and Sophie was cunning as a high-powered lawyer.

Sophie was quiet for long moments, as though deep in thought, then said, "It's sad when people are alone in the world. Gaynelle was all I had left—till Jamie. Now you want to take him away from me."

Lauren's hand began to shake, and Jamie's blue eyes went wide in wonder over where her smile had gone, along with her teasing baby talk that always made him giggle.

"Maybe—" Lauren hesitated, thinking how Sam might want to strangle her for saying it "—you can come and visit him in Atlanta. And when he's older, he can come and visit you."

There. She had said it, and she was glad, because she had darted a glance at Sophie and had seen the glimmer of hopeful tears in her eyes. Her unauthorized invitation had given Sophie hope, and Lauren felt no guilt, because maybe it would ultimately turn out that way. Sam was not cold-hearted.

"I don't know," Sophie murmured. "It might be best if I just got out of his life completely—*if*," she added sharply, "I ultimately decide Jamie is better off with you and Sam. I haven't made up my mind yet."

Lauren didn't say anything. After all, what could she say? It was up to Sophie whether or not she wanted to go to war with Sam...and war it would be. Lauren had no doubt about that. Nothing would stand in the way of him having his son, no matter how much it cost.

As she and Sam pushed Jamie in his stroller around the quaint little village of Coronado, Lauren knew it was not her imagination that there was a new, intimate awareness between them. She could tell he felt it, too, not only in the warm, caressing way he looked at her but also by how his touch would linger when they brushed against each other.

It was only going to make it that much harder to say goodbye. Why had she been so weak as to allow the intimacy?

Why, indeed, she scoffed inwardly.

As if she'd had a choice.

Her body had betrayed her and would do so again and again. Knowing that, she could only pray that Sophie would soon make her decision…and set them free from the velvet cocoon that held them captive.

"Do you want to go over to the beach beside the Hotel Del and watch Hell Week?"

They were having dinner on the patio, Lauren's favorite spot. There were no bugs on Coronado. No flies, gnats, or mosquitoes to annoy them. Just swaying palms, fragrant jasmine, sweet clematis. The breeze from the ocean was cool, and they wore sweaters, but it was not chilly enough to keep them inside.

Bemused, Lauren looked up from her shrimp cocktail. "What is Hell Week?"

"It's the culmination of BUDs training for the SEALs. It stands for Basic Underwater Demolition Seals. It's called Hell Week, because it is. I know. I went through it. Tonight they'll be doing an exercise where they try to land rubber rafts on those sharp rocks below the Hotel del Coronado. Lots of people always gather to watch.

"You've seen it, haven't you, Sophie?" He politely included her in the conversation.

"Yes," Sophie replied. "A long time ago. I felt so sorry for those boys and don't want to see it again. But you two go ahead. I'll stay here with Jamie. Enjoy yourselves."

Sam looked at Lauren and winked.

More and more lately, Sophie was acting nicer to them. It was a good sign.

Lauren held up crossed fingers when Sophie wasn't looking, and Sam did the same.

It was a good sign.

Perhaps the end was in sight.

An hour later, Sam and Lauren were gathered on the beach along with a few dozen other curious onlookers.

It was quite a sight to see—worn-out and exhausted young men trying to finish the end of what had to be the most challenging and grueling week of their lives.

Sam explained that the SEALs were deprived of sleep as they were put through the torturous exercises. The attrition rate sometimes climbed as high as eighty percent. "But it's necessary. They've got to be tough to make it. It's what the SEALs are all about."

Lauren was deeply impressed. Not only by what she was witnessing but knowing that Sam, himself, had made it through such demanding training. He was truly a unique and marvelous man.

He held her hand. It seemed natural that he do so. And all the while, Lauren was reminded of his hands upon her body last night, bringing joy unsurpassed.

When the exercise finally ended, they began walking down the beach by silent consent. The wind off the water was cold. Lauren pulled her jacket tighter about her, and Sam put his arm about her to lend her his warmth.

They talked of anything and everything, and before they realized it, they had passed from the glow of the hotel and into darkness, save for the moon's milky path upon the ocean. No houses were around them. They were all alone.

"Want to watch the moon awhile?" Sam asked. Without waiting for answer, he sat down on a rock, pulling her with him.

But they did not watch the moon.

With a soft groan, he pulled her to him and kissed her. At first, their lips were soft as they touched, then deepened as the tip of his tongue melded against hers. With a delicious sigh, Lauren opened her mouth to receive his sweet assault.

Sliding his hands beneath her jacket and sweater, he

filled his palms with her breasts, fingers kneading gently. His thumbs found her nipples and began to massage slowly at first, then harder, around and around. At the same time, his tongue was likewise rotating, driving her mad with delight.

With a quick yank, she pulled her clothing upward, along with her bra, then boldly cupped his face and drew him downward.

He was on his knees before her, sucking each breast in turn as he maneuvered to unzip her jeans. She lifted her hips, so he could ease them down along with her bikini panties.

His fingers dove into the thatch of dark curls, easing inside her.

Lauren arched her back, hot needles of pleasure stabbing into her belly. They were going to make love in the sand, and she did not care, knowing there was no way they could ever make it back to the house and to bed. The fire was raging, and soon it would be out of control.

But it was her turn to inflict pleasured anguish...her turn to make him writhe in sensual rapture.

Before he had a chance to wonder what she was doing, Lauren had pulled away to drop beside him onto the damp sand.

He chuckled softly, a bit shyly, as she unbuckled his belt. He had to help her with the zipper, and then the whole of his manhood was in her hands...her lips closing about him.

He gasped as she drew him into the buttery warmth of her mouth. Her tongue licked up and down, her lips soft, caressing, and as the waves crashed upon the shore below them, his own crescendo was building, hurtling to explosion.

He could stand no more.

Stretching out in the sand, he rolled her beneath him, spreading her thighs. He drove into her to fill her with one mighty thrust, reveling in the feel of her closing hot and tight about him.

Her legs squeezed. Her heels dug into his buttocks, urging him onward. He could feel her nails all the way through his thin jacket as he pushed in and out of her, harder, faster, forceful, slamming her into the sand as she clung to him. Her ecstatic face was bathed in moon glow as she lifted her bottom to meet his every push.

It was coming.

He could not hold back, could only hope she was ready, for he wanted to share the divine moment of supreme climax. He wanted her flesh in tune with his, every nerve melding before shattering to make them one...if only for an instant.

Then he felt her shuddering against him and knew she would journey with him to that utopia of bliss.

He pushed even harder, and she met him in tiny but mighty undulations, her heels digging in yet deeper to lock him against her.

A falling star ripped across the sky, but neither saw, for they, themselves, were momentary comets, soaring through space in a heated rush to touch the zenith of their desire.

After long moments of tender quiet, when they clung together in the sand, Sam was the first to speak, sounding slightly amused amidst his concern. "What I want to know is how we explain going home looking like we were part of the amphibious landing, too."

Playfully, brazenly, Lauren traced the lines of his face in the moonlight. "She doesn't stay up very late. Another hour or so at the most. If we don't go back till then, she won't see us, and we won't have to explain."

He raised an amused brow. "And what do you propose we do in the meantime to keep warm?"

She reached downwards to caress him and felt him spring alive. "I can think of something."

He grinned as he lowered his mouth to hers. "Lady, I think you just read my mind."

Chapter Thirteen

Lauren felt as though she were living in paradise.

Coronado, with its flower-bedecked houses and tree-lined streets, combined with the glorious weather, was only frosting on the cake when compared to the happiness and joy in which she reveled while basking in the midst of playing the greatest role in life any woman could ask for—that of wife and mother.

And the absolute and only shadow over such bliss was, of course, Sophie.

It seemed as though she were always around, even though she pretended to be pursuing her own interests while handing over complete care of Jamie to Lauren. She would say she had a tennis date at ten in the morning, only to pop back to the house an hour later, claiming to have forgotten something. Or she would announce plans for bridge with her friends in the evening, then show up unexpectedly way before the game should have ended.

In short, Lauren never knew when she would appear, and this kept her on edge.

"You've nothing to worry about," Sam assured her over and over. "You're doing a marvelous job. I'm no expert on babies, heaven knows, but I honestly don't see how anybody could give Jamie better care than you do. If there is such a thing as perfection, you're it, Lauren, so relax."

So she tried to take one day at the time, knowing it would all come to an end sooner or later...even though Sophie refused to discuss when that might be.

Secretly, however, Lauren had to admit she really didn't care, because she was so content. Besides, it was easy to drift into a fantasy world and pretend she *was* Sam's wife and Jamie's mother.

But sometimes she felt guilty to think that way. After all, it was difficult for Sam. He needed to get back to his job, and there had been times when she wondered how much of a hardship it was going to be for him to pay her the money he would owe her when it was all over. She had even toyed with the idea of saying she would only take half. After all, it just didn't seem right, somehow, to take such a huge sum for doing nothing more than simply *loving*.

She knew that's why it was all so easy for her. Nothing was a chore with Jamie, because she loved him.

And, for the same reason, playing the role of Sam's wife was anything but work.

Their nights, since they had succumbed to the rumbling fires of desire, exploded with all the fury of a volcano. Passion swept, spewed and whirled about them in delicious consummation. They could not seem to get enough of each other.

Their closeness and awareness spilled over into their days, of course, and Lauren pondered whether Sophie noticed and thought it was merely for her benefit. If so, it could work against them. After all, Sophie might think they were actually trying to cover something up.

The only thing Lauren was trying to cover, however, was not letting Sam know that she wasn't acting, that she did not look upon the situation as something to get through so she could get on with her life—a life that did not include serious involvement with a man.

The sex was good.

No, it was better than good.

It was wonderful.

And not entirely because Sam was a tender and caring lover, which he was. Always he made sure her needs were met and satisfied.

It was, she knew, because she loved him.

And if she'd learned nothing else the past weeks, she now knew that nothing could surpass the joy of making love to someone she truly loved.

The only thing that could surmount it would be if she could believe Sam loved her in return.

So, to ease the pain of knowing it would soon be over, Lauren tried to focus on helping Sam learn as much as possible about caring for Jamie. She told him he would need to duplicate all the equipment Sophie had bought for him, though it did not have to be as expensive. Jamie did not, she pointed out, need a three-hundred-dollar stroller. There were many models much cheaper that would do just as well. The same was true of high chair and crib.

By keeping the conversation strictly on Jamie—when they were not in bed and making love, of course—Lauren felt she was able to keep things in perspective. On the surface, anyway. In addition, she felt more in control of her feelings and could hide them from Sam by maintaining a businesslike demeanor.

One morning when Sophie had left to go shopping, and Lauren had just finished giving Jamie his breakfast, Sam sneaked into the kitchen without her hearing him. She was standing at the sink, washing up the dishes as she talked to Jamie, describing how they were going to spend their day.

Jamie, understanding only that he was with someone he

had come to love and depend upon in recent weeks, banged happily on the tray of his high chair, chubby legs swinging merrily.

"We're going to give you your bath, dress you in one of those cute little sunsuits your daddy bought you, and then we'll stroll to the playground so you can swing. I might even let you get all messy and sticky with an ice cream cone, too. Would you like that—"

She squealed as Sam grabbed her from behind, wrapping his arms around her waist as he pulled her against him to nuzzle the back of her neck with warm lips.

Lauren masked the thrill of his touch with anger and viciously scolded, "Stop it, Sam. You nearly made me drop one of Sophie's crystal juice glasses.

"What's wrong with you, anyway? She left ten minutes ago. You're putting on a show for nothing."

Her back still turned, she could not see the hurt look on his face.

"Sorry," he mumbled. "I didn't hear her leave."

"Well, she did. Ten minutes ago."

"You said that."

Hearing the edge to his voice, she glanced about, but he had already turned his attention to Jamie.

"What do you say, big boy? Did you get enough to eat this morning, or are they still trying to starve you to death with all that yucky strained stuff they call food?"

Jamie giggled and waved his arms, wanting his daddy to take him.

As testily as he had spoken to her, Lauren responded, "He's getting junior foods now. He gets exactly what his pediatrician says he's to have."

Sam was unfastening the tray that held Jamie in his seat. "Yeah? Well, none of that stuff looks appetizing to me. If I had my way, I'd take him out for an Egg McMuffin or a sausage biscuit." He rubbed noses with Jamie. "How would that be?"

Jamie squealed as though he thought that would be wonderful.

Lauren, however, had gone into a witchy mode to hide her true feelings. "Good grief, Sam," she snapped. "Is that what you're going to do the minute I'm out of the picture? Feed him fast food and forget things like a balanced diet?"

Sam recoiled at her waspish tone. Last night, they had been as close as two people could be, and now she was treating him as though he were an enemy. "Hey," he snapped right back. "I'm only kidding, but when he gets older, yes, I'll let him eat fast food. I want him to grow up like a normal little boy. If you and Sophie had your way, he'd never have any fun."

She whirled about, soap suds slinging from her hands. "How can you say that? I spend all day, every day, seeing that he has fun. I play with him all the time. So do you. And I've never said a word about it, and—"

She fell silent, biting her lip so hard, she tasted blood. She did not want it this way, did not want to fight to mask her true emotions. It was like knowing someone she loved was going to die, and wanting it to go on and happen so closure could begin.

Yes.

It was true.

Despite living in paradise, she wanted closure...healing...to begin.

"I'm sorry," Sam said lamely as he lifted Jamie into his arms. "You seem so cranky this morning that I guess I was just striking back."

"Well, I didn't mean to be," she lied.

Holding Jamie, he walked to where she stood and touched her shoulder with his free hand.

She did not turn around, for in that moment she did not trust herself to look at him.

With a sigh, he told her, "Lauren, I don't like this dragging out any more than you do. It's rough, I know, but I'm really starting to believe it's all just a sick game with Sophie. She likes controlling our lives. She's also banking we'll give up and go away, but if she doesn't get tired of it soon, I could lose my job.''

''And she'll kick us out and laugh about seeing us in court,'' Lauren said lamely.

''Maybe it's time I issued an ultimatum of my own.''

''Such as?'' She dried her hands on a towel and poured them both a cup of coffee.

He waited till they were seated at the table, Jamie on his knee, before explaining. ''The way I see it, we've given her enough time to make up her mind. So I'm going to tell her that if she hasn't decided by this weekend, I'm taking Jamie and leaving Monday whether she likes it or not.''

''But—''

He held up a hand in a plea to allow him to finish. ''I know what you're going to say—that she'll run to the phone and call her lawyer and have me stopped at the airport on Monday, but we're actually going to leave Sunday morning.''

Lauren was stunned. ''You're really going to run away?''

''I have to.'' He shook his head in disgust. ''Damn it, I hate to have to do it this way, to be made to feel like a criminal in order to have my son, but it seems I really don't have any other choice.''

Lauren made no comment, not wanting to either agree or disagree, telling herself it was not up to her to judge his decision. ''So how do you plan to do it?''

''Well, I think when I put it to her that this is it, that I'm not waiting any longer, I'll be able to tell by her reaction what her answer is ultimately going to be. If I sense she's going to say no, then we'll start getting ready to run. If we can make it back to Georgia, she'll have a tougher time fighting custody all the way from California.''

''And the trust fund?''

He shrugged, but Lauren did not miss the shadow of sorrow that crossed his face as he said, ''I'll try to make it up to him in other ways and hope the day never comes that he resents me for causing him to lose a fortune.''

"I don't think you have to worry about that." Lauren's heart was warmed to see the adoring way Jamie was gazing up at his daddy's face and how he was patting his cheek with his little dimpled hands. She could not imagine Jamie ever regretting being raised by his father, as opposed to having a lot of money. Still, she could understand Sam's concern after his own, sad experience, especially when he'd not known about his own inheritance. Now the decision was being made for Jamie, so everything had to be taken into consideration before burning any bridges.

"It's a chance I've got to take," Sam continued. "So here's what we'll do. Day after tomorrow—Saturday— we'll make like we're taking Jamie to the park, only I'll take the ferry into San Diego and go to the airport and rent a car. I'll drive it back and park it a few blocks away. That night, after Sophie has gone to bed, we'll quietly pack our things and take Jamie and slip out of the house and walk to the car.

"And we're on our way," he finished with a grin and a triumphant wave. "By the time she wakes up and realizes we're gone, we'll be miles away."

Lauren could not share his optimism that it would work, hating to point out, "The law will think to check on whether you rented a car. It won't take long for them to track you down, because you've got to give your driver's license number. The highway patrol will be after us within hours."

"True," he conceded, "but they won't be after us as fast as you might think. It will be Sunday morning when she finds out we've left, remember? And she will first have to track down her lawyer, which might not be so easy on a weekend. Then he's going to have to get the necessary papers filed to get a warrant for me before the law can be notified to start searching. At the earliest, it wouldn't happen till afternoon. We'll be hundreds of miles down the road by then, and we won't go the regular route, anyway. I've already checked a map. We'll keep to the side roads, off the beaten paths.

"We can do it, Lauren," he said, giving her arm a squeeze.

She did not say anything, staring instead into her nearly empty coffee mug and thinking again how she never should have gotten involved. She had, sadly enough, not only sold her heart for ten thousand dollars but would now become a fugitive, as well.

Sam watched her in silence for a few moments, then said, "I know what you're thinking."

"You do?" She did not look up.

"Yes, because I think we share the same doubts—that this was a dumb idea, and how it would have been easier if I'd just kidnapped him to start with."

But oh, how Lauren wished it did not have to be this way, for she had, despite everything, grown fond of Sophie and knew how it was going to hurt her to lose Jamie.

He downed the rest of his coffee before confiding, "You know, I have to admit there was a time, especially in the last couple of weeks, when I thought she might actually give in and say 'Okay. You two are great together. You'll make wonderful parents. Take Jamie and go, with my blessings.' But when she kept dragging it out, I finally realized she's still stubborn enough, and stupid enough, to think I'll give in and say to hell with it."

"I never thought for a minute you'd do that."

"I never thought that about you, either, and I want you to know how much I appreciate all your efforts. You've done everything you could to make it all go well, and I've enjoyed just being with you. I want you to know that.

"Know, too," he added, after drawing a deep breath and letting it out slowly, "that the rest of it—what we've shared, you know, between us—wasn't expected, but it was nice, and..." He fell silent, unsure of what else to say about the most wonderful experience he'd ever had with a woman.

She lowered her eyes to stare into her mug once more, her stomach suddenly tied in knots. It was as though he were already saying goodbye, and, oh, how it hurt.

But she was not about to let him know that, not about to make a fool of herself. She might walk away with her heart secretly in tatters, but she would hold her head up. Never, ever, would he know she had been so stupid as to fall in love with him after he'd made it perfectly clear from the very beginning that he was not interested in her romantically.

Giving her head a reckless toss, she forced a smile and quipped, "Hey, you don't owe me anything except a check for ten grand, Sam. Everything else was just for fun."

She snatched up their mugs and went to the sink, keeping her back turned and her voice even as she fought inner tremors to add, "That's what's been so great about all of this—the way we've behaved so maturely. We were able to have some fun without taking it serious, and, gee, wouldn't it be great if all relationships could be that way when a man and woman wanted them to be?"

"Yeah, wouldn't it?" He got up and walked out as he said, "I'll go give Jamie his bath while you finish cleaning up. Then we'll head for the park. You'll probably want to go to the pay phone, too, and call Midge and let her know you'll be home soon."

Only when he was gone did Lauren yield to the tears she had been fighting.

How she wept, shoulders shuddering as she clung to the counter for support. She loved them both so very, very much!

Suddenly the back door creaked and panic washed.

Sophie was back.

Thinking quickly, Lauren opened the vegetable bin under the counter and snatched up a large onion. Grabbing a knife, she began chopping it almost viciously, so that when

Sophie finally walked into the kitchen, she was able to look up at her with a sheepish grin as tears streamed down her cheeks, and proclaim convincingly, "Onions always make me cry, darn it."

Sophie tossed her bag on the counter and looked at her with narrowed eyes as she curtly demanded, "What, pray tell, are you doing peeling onions at this time of day?"

Lauren later thought how the lie that suddenly came to her had to have been a special gift from her guardian angel. "Sam wanted an omelet, and he likes onions."

Sophie made a face. "I still say it's too early for onions. Never could understand people wanting them in their omelets. Or green peppers, either, for that matter. It's not good to put all that spicy food into your stomach so early in the day. Where is Sam, anyway? And where's Jamie?"

"He's giving him his bath. Then we're going to the park. I thought you were going shopping," she added, knowing her return had been another ploy to try to catch them off guard.

"I left my shopping list. I'll be leaving again soon. I'll be away tomorrow, too. I'm going into San Diego to have lunch with my attorney."

Lauren did not miss the implication behind her words. Lunch with her lawyer meant a business conference, but what *kind* of business? Relinquishing custody of Jamie to Sam, or preparing to do battle to keep him herself? She was not about to ask, even though she burned to know.

"I like bathing Jamie," Sophie said quietly when a few moments had passed and neither of them had spoken.

"So do I." Lauren turned to go, anxious to escape. She was never comfortable around Sophie, especially when Sam was not there. "I think I'll give him a hand."

"Oh, let Sam have him to himself for a while. You and I can enjoy the patio. I see there's still coffee in the pot. I'll pour us both a cup, and we can go outside. It's a beautiful morning."

Lauren knew it would not be wise to decline and doggedly followed her.

Once settled amidst the sweet fragrance of the many flowers and the gentle breeze from the ocean across the way, Sophie suddenly surprised her by bluntly declaring, "I realize it's time all of this came to a head, Lauren. I want you to know that I will be making my decision quite soon."

Lauren dared to probe, "May I ask which way you're leaning?"

Sophie gave a long sigh as she leaned her head back against her chair and closed her eyes for a moment before meeting Lauren's anxious stare. "I don't want to say anything until after I have spoken with my attorney."

Lauren felt sick to her stomach. It could only mean Sophie didn't want to admit she was denying Sam custody till everything was in place for legal combat.

"You know," Sophie went on, "I happen to love Jamie very, very much. He's all the family I have left in this world. I had a sister, but she died when she was young and had never married. There were a few cousins, but we were never close. For all I know, they're dead, too. Jamie is all I have," she repeated.

"Yes, I know," Lauren said woodenly. Oh, why wasn't Sam here? And why was Sophie singling her out for this?

Because she thinks you're involved, too, dummy, a little voice inside nagged. *She thinks you're going to be Jamie's mother, a part of his world for the rest of his life. She doesn't know you're going to ride off into the sunset with ten thousand dollars and a smashed heart.*

"I only had one child, you know," Sophie said in a strange, faraway voice as she stared beyond Lauren. It was almost as if she was actually able to see into the past. "A son—Gaynelle's father. When he died, I think I turned into an old woman overnight. Everything in me just shriveled."

"You...you aren't that old," Lauren said uneasily. She

couldn't help but feel sorry for her. Losing her only son and granddaughter had to be a terrible tragedy.

"My husband and I loved each other very much. We wanted more children, but the good Lord didn't see fit to give them to us, so we cherished the one we had. And Jamie looks so much like him," she said, suddenly bright, her eyes shining, as she turned to Lauren once more.

Lauren thought Jamie was the image of Sam, but if Sophie saw otherwise and it made her happy, so be it.

But then Sophie's glow faded as she lowered her voice to admit, "I don't mind telling you that I was very upset when Sam tracked me down. I'd hoped I wouldn't hear from him ever again."

Gingerly, Lauren reminded, "But Sam was thrilled when Gaynelle asked him if he would want to adopt their baby. It's only natural he would have followed up on her offer."

"He should have left well enough alone," Sophie said with teeth clenched, hands squeezing her coffee mug.

Lauren knew it was time for the conversation to end. Nothing good was going to come of it now. "I think I'd better go see if I can help with Jamie's bath." She stood.

Sophie went on as though Lauren had not spoken. "Anybody wild enough to get involved with Gaynelle isn't good father material. Sam might think he is, because right now it's all a lark, and Jamie is such a little sweetheart. Any man would be proud to have him for a son. But down the road, Sam might be tempted to go back to his old ways of partying and cavorting around, and I was thinking maybe I should—"

"Oh, that's just not true, Sophie," Lauren cried, unable to keep still any longer. In the past, she would have kept her mouth shut, figuring Sam could fight his own battles. Now, however, loving him as she did, she could not allow such remarks to slide by. "Granted, Sam might have been a bit irresponsible in his personal life at one time, but no more. All he wants now is to take care of his son and see that he's raised properly. You will never have to worry about Jamie being neglected.

"*Never,*" she repeated more forcefully.

Sophie was taken aback, her face going pale as she blinked in disbelief that someone she had regarded as rather meek could now come across as fierce as a mother bear defending her cub.

Finally getting over the shock of Lauren's explosion, Sophie cleared her throat and said, "Well, I was only going to say..." But she trailed to silence. Staring down at her hands, she shook her head and murmured, more to herself than Lauren, "Nothing. Never mind. I don't suppose it matters."

Lauren, concluding she'd been about to continue denouncing Sam, did not prod her to finish what she had been about to say. She did not want to hear it. "If there's nothing else, I'd really like to help with Jamie's bath."

"Yes, so would I," Sophie said, her voice breaking.

Lauren turned and rushed inside, fearing if she did not escape then and there, she would burst into tears again.

It was just all so sad, even for little Jamie, who loved his great-grandmother but would probably never see her again.

Sam, Lauren quietly, painfully, acknowledged, was the only one who would come out smiling. He would have his son and could look forward to a wonderful future. And someday down the road he would meet the right woman, fall in love, get married and maybe even have more children.

Thinking about it, Lauren suddenly felt an odd kind of kinship to Sophie, for they were the ones who were going to be left to try to pick up the pieces of their lives.

Sam was drying Jamie when Lauren entered the nursery. Glancing up at her, his smile faded as he saw her expression. "Is something wrong?" he asked warily.

She recounted her conversation with Sophie and how she

had indicated she might be ready to announce her decision after lunch with her attorney on Friday.

Lauren saw his jaw tighten as he powdered Jamie in silence.

"Very well," he said finally, grimly. "We'll just be ready to leave a day early."

"Like criminals," she said dryly.

"I don't see it that way, Lauren. All I'm doing is taking my son home with me. I only hope the law in Georgia backs me up. I called my lawyer a little while ago, and he says I've got a good case.

"We're going to make it, Lauren," he said in a happy rush, lifting Jamie up into his arms with a hug that made him squeal in protest. "It's going to be okay."

For you, maybe, she cried in her heart, *but not for me.*

Chapter Fourteen

Sam decided to leave the rental car in the Del's parking lot. No one would think anything about a couple and a baby leaving from a hotel in the wee hours of morning, but a passerby might think it odd to see them in a park at such a strange time.

Sophie's house was less than five minutes away, close enough that Lauren could walk as he carried Jamie in his car seat. He did not want to risk picking them up in the car, lest Sophie hear and look out to see what was going on. It was better to just steal away into the night. He also planned to sneak their luggage out after dark to hide in the shrubs, which meant he would have to make several trips back and forth from the car to retrieve everything.

But it didn't matter.

He only wished there were some other way. Sophie loved Jamie, and he hated to hurt her, but Jamie was *his* son, and nothing was going to stand in the way of his having custody.

And then there was Lauren.

Sam didn't like thinking about that part of it...how once they were back in Atlanta they would not be seeing each other again. Oh, sure, she'd probably call a few times to be polite and ask how Jamie was doing. And she'd say things like to let her know if he needed help. Lip service only. She wouldn't mean it.

But she did care about Jamie, and it wasn't an act. She genuinely loved the little fellow. Who wouldn't? And no doubt she would miss him, but Sam doubted that would last very long. Lauren was a terrific young woman with so much to offer the man lucky enough to win her heart.

Her heart, however, was locked up tighter than the Federal Reserve, and, oh, how Sam envied the man who might one day find the key to unlock it.

So many times in the past week he had come dangerously close to admitting he was falling in love with her. He was tempted most, he supposed, during those soft velvet moments after the sweetest lovemaking this side of heaven. As they lay locked in each other's arms, their bodies slick with perspiration, hearts thundering like a spring storm in Georgia, it was the perfect ambience for soul-rendering confessions of adoration. But even as he fought to muster the courage, he could feel that invisible barrier rising once more. The moment would pass...the words gone unspoken.

As he walked along the flower-bordered sidewalk, a warm sun streaming down, Sam wondered if, down the road, he would regret not taking the plunge and baring his soul to her. And, as always when he thought about it, he was struck to painfully remember the night when he'd so foolishly yielded to his feelings for Gaynelle—feelings that he now, however, knew were not genuine. They had been, instead, the wishful thoughts of a lonely man desperately seeking love and all that went with it—commitment, the feeling of belonging to someone, home, family. A life.

Never would he forget how Gaynelle had reacted.

She had laughed at him.

Not merely snickered or giggled.

She had thrown her head back and laughed loudly and raucously.

He had chosen a romantic setting—a cozy restaurant, roving violinists and candlelight. And, yes, champagne...but very *special* champagne, because he had managed to slip a diamond ring into her glass. Then, handing it to her, he had whispered, "Gaynelle, I'm asking you to marry me."

Later he wondered whether it was the sight of the ring in the bubbling champagne or his proposal that she found so hilarious. He never asked. He only knew that when she was able to find her voice amidst the laughter she had cried, "Oh, Sam. You are such a romantic fool. Don't you know a husband is the last thing in the world I want?"

Never had he known such humiliation, and, to save face, he had lied and pretended relief, saying he only did it because he thought she was expecting him to propose, but, actually, marriage was the last thing he wanted, too.

He didn't think she believed him and supposed it didn't matter. The damage was done. He returned the ring and got his money back, and their live-for-today-to-hell-with-tomorrow life-style continued—till she told him she was pregnant.

Again, he had been so foolish as to throw himself at her feet, begging her to marry him for the baby's sake.

And when she had once more refused, saying she intended to have an abortion, he had actually, and unashamedly, wept.

Later he had admonished himself for allowing things to go so far between them, because Gaynelle had always been open and honest about her determination to remain single.

And, likewise, Lauren had been equally candid as to her feelings where romance was concerned.

So he was not going to make a fool of himself again.

He would keep his mouth shut.

He would take solace in being a good father to Jamie,

which was another reason he was so determined to whisk him away. It was going to be painful enough to say goodbye to Lauren without leaving his son behind, hoping he could one day win him through the courts.

Sam was taking no chances, regardless of the consequences, even though he did not like going about it as he felt forced to do. He had never been a sneaky sort of person. Neither had he ever intentionally broken the law. He preferred to do things the right way and had always stood up for what he believed in, ready to fight for it. That's why he had wanted to be a Navy SEAL. He was, he was proud to think, an honorable and courageous man.

And now he was running away like a thief and a coward…because, God forgive him, he just didn't see any other way.

Sam could not, would not, risk losing his son.

Jamie was all he had in this world.

Rounding the corner, Sam felt a happy rush at the sight of Lauren and Jamie. Lauren was sitting on a bench in front of Sophie's house, and Jamie was in his stroller, playing happily with what appeared to be a new toy.

"So you're still spoiling him," Sam chided good-naturedly as he lifted Jamie from the stroller after giving her a perfunctory kiss should Sophie be watching. Not that it mattered what she thought anymore. He was leaving, regardless. He just wanted an excuse to kiss Lauren.

"It's musical, see?" Lauren took the little bear from Jamie's hand and squeezed it. "It plays Brahms's Lullaby. Jamie hasn't figured out yet that he has to mash it to make music, but he will, because he's so bright."

"Of course, he is," Sam said proudly, kissing both his cheeks.

Jamie's attention was on his daddy, the bear forgotten, so Lauren put it in the stroller.

Sam sat down next to Lauren. "So where's Sophie?" he asked solemnly, adding, "I'd like to get the big scene over with as soon as possible."

Lauren frowned. She was beginning to worry, because she hadn't seen Sophie since breakfast. "I don't think she's back yet."

It was Sam's turn to frown. "She should be. It's nearly five o'clock. Didn't you say she was meeting her lawyer for lunch?"

"That's what she told me."

He swore under his breath before voicing his fear that she had changed her mind and planned to drag things out awhile longer. "She's got to be doing it just to be hateful," he fumed. "She's had plenty of time to reach a decision, but lately I've started thinking she was lying and knew all along she'd never give Jamie up without a fight no matter what she thought of us and our marriage. She just figures it will make her case stronger, to be able to say she gave me a chance to prove myself, only I failed."

Lauren saw his clenched jaw and the steely set to his eyes. She moved to take Jamie from him, but he held tight, kissing the top of his head as he whispered that, no, he wanted to hold him.

As much as she hated to admit it, Lauren suspected Sam's theory just might be right. Sophie had been acting so strange the past few days, as though she were terribly nervous about something. Perhaps she feared the ultimate confrontation sure to come when she said no.

Yet, Lauren was bothered by something else about Sophie. Something almost humbling and pitiful, which didn't make sense. No longer than the few weeks Lauren had known the woman, she had been impressed by her spunk, her spirit. She was a fighter, through and through.

So why all of a sudden did she seem to be wilting like a thirsty flower on a dry summer day?

"I got the car okay," Sam said. "I left it at the hotel. It won't take us long to walk there."

Lauren cast a wary eye skyward. "That's good, because the weather report is calling for rain. Maybe I should sneak one of Sophie's umbrellas out of her closet just in case."

"She might miss it if she goes out later."

"Why would she go out?"

"She probably wouldn't. I just don't want to take any chances, Lauren. Not now. If it rains, I'll take Jamie and run, and you can walk fast."

"What about our things? They'll get soaked out here in the bushes."

"Sorry, but it can't be helped. I'll start as soon as it gets dark."

"Well, watch out for Mr. Godfrey." She waved at Sophie's next-door neighbor, who had just come out on his porch to pick up his evening paper. "I noticed when he turns in his driveway at night his headlights shine over here. If you happened to be hiding the luggage, he'd see you and probably pick up the phone and call Sophie to find out what was going on."

"I'll be careful. How is his wife doing, anyway?" Sam had met the old gentleman one morning, and he had told him about her having had a stroke.

Lauren related what little she knew. "It's doubtful she'll ever get any better. She'll probably have to stay in the nursing home. And it's a pitiful situation. Sophie says it's just the two of them, no children, no family. They've been married sixty-five years. Sophie gave a little dinner party for them on their anniversary last fall."

"It'd be a blessing if they died together, wouldn't it?" Sam mused aloud. "That's what marriage is all about. Till death do we part and all that."

Lauren looked at him, bemused. It was strange to hear him say such a thing, feeling as he did about marriage and wanting no part of it. He had actually sounded wistful.

Several moments passed without either of them speaking. Jamie bounced in delight to watch the butterflies dancing about the hibiscus bushes, prompting Sam to remark, "He's going to miss the butterflies. I guess I'll have to hurry up and find us a place with a yard by spring so I can set some flowers out to draw them."

Lauren murmured, "That would be nice," then added, "He's going to miss Sophie, too. For a while, anyway."

Sam asked sharply, "Do you really think so?"

"Of course. She's cared for him since he was born."

"But you've been looking after him for over a month."

"What's one month versus six? Like it or not, they're bonded, Sam. Haven't you ever noticed how his eyes light up when she walks into a room, how he holds his arms out for her sometimes, even when I've got him?"

"Yes, but he'll be happy with me. He loves me."

"Of course, he does. Babies love everybody who's kind to them. He'll miss her, but, eventually, he'll forget her. And me, too," she added pensively.

Sam was quick to remind her, "You know, I'm hoping you'll stay in touch."

Lauren knew he was expecting her to politely assure him she would certainly be around from time to time but could not bring herself to lie.

When she didn't say anything, Sam returned to discussing Sophie's whereabouts. "I can't imagine what's keeping her. Surely she hasn't been talking to her lawyer all this time."

"Maybe she met a friend and went to a movie. She's been able to get out more with us around to look after Jamie, and she's probably enjoyed her freedom, even though it's bound to upset her when he's no longer around."

Sam was neither surprised nor upset by Lauren's focused empathy for Sophie, because, despite everything, he felt the same way. "It's just a shame things couldn't have been different, so she could be part of the family, too. But now I believe she'll hate me too much for that to ever happen."

Lauren thought a moment, then said, as though it had just dawned, "You know, she doesn't really seem like the hating kind."

"What do you mean?"

"Well, think about it. She's not really a bad sort. She

puts Jamie's welfare above everything else. She can't be faulted for a thing where he's concerned.'' She turned to meet his steady gaze. "What if we're wrong about her? What if this wasn't contrived, after all?''

"I don't see what you're getting at.''

"Maybe she really *was* trying to see if you could give Jamie a good home. True, she was hoping you wouldn't agree to her so-called test and say to hell with it, but since you didn't, maybe she was hoping to find that you actually would make a good father.''

Jamie was starting to fret. The butterflies had flown away, and it was time for his supper. Sam began to jiggle him on his knee as he listened to Lauren.

"What if,'' Lauren continued to speculate, "she tells you tonight that she's decided favorably? Wouldn't you then want to include her in Jamie's life?''

"Of course, I would. But I'm afraid I just can't share your optimism, because if that were the case, why would she have wanted to talk to her lawyer? It looks to me like she wanted to make sure she was ready to go to war before firing the first shot.''

"You're probably right, though I have to say she was acting sort of funny. Sad, kind of.''

"Well, that doesn't make sense. She should be gloating to think how she made a fool of me.''

Lauren put her hand on his knee. She felt so bad for him. "But she didn't make a fool of you, Sam. You proved exactly what you are—a man who loves and wants his son and who was willing to try his best to prove it. You've nothing to be ashamed of. I'm just sorry you think you have to resort to what can only be called kidnapping.''

He gave her a sharp look but laughed as he said, "Boy, you really know how to make a guy feel good. First you tell me how great I am and then remind me I'm about to become a criminal.''

"Well, you *are* breaking the law,'' she reminded him.

"Do you see any other way?''

"Yes," Lauren said bluntly. "Fight her. You know you'll win. We've talked about it before. You're Jamie's natural father. Your own lawyer has told you that, hasn't he?"

"In so many words, yes, but he can't guarantee it. Nobody can. And we've also talked before about how it will be decided here, in Sophie's backyard, so to speak. So when I think of the time involved, and the money, I'd rather do it my way—even if it is, technically, against the law.

"Something else," he continued. "Sophie went to court and had herself appointed legal guardian for Jamie right after Gaynelle died."

"I hadn't thought of that."

"Oh, she let me know that the first time I called her. She's thought of everything. That's what's got me worried now. There's no telling what she'll do."

"First of all, she'll try to have Jamie brought back to California. If she succeeds, what then?"

"I don't want to think about it," he said wearily. Jamie's fretting was increasing, and Sam started to rise. "I think we'd better get him fed."

Lauren caught his arm to hold him back, and yielded to what had been on her mind the past several days. "I want you to know I don't expect you to pay me all the money. It wouldn't be fair...not when it didn't work. And who's to say it wasn't my fault, anyway?"

He put Jamie against his shoulder and patted his back to try to quiet him as he looked at Lauren with stern eyes. "None of this is your fault. You've been wonderful. Sophie had her mind made up all along, only I was dumb enough to hope there might be a chance. So don't let me hear you talk nonsense again, okay? You earned that money. Every dollar of it. And you're going to take it as soon as we get back to Atlanta. Understood?"

"I'm just not sure—"

"Well, I am." He cut her off. "And something else, too, Lauren. I want you to know the time with you has been great. I've enjoyed it. And under different circumstances, who's to say—''

"Yeah, who's to say?" she quipped with a crooked smile to hide the way she was melting inside. Dear Lord, she had to be as cool about it as he appeared to be. "Maybe in another life I'll consider going to bat for the fourth time. Who knows?''

"Yeah," he matched her nonchalance. "Who knows?''

Sophie finally returned just before dinner.

Lauren had prepared a tuna casserole and salad, and she and Sam were enjoying a glass of wine on the patio while waiting for her.

"I'm not hungry," Sophie said when Lauren told her everything was ready. "I don't feel well. I'm going to bed early.''

Lauren and Sam exchanged puzzled glances, then Sam cleared his throat and mustered the nerve to say, "Well, I'm sorry you're feeling bad, Sophie, but I was wondering if you wanted to talk to me. Lauren said you were meeting with your lawyer today, and that you thought you were about to make a decision about everything.''

"I did meet with him," Sophie acknowledged, "but we'll have to talk at breakfast. I..." She faltered. "I have some things I need to think about and, as I said, I just don't feel very good.''

"Something is definitely wrong," Lauren said after Sophie had gone to her room. "What if I go and talk to her? Maybe she'll tell me what it's all about.''

Sam gave his head a vehement shake. "No. She's just not wanting a fight this late at night. Her mind is made up against me. All I want now is to get away from here as soon as possible.''

A few hours later, all was ready, and they settled down to sleep until they could be sure all was quiet in the neighborhood. Sam did not want to chance anyone seeing them and felt 4:00 a.m. would be the best time to venture out.

Lauren knew it would be their last night to share a bed. They had talked about how they would take turns driving during the long, grueling trip to Atlanta and go straight through. It would be rough, but as long as Jamie was all right, they would not make any stops except for food, gas and personal needs.

She had turned on her side, away from him, hoping sleep would come so she would not just lie there in misery to think about how she would never again awaken with her head on his shoulder or feel his arms about her.

But when he pulled her against him, she could not resist. With masterful hands, he stroked from her shoulders to her buttocks, and she shivered deliciously to his touch.

Finally, he rolled her toward him, and she threw back her head as his mouth moved to her breasts, and she trembled even more to anticipate the splendor she knew awaited.

"It's been so good with you," he murmured, his lips darting from one nipple to the other, curling his tongue about to taste and tease. "Every moment holding you has been paradise." He licked the globes of her breasts, her skin like velvet to his sweet caress, making him mindless with desire.

Outside, the rain began to fall, and the wind started blowing, but the storm without was nothing compared to the tempest within as Lauren arched against him wildly, eagerly.

He cupped her head and kissed her mouth and knew he would want her every day and night for the rest of his life.

He drew her against his naked body, and she pressed even tighter against him, reveling in the warmth and feel of his hard, muscled thighs, wanting to feel him deep inside her.

Touching his hair, his face, she danced her fingers downward to caress his perfectly molded buttocks and pull him to the essence of her womanhood.

She loved him.

Oh, how deeply and completely she loved him.

Gently he moved her legs apart and rolled to hover over her.

Lauren was glad it was dark…glad he could not see the tears welling in her eyes to think how this would be the last time he would ever enter her…the last time they would become one in the glory of their passion.

She raised her hips to meet his first, mighty thrust.

When it was over, when they had reached the stars once more in unison, they clung together tightly, neither wanting to be the one to let go.

Finally, Lauren could stand it no longer, fearing she would burst into tears to open the floodgate of emotions and confess that she loved him with every beat of her heart and always would.

She pulled away.

Sam let her go.

He was waging a battle of his own as he fought to keep from telling her that somewhere along the way he had cast aside his cynicism about love and was throwing himself at her feet to declare he had never loved a woman more…would never again.

But Gaynelle's laughter echoed yet in his ears…in his soul.

And Lauren's pride would not allow her to bare her heart.

So the words went unspoken.

The rain was coming down harder, and Lauren thought of how they were going to get drenched if it didn't let up by the time they made their way to the car. They could cover Jamie with a blanket, and Sam could run with him, but his things would be soaked. His toys, his new musical bear.

The bear!

Lauren bolted upright.

"What is it?" Sam asked sharply.

"Nothing. I'll get it." She scrambled out of bed.

He sat up. "Where are you going?"

"I'll be right back." It was her fault, so she was not about to let him be the one to get soaked. She should have remembered the stroller, and the bear, and brought both inside, but it had slipped her mind. They weren't taking the stroller, so she'd not thought about it. And in all the turmoil, she had forgotten the bear, as well.

Before Sam could stop her, she quietly hurried from the bedroom to tiptoe down the hall to the foyer.

Praying the front door would not squeak, she opened it and stepped onto the porch. She could not see her hand in front of her face but knew exactly where the stroller was—next to the bench that sat on the grassy strip between sidewalk and street.

Taking a deep breath, she plunged into the torrential downpour.

She slipped, almost fell, but kept on going.

Suddenly the street was illuminated by the glare of headlights as a car came speeding around the corner. She could see the stroller, with the soaked bear propped in the seat. It was only a few feet away from her. She would grab it, and—

Over the sound of pouring rain came the squeal of brakes and tires singing over the water as the car began to hydroplane, skidding straight toward Lauren.

She glanced up but was blinded by the glare of the lights bearing down on her. She stumbled backward in a frantic effort to put something between her and Mr. Godfrey's out-of-control car. The bench. The palm tree. The stroller. Anything.

And then there was a loud, sickening thud as the car plowed into the tree.

Lauren screamed.

And then she knew nothing.

Chapter Fifteen

Sam had to take the time to find his pajamas and put them on before he could follow Lauren. Consequently, he had just stepped out on the front porch when the car slammed into the palm tree. In the same blinding instant, he saw Lauren in the glare of headlights as the tree came crashing down on top of her, knocking her to the ground.

"God, no!"

He bolted down the steps, almost falling in his haste.

She was buried under thick palm fronds, and he clawed frantically at the ragged branches. Over and over he called her name, but there was no sound except for the pouring rain and the still-running engine of the wrecked car. Then dogs began to bark, and doors were opened in houses up and down the street as neighbors, having heard the crash, spilled out to see what had happened.

Sam, still fighting to get to Lauren, called into the darkness, "Please. Somebody call 911—now!"

He worked in the crooked glow of the smashed headlights that shone crazily into the debris. Finally he was able to reach Lauren. Touching his fingertips to the pulse in her neck, he whispered a prayer of thanks to find it. She was alive, thank God.

Now the question was whether she was badly hurt, but he was afraid to move her, knowing if she had any kind of spinal injury, it could cause more damage. Despite his emergency medical training in the SEALs, he realized it was best to wait for the paramedics, who would have the proper equipment.

He removed more branches to check whether she was bleeding. All he saw was what appeared to be some pretty bad scratches, but there was no profuse blood. Obviously, the tree had served as a buffer between her and the car; otherwise, it would have been a lot worse.

"Lauren, can you hear me?" he whispered against her ear. "Lauren, honey, please be okay. I love you, sweetheart. I love you so much. You've got to be all right."

He felt shaking hands clutching his shoulder, and then a woman's frantic voice. "Sam. Oh, Lord. Tell me she's not—"

He was holding his hands over Lauren's face, trying to shield her from the rain as much as possible. Sophie had come up behind without him noticing. "No, she's not dead, but she's unconscious, and I'm afraid to move her."

"What...what can I do?" She was sobbing.

"Go back to the house and call 911 for an ambulance, then bring me an umbrella.

"And be careful," he called after her. "The sidewalk and steps are slick in the rain."

One of the neighbors appeared, a man who lived in the house on the other side of Sophie. "My wife called for an ambulance. It should be here any minute. Is there anything I can do?"

Sam told him to check on the driver of the car.

The man hurried to oblige and returned in a few seconds

to report in a panic, "It's Bob Godfrey. He's slumped over the steering wheel. I think he's dead."

"Maybe not." Sam knew he should see if there was anything he could do but hated to leave Lauren. She was his love, his life, and even though she'd never be his, he could not stand the thoughts of her suffering.

Sophie returned to advise, "I called 911, but they said someone had already reported it. They're on their way. Here's the umbrella."

"Hold it over her, Sophie. Keep her as dry as possible."

He ran to the car to check Mr. Godfrey, and this time when he felt for a pulse he did not find one. There was nothing he could do, nothing anyone could do. The man was dead.

He hurried back to where Sophie was kneeling beside Lauren and shielding her with the umbrella.

"She hasn't moved or made a sound," Sophie said worriedly.

Sam dropped to his knees, feeling for Lauren's pulse again. It was still strong. A good sign.

"What was she doing out here in all this rain in the middle of the night?" Sophie asked.

Sam explained, "I'm not sure, but I found this musical bear she bought Jamie outside. Maybe she had realized she left it out in the rain. She was in the wrong place at the wrong time—she was out here when Mr. Godfrey had his wreck."

"Oh, that's Bob?" Sophie cried in dismay, previously unaware her neighbor and good friend was involved. "Is he hurt bad?"

Hearing sirens in the distance, Sam said, "The paramedics will check him." He wasn't about to give her the news himself. "I think you should go inside and get some dry clothes on. There's nothing you can do here."

"You…you're probably right," she said tremulously, struggling to stand. He caught her arm and helped her up as she urged, "As soon as the ambulance attendants check her, you come tell me how she is."

Patiently, he explained, "They won't be able to tell us anything. We're going to have to wait till we get her to the hospital and let the doctors check her over there."

"I want to go to the hospital, too. I'll call Gertrude to come stay with Jamie."

He was no longer listening to her, because the ambulance was braking to a stop. Three paramedics were on board and leapt out with flashlights and medical kits. Two ran to the car, the other spotted Sam and Lauren and rushed over.

Right behind them were two police cars, blue lights flashing.

Sam explained what he thought had happened as the paramedic opened his kit and took out stethoscope and blood-pressure cuff to begin his cursory site examination.

One of the other attendants walked over. "What have you got here, Dave? I'm afraid the driver is dead. No visible sign of injury. Looks like a heart attack."

Sophie, still standing there, moaned and cried, "Oh, no. Oh, no."

Sam grasped her by her shoulders and gave her a little shake as he urged, "Please go change into dry clothes, Sophie, or you're going to be sick."

Crying, she finally turned to disappear into the darkness.

The paramedic named Dave told his partner, "Her BP is one ten over seventy. Pulse eighty. Respiration satisfactory."

His partner knelt on the other side. With his thumb, he gently opened Lauren's eyelids in turn to examine with his flashlight. "The pupils constrict. Doesn't look like head trauma." He took a pin from the kit and pressed it to Lauren's nail bed, and she flinched. "Good motor response. I think she's just knocked out. Or maybe she fainted. Hell, if I saw a car coming at me like that, I'd probably pass out, too. We'll use the backboard to be on the safe side in case there is injury, though."

Sam helped them slide her onto the board. He took the head blocks from Dave and said, "I'll do it. I know how." And, as he positioned her neck between the thick, orange blocks, he took the opportunity to press his lips against her ear and tell her once more, "I love you, honey. Please be okay. I love you so much."

When she was finally loaded into the ambulance, Dave advised Sam, "We'll take her on in. We can't move the driver till the medical examiner gets to the scene to do his thing."

Sam had started to climb into the back of the ambulance with Lauren, but Dave said, "Sorry, buddy. I'm afraid we've got a law in this county that says nobody rides but the patient and us. You'll have to follow in your car."

My car, Sam thought wryly, *is parked at the hotel lot in readiness for my getaway.*

He was further jolted to remember the hidden luggage. In the morning, Sophie would see it and know he had been planning to run away.

"Damn it." He swore under his breath, frantically trying to figure a way out of the mess. He wanted to be with Lauren. Oh, man, did he ever want to be with her.

And not just for now but always.

"Hey, I'm really sorry," Dave said as he gave Sam a friendly pat on the back. He thought his cursing was due to being refused transport in the ambulance. "Just come on behind us, okay?"

"Yeah, sure." Sam glanced about. The crowd was starting to break up. As far as they were concerned, the show was over, and it was still raining, and they were getting wet. The police were not going to let anyone gawk at Bob Godfrey's body, so there was no need to hang around.

There were four suitcases, and the police weren't paying any attention to Sam. As soon as the ambulance was gone and no one was looking, he grabbed two of them and took them around to the back of the house. Leaving them on the porch, he eased inside to check on Sophie's whereabouts and was relieved to hear her on the phone talking to Gertrude. Moving swiftly, he had all the luggage back in his room by the time she hung up.

"You didn't go with her?" she asked, stunned that he was still there. He explained there was no room and needed to borrow her car, but she shook her head. "Wait for me. Gertrude is on her way over. I'm going with you.

"Now don't worry," she added, turning toward her room, "I'll hurry. I know you have to be there as her husband to get her registered and all."

Her words struck a chord as Sam realized there were going to be all kinds of complications as to how to register Lauren. She was Lauren *Gentry*—not Rutledge, and if Sophie were there to hear it…

He wasn't taking any chances.

Even if he was planning on running away, it still wouldn't do for Sophie to discover he and Lauren were only pretending to be married. She would kick him out, and he'd play hell with Sophie, getting his hands on Jamie to take him with him.

Grabbing the car keys from the hook by the door where Sophie always left them, Sam was out of the house like a flash. He would worry later about her being upset to find he'd gone on without her.

At the emergency room, he asked to see Lauren but was sent, according to routine, to the admitting office. There he gave Lauren's real name and signed that he would be responsible for the charges. She probably had insurance, but he didn't want to be bothered worrying about it now.

As he scrawled his signature, the secretary asked, "Are you a family member?"

He raised his eyes from the admissions form to look at her as he asked politely, "Does it matter? I signed for financial responsibility."

"Well, if you're the next of kin, it needs to be stated, because I see your last names are different."

He told another lie, figuring it didn't matter, and besides, it might be best in case someone left Lauren's chart lying around and Sophie were to see it. "I'm her husband. She kept her maiden name when we got married."

The secretary nodded with an approving smile. "I did the same thing. Lots of women do these days."

Finally he was taken to the curtained cubicle where Lauren was still strapped to the backboard, which had been placed on a stretcher. A doctor and nurse were in the room. "Is she going to be okay?" he asked at once.

"I think so," the doctor said without looking up from his clipboard. "We're getting ready to take her to X ray as a precaution. If nothing is cracked or broken, she's still going to be very sore, judging from the bruises I'm seeing. And she's got some nasty scratches we need to get cleaned up. A few might need bandages. But, all in all, I'd say she's a very lucky young lady."

Finally he lifted his eyes from his charting to look at Sam and curiously ask, "Which one are you—Sam or Jamie?"

Sam, stunned, could only stand there, wondering how the doctor knew the names.

"Uh-oh. Did I goof?" The doctor's tone of voice indicated he didn't care if he had. With a shrug, he explained, "She came to for a few minutes and called for both of you, then fell asleep again."

Annoyed, Sam stiffly repeated the well-worn lie. "I'm Sam. Her husband. Jamie is my—" he was quick to amend "—*our* son."

"I see," the doctor said tonelessly.

The nurse smiled.

Sam gritted his teeth. He had enough on his mind without total strangers implying Lauren had two lovers, for Pete's sake. "Well, how come she's still unconscious?" he then asked sharply.

The doctor casually explained, "I gave her a sedative. There's always the risk of shock in accidents like this. We need to keep her still. She'll sleep through the X rays, and that's good.''

When the doctor and nurse left, and he was finally alone with Lauren, Sam moved to stand beside her. He felt so helpless, and his heart was full to bursting with his love for her.

He began to stroke her cheek gently, tenderly, all the while crooning to her, ''You're going to be okay. Just rest and take it easy, honey. It's going to be fine.''

An aide came and rolled her out, and Sam began to pace about restlessly as he wondered how it was all going to affect his plans. Probably Sophie would now delay announcing her decision until Lauren was back on her feet. There would be time to make new arrangements to get away. The main thing, though, was for Lauren to get over this and be okay.

Hot tears squeezed at the back of his eyes, and he clenched and unclenched his fists as he shuffled about the tiny cubicle. He'd had no doubts he had feelings for her before, but seeing her as he had, not knowing at first if she were alive or dead, had wrenched his guts to the core.

He wished he did not love her, wished he did not have to deal with the anguish of trying to get over her, and something told him that was not going to happen, anyway. He was never going to be able to get her out of his mind…his heart. She was now a part of him, but there was nothing he could do about it.

Because Lauren did not want commitment.

Neither had Gaynelle.

And he could not bear to hear the laughter again.

Suddenly the curtains swished open and Sophie burst on the scene to angrily cry, ''You left without me. I had to take a cab. Then I had a time finding you, because admitting didn't have a Lauren Rutledge. I didn't know she's one of those modern women who keep using their maiden name after they get married.''

Sam threw up his hands in apology. "Sorry," Sam apologized. "I was just trying to get here as fast as possible."

"I suppose I can understand that," she said grudgingly, "but I was worried, too. I still am. Where is she?"

Sam told her what little he knew, emphasizing that the doctor seemed optimistic Lauren would be all right.

"Thank the Lord," Sophie said with a grateful glance toward heaven before proceeding to share the information she had received from Gertrude. "Bob Godfrey should never have been driving himself. His wife had just died at the nursing home and, no doubt, he was beside himself with grief, and that triggered a fatal heart attack. He had one a while back."

Sam was washed with pity for the old man, but at least he was at peace now and the accident was not as bad as it might have been.

"Sam, we need to talk."

Something in her tone caused him to look at her sharply and, seeing the grim expression on her face, his heart skipped a beat. Surely she was not going to pick now to tell him she was not going to relinquish custody. "Later," he said tightly, turning away.

"No." She swung her head stubbornly from side to side. "We need to talk now."

"Sophie, I've got a lot on my mind."

"So have I. These past weeks haven't been easy on me, either, Sam, watching you and Lauren, trying to decide if you were sincere, if your marriage is solid—"

"Sophie, I—" He swallowed hard. God, he did not want to hear her say it. Not now. He needed time to think and plan, because he had to take Jamie and run. Fast. Only, he couldn't abandon Lauren, and there was no telling how long it would be till she was able to travel.

"Sam, I really want to get this over with."

He met her determined gaze with one of his own. "And I want to wait till my nerves are a little more settled, Sophie. I've got a lot on my mind right now. I can't deal with—''

''You can deal with this.''

''But—''

Again, the curtain opened with a swish as Lauren, on the stretcher but minus the backboard, was pushed back in.

''Here we are,'' the nurse cheerfully announced.

Sam grinned all the way to his heart.

Her eyes were open.

She was awake.

''You're going to be okay,'' he said, beaming. Then, brows drawn together, he looked to the nurse for confirmation. Seeing her nod, relief returned in a sweeping rush. ''Thank God.''

Only then did Lauren notice Sophie. ''You came, too. Thank you. But where's Jamie?'' She raised her head from the pillow but relaxed as Sam assured her he was in good hands.

''Just rest.'' He urged. ''You had a bad fall.''

''I'd like to get out of here.'' She looked at the nurse. ''How long do I have to stay?''

''The doctor would like to keep you for observation for a little while, anyway. I'd say at least till around lunchtime.''

The nurse left them, and Sam said, ''Well, I'll hang around and keep you company.'' Fishing in his pocket for the keys, he held them out to Sophie. ''Here. You take your car. I'll bring Lauren home in a cab.''

With a stubborn lift of her chin, Sophie firmly said, ''I'm not leaving till we talk, Sam, no matter how long it takes.''

Lauren, a chill of foreboding creeping up and down her spine, looked from Sophie's determined face to Sam's worried expression. ''What's this all about?''

''It's okay.'' Sam patted her shoulder, knowing there was nothing to do but get it over with.

His eyes were steely as he finally turned to Sophie. ''All

right. But not here. Lauren needs her rest. Let's go get a cup of coffee.''

Lauren watched them walk away and wished she could go, because somehow she knew this was it, and she wanted—needed—to be with Sam when he heard Sophie's decision.

But why had Sophie picked now to do it, Lauren wondered groggily as the sedative began to claim her once more. Had she found the luggage and discovered they had been planning to flee with Jamie, and wanted to tell Sam he was no longer welcome in her home? Had she already been on the phone with her lawyer to start the legal process to block Sam from taking him?

Lauren fought the dizziness that was creeping over her. She wanted to stay awake, wanted to be there to comfort Sam when he returned. It just wasn't fair. Not any of it.

But thinking that way only served to make her feel guilty and ashamed. After all, her life had been spared. Had that palm tree not been precisely where it was, the car would have struck and killed her. So she was blessed to be alive.

Staring at the glaring light above, she was reminded of stories she'd heard about great white lights and near-death experiences and wondered if she might have just been through something similar herself.

She recalled hearing a voice, a man's voice, avowing his love.

Had it actually been her guardian angel?

And did women have *male* guardian angels?

She did not know, but it had seemed so real.

And now that she thought about it, the voice had sounded like Sam's—only, it couldn't have been him.

Because he didn't love her.

He wasn't ready to love any woman anytime soon.

Perhaps, it had only been her dazed mind playing tricks on her.

Wishful thinking.

Hopes.

Dreams.

Nothing real.

Probably he secretly despised her now anyway. After all, it was her fault that he was trapped, because if she hadn't forgotten the bear, they would be well on their way.

The three of them.

Now, however, if Sophie was lowering the boom, as Lauren feared she was doing, there would not be another chance to take Jamie and run. Sam was going to have to fight it out in court, at great expense, inconvenience...and heartache, as well.

Lauren gave her head a vicious shake, willing the drowsiness to go away. She needed to be fully lucid to give Sam the moral support he was going to need so desperately.

And she also wanted to tell him she was not going to accept the ten thousand dollars. He was going to need it for legal fees and, because she secretly loved him, it would be her way of helping him, even though they would never see each other again.

It was just something she felt she had to do in hopes it would ease the burden of her heavy heart.

Finally Lauren lost the fight against the sedative and unwillingly drifted away.

When she awoke, she thought she was dreaming because, through a hazy, sleepy fog, she imagined that Sam was standing beside her.

But that was not what puzzled her.

It was his eyes, glowing like lights on a Christmas tree.

And his smile, which seemed to spread from ear to ear.

Then he bent to kiss her, and she knew, with a thrilling rush, that it was, indeed, real.

"She said yes," he said hoarsely, his voice cracking with emotion. "Can you believe it, Lauren? She said yes."

Lauren blinked, at first not understanding, for her head felt heavy, leaden, from the drugs. She struggled to get up, and this time Sam did not try to hold her back. Instead, he grasped her shoulders to help her into a sitting position.

At once, her mind felt clearer, and her eyes were focusing…and that was when she saw the tears.

Sam was crying, tears streaming down his cheeks, even though his eyes were still shining, and his grin threatened to split his handsome face.

"What…what did you say?" she dared ask, praying all the while she had heard right—and if she had, that it meant what she thought it did.

"Sophie said yes, Lauren." His voice cracked with emotion. "She's agreed to let me have Jamie."

Chapter Sixteen

"I hate for you to fly back by yourself, Lauren."

Lauren was sitting in the rocker with Jamie cradled in her arms. She did not look at Sam, having avoided eye contact with him since coming home from the hospital three days ago.

"Lauren, are you even listening to me?"

She shook her head and smiled down at Jamie. He had fallen asleep while taking his bottle. A tiny milk bubble appeared at the corner of his rosebud mouth, and she dabbed at it lovingly with his bib. Such an angel. Precious beyond words. Truly a gift from heaven above.

She wondered if he would look like Sam when he grew up. His eyes were blue, and his hair was a straw-colored blond. *If you do look like your daddy, little guy,* she told him silently, *you're going to be a real heartbreaker.*

Sam walked to the rocker and dropped to one knee. "Are you sure you can't wait and go back with me and Jamie?

It shouldn't be but a couple more weeks. Besides, what will I tell Sophie?''

Lauren drew a deep breath to steady herself, for it was terribly unnerving to have him so close. He was touching her, too, his hand on her knee. It might as well have been a burning coal, for the heat was overwhelming.

Finally she was able to trust her voice to speak. ''We'll tell her I want to go back early to get everything ready for Jamie. She'll understand.''

The phone rang, but they ignored it. Sophie would answer elsewhere in the house as she always did.

Sam dared hope Lauren's reluctance to say anything meant she was having second thoughts. ''Come on,'' he coaxed with a grin, giving her knee a shake. ''You know you'd rather squeeze into the coach section with me and the tiger here.''

''I'm not flying first-class,'' she reminded.

''I know. What I mean is, you might not get to sit next to somebody with a baby fussing and crying from coast to coast. Not to mention a smelly diaper.'' He wrinkled his nose in mock disgust. ''You'll miss all the fun.''

She managed to smile at his humor and said, ''Jamie is a good baby. You'll be fine with him. Besides—'' she lowered her voice lest Sophie was within hearing range ''—you've got to get used to taking care of him yourself, at least until you find a nanny.''

''I know.'' He sighed and got to his feet. ''But I wish you'd consider hanging around a while longer.''

''I've thought about it,'' she lied. The truth was, she couldn't wait to leave, because each day was now agony to know it was all coming to an end. She supposed it was like looking forward to a root canal—wanting to get it over with so the healing process could begin.

''At least wait till after I talk to Mr. Snead.''

''I'm packed, and I have my ticket for today. And I really do need to get back, Sam. Remember, when I called Midge she told me about an opening for a sales rep for a dental supply company. I think I'd like to try that, so I need to get back and make my application.''

"Couldn't you do it by mail?''

She could—but it was her excuse to go ahead and leave. "I'm afraid not,'' she lied again.

"Well, if your mind is made up.''

"It's best.'' She bent to kiss Jamie and bit back tears.

"Sophie's been real good about all this,'' Sam said. "I'm just glad she never found out I was planning on running away with him.''

"I know. And I'm also glad she didn't discover we're really not married. Have you thought anymore about how you'll break it to her later?''

He shook his head. "Strangely enough, she hasn't mentioned the future. It's like once I leave here with Jamie, that's it, and we won't hear from her again.''

"Have you discussed it with her?''

"No. I guess I'm being a coward about it. I mean, I'll stay in touch with her, of course, but I'll probably wait a while so it won't look suspicious when I tell her we got a divorce.''

Lauren winced. *Divorce* was a word she did not like and prayed that if she ever did get married, it would be for keeps. So many of the children she had grown up with in foster homes were there because of broken homes. "How long will you wait?''

He pursed his lips thoughtfully, then said, "Maybe Christmas. It's a long way off, and it'll be a good time to contact her. She'll be lonely, not having any family.

"It's a shame about the Godfreys,'' he added. "I think they were pretty close.''

"They were. She's bound to feel extra sad once you and Jamie are gone.''

"She's dreading it, for sure. Maybe Mr. Snead will wrap things up quick so we can get it over with. As I understand it, I have to undergo a DNA test so he can file an affidavit of paternity with the court. Then, as soon as he can get it on the docket, we'll have a hearing before a judge to make it all legal. There's also the matter of the trust fund. Sophie wants that taken care before we leave the state. We've agreed to have her bank in San Diego act as trustee.''

"Jamie is going to be rich one day. I'm glad."

"She's setting it up so it can be used for his education. He'll get the bulk of it when he's thirty."

"Did you agree with that?"

"Yes, I did. I figure he'll be old enough by then to know how to handle it. He'll be out of medical school, too, and—''

"Medical school?" Lauren echoed, stunned. "Don't tell me you're going to be one of those parents who maps out their child's life for them and makes them miserable trying to live up to all your expectations."

He laughed, and she knew he was only joking. "I hope you know me better than that."

Sam was standing at the window, looking out at the lovely blue-and-gold day, but suddenly whirled about to declare, "I'd really like to stay in touch with you, Lauren. You've been so wonderful through all this. And I know you're crazy about Jamie. I feel I owe it to you to stay friends, and…'' He trailed off to silence. Somehow it wasn't coming out right. He knew what he wanted to say but didn't exactly know how. It just wound up sounding patronizing.

Which was how Lauren perceived it. She felt he was only being polite, and she didn't want that. She hedged by flippantly saying, "Oh, I'll check in from time to time to see how you two are doing."

Another lie.

Silence then descended like a shroud as they each were lost in their own musings.

Lauren was trying not to think about the moment at hand but still wished time would pass quickly so she could escape the torment. The past few days had been rather tense. Sophie had little to say and devoted almost every waking hour to Jamie. Lauren knew how she felt, because she would have liked to do the same. She had to pretend, however, that because she was soon going to have him all to herself, she was glad for Sophie to take over.

Lauren had also used the excuse of feeling sore from the accident to keep from sleeping with Sam. He obliged by sleeping on a cot in the nursery. The truth was she feared she would burst into tears and cling to him if he made love to her again. So she had kept her distance, but, oh, how hard it had been.

Sam endeavored to end the awkward moment. "I called a Realtor I know in Atlanta, and she says she's got a small house that would be perfect for me."

"What section?" Lauren hoped it was nowhere near her condo, even though she would not be there much longer.

"Buckhead."

She was glad. She never went to that area.

"I've been cleared for the permanent desk job, too," he continued. "There might even be some days I can work at home, if I get a computer, which I'll do, of course. According to the Realtor, the house has a third bedroom I can use for an office. It's got a nice yard, too. I can put up a swing set when Jamie's a little older."

"That will be nice," Lauren murmured, dying inside to think how she would not be the one to push Jamie in his swing and hear his laughter as he swished through the air.

"If it works out, I'll rent with an option to buy."

Lauren glanced at the clock on the bedside table. If she had to keep listening to Sam's plans for a future that did not include her, she was going to scream. "I know it's early, but maybe we should go ahead and leave for the airport."

Sam's shoulders were drooping as though he bore the weight of the world, but he made his voice light and said, "Yeah, I guess so. I'll put your luggage in the car."

Lauren wished Jamie were going, but Sophie had insisted

on keeping him, saying she and Sam needed some private time.

So now the dreaded moment was upon her—she would have to say farewell to the child she could not love more had she given birth to him herself. But would wait until Sam left the room. She was going to break down and cry, she knew, and did not want him to see her.

Sam was almost to the door when Sophie came rushing in. "Mr. Snead's secretary called and said if you can be at his office in half an hour—he can see you today."

"I'll just wait till my appointment tomorrow," Sam said. "I need to get Lauren to the airport."

Sophie argued, "He can't see you tomorrow. That's the reason for your having to rush over there now. His secretary says he's been called out of town on an emergency and has to leave this afternoon. He won't be back for a week. If you don't go, it will mean waiting a week or more to start the proceedings."

"Well..." He hesitated, looking at Lauren.

She waved him away, knowing he was only being polite to want to see her off. "Go ahead. I'll get a cab."

"No, you don't have to." Sophie explained, "I've already called one for Sam. It should be here in a few minutes. We have time for me to drive you to the airport."

She turned to Sam just as a horn blew in front of the house. "That will be the cab. You need to hurry."

She was practically pushing him out the door, and Lauren focused on Jamie, not trusting herself to look at Sam for fear she'd burst into tears.

Suddenly Sam balked. "Sophie, go tell the cab I'm on my way. I want a minute with Lauren."

"All right. But hurry." She scurried out.

Lauren knew she had to hang on to her composure during their last moments together. Pasting a smile on her face, she said, "Well, I'm glad everything turned out like you'd hoped."

Sam gestured helplessly. "I don't know what to say,

Lauren, except that I appreciate everything you did. And remember, I'm hoping you'll stay in touch. For Jamie's sake," he added, clinging to his pride to the last instant.

Lauren stood, holding tight to Jamie. "I'm glad I was able to help. You'll make a good father. Jamie is a lucky little boy."

Sam took his wallet from his hip pocket. "I was able to get your money for you yesterday. The bank in San Diego called my bank in Atlanta, and I was able to transfer my savings to a cashier's check." He handed it to her. "You can cash it when you get home.

Lauren made no move to accept it. Her arms were filled with Jamie. She also wanted to argue about the amount but had decided he would insist on her taking all of it.

Her purse was on the bed, and he put the check inside and stood back. "Well, I guess this is it."

Lauren was glad she had Jamie. Otherwise, she might have thrown herself in Sam's arms, and that would never do. She had been paid for her services. Her job was finished. There was no need to make a fool of herself by admitting she had fallen in love with the boss.

He stepped closer, and for an instant, she thought he was going to wrap both her and Jamie in his arms for a big family kiss as they had done in the past...for Sophie's benefit, of course. Only, now it wasn't necessary, and, instead, he gave her shoulder an awkward pat and lightly said, "Well, you be careful going home. I'll call you when I get back and give you my new address and phone number. It shouldn't be but two or three weeks."

"Sure. Fine. You be careful, too." But all the while she was thinking how if he did call he would get the phone company's recording that her number had been changed to unlisted, because that's what she intended to do right away. And if he went by the clinic, she would make sure no one told him where she had gone to work. She also planned to move as fast as possible. There was just no way she would torture herself by having contact with him.

* * *

Sam walked out the door, head down. He knew his eyes were misty and he did not want her to see.

The past few days had been a blend of heaven and hell. Heaven, because Sophie had given her consent.

Hell, because his time with the woman he had come to love was over.

Sophie was waiting in the foyer, but he didn't look at her, instead breezing by with the suitcases. He had earlier parked the car in the driveway out front.

"I gave the cabdriver Mr. Snead's address," she said, following him out to the porch. "As soon as I see Lauren off, I'll drive over to pick you up. It's probably best I go along, anyway, in case he needs me to sign anything."

"Thanks. I'll see you there."

He put Lauren's bags in the trunk, then got in the cab.

Settling back, he closed his eyes and felt the beginnings of a headache. Lord, he was truly a maelstrom of emotions. He should have been over the moon with joy, yet he felt as if someone in army boots had stomped all over his heart.

He should have kept it all strictly business, damn it.

He should have done what he thought about in the beginning—act like a jerk when he and Lauren were alone, be hard to get along with, make her draw away from him so there'd be no way they'd become close.

But he hadn't been able to do that, because Lauren was so easy to love. He just couldn't help it, no matter how much he argued within himself.

And, oh, what an actress she was. Truly she had missed her calling, because there had been times when she'd slipped into the role so deeply that he had actually dared to believe maybe she loved him a little, after all.

Especially when they were making love.

Warm and giving, passionate and sensuous, Lauren was the perfect lover.

Yes, painful though it was to admit it, she was one hell of a fine actress.

He did, however, take solace in one thing—he hadn't made a fool of himself.

He had succeeded in resisting the burning urge to admit to her what he was feeling and ask if she might care, if only a little. If so, then it would be a beginning.

But, thank God, he'd kept his mouth shut, because even though he was hurting like hell to lose her, at least he hadn't had to endure the possible anguish should he have heard the laughter...*again.*

Lauren sat in the back next to Jamie, who was securely fastened in his car seat.

As they crossed the Coronado Bridge into San Diego, she tried to focus on the beauty spanning all around rather than awareness that she had but a little while left with Jamie. It was bad enough walking away from Sam. Leaving Jamie, too, was more than she could bear.

Sophie had not spoken since they had left her house but suddenly said, "I'm going to have the car seat shipped to you."

"That's very nice of you," Lauren said, thinking how she probably should have said no, that she and Sam would buy a new one, there was no need for her to go to the trouble and expense. But she wasn't sure how Sam was fixed for money. Maybe he couldn't afford it.

"Actually, I plan to send everything. Crib. Changing table. High chair. All of it. I won't have any use for it now."

Lauren noticed a strain in Sophie's voice and felt a secret bond to know she was suffering, too. "That's nice of you," she repeated dryly.

"I wish you didn't have to go back early."

"Well, as I said, I really need to get back to work. One of the girls quit without notice and left them shorthanded." She felt guilty to think how easy the lies came now.

"I wish you could just stay home with Jamie."

"That would be nice," Lauren said, fighting to keep her voice even.

"Well, I understand how it is with young folks. It takes two incomes these days to make ends meet. It's just a shame Sam turned down my offer."

"What offer?"

"I told Sam how I've got money of my own, and if he'd let me, I'd like to match whatever you'd make working so you could stay home with Jamie till he's old enough to start school. He said he couldn't let me do that. Didn't he tell you?" Sophie cut a glance at Lauren in the rearview mirror.

"Uh..." Lauren hedged before lying once more. "He mentioned it. And I agree. It wouldn't be right."

Sophie gave a snort. "I don't see why not. It's my money to do with as I see fit, and I can afford it."

"Well, it's generous of you, but..." Lauren let her voice trail off. She didn't know what else to say.

Jamie squealed and bounced in his seat. He loved to ride.

Lauren devoured him with her eyes, wanting to seal the image in her mind, and heart, forever.

Finally they arrived at the airport. Sophie pulled up for curbside check-in, saying, "You can go with me to park the car and help bring Jamie back."

Lauren was quick to protest, "But you don't have to do that. I can say goodbye right here, and you can hurry and join Sam."

"Sam will be fine, and I know you want to spend an extra few minutes with Jamie. After all, it may be several weeks before Mr. Snead wraps everything up."

Lauren made no further protest. The truth was, she did want the extra time. After all, it would have to last her the rest of her life.

"I have a surprise for you," Sophie said when they were seated at the gate where Lauren would board the plane for Atlanta.

Lauren watched with interest as Sophie took a plastic bag from the rack under the stroller. Inside was the bear she had nearly gotten herself killed retrieving. In all the turmoil of the past days, it had slipped her mind, but now she was delighted to see it.

"And it still works," Sophie said triumphantly, giving it a squeeze.

Jamie heard the music and reached for it with a big smile.

"I don't believe it," Lauren said in wonder. "Thank you, Sophie. I really wanted him to have it. He seems to love it."

"He loves you, too. He's going to miss you."

Lauren swallowed past the lump in her throat and managed to say, "He's a wonderful little boy. I'm going to miss him, too."

She was paying attention to Jamie and did not realize Sophie was crying till she heard her sniffing. Touching her arm, she asked, "What's wrong?"

"Don't you know?" she whispered hoarsely, searching Lauren's face. "It's tearing me apart to think that after a few more weeks I'll probably never see him again. He's my breath of life. He's all I've got."

"Then tell Sam how you feel. I'm sure he'll understand and work something out for you to visit."

"Oh, I wouldn't dare. Not after all the mean things I said in the beginning and what I put you two through. Like when I saw Jamie was cutting a tooth. I kept quiet so you'd maybe feel bad not to have realized it yourself and you'd give up and go home. I see now how silly that was, and I want you to know I'm sorry."

Lauren smiled. "It's okay. It just made me want to try harder."

"Anyway—" Sophie went on "—that's why I put off saying anything about having made up my mind favorably. I was trying to muster nerve to talk to Sam about letting me see Jamie through the years."

Lauren, surprised, reminded, "But you said you had to

talk to your lawyer first. I thought that meant you were going to refuse.''

Sophie's eyes went wide. "Oh, no. That wasn't the reason. I wanted to tell Mr. Snead what I'd decided and ask if there was anything that could be done legally to give me visitation rights, but he said there wasn't. When I heard that, I wanted more time to try and get my nerve up to talk to Sam about it. That's why I said I wanted to wait till morning, only, after you were nearly killed, I knew it was time to stop procrastinating and let you two get on with your lives. But I still couldn't bring myself to mention anything else to Sam.

"I guess," she said, dabbing at her eyes with a tissue, "I was afraid he'd say no, so I didn't say anything."

Lauren's heart went out to her, and she felt like crying herself as she implored, "But you have to talk to him, Sophie, and let him know how you feel. How's he ever going to know if you don't tell him...if you don't ask?"

Sophie was quiet for a moment as she thought about it, then conceded, "Maybe you're right. But you can tell him," she went on brightly, hopefully. "Tell him we had this talk. Tell him how I feel. Maybe he'll understand why I couldn't ask him myself."

Lauren could not let her know that was not possible, because she would not be seeing him again. "No," she said firmly. "It's best you do it, Sophie. Do it today."

An announcement was made that Lauren's plane was about to begin boarding.

"I guess it's time," she said lamely. She leaned to kiss Jamie's cheeks in turn, whispering in each ear how much she loved him...how much she always would.

She stood and shook Sophie's hand. "Tell him," she repeated. "It never hurts to ask."

Sophie, blinking back fresh tears, shrugged and said, "He'll laugh at an old fool like me."

"No, he won't. Sam isn't like that. And even if he did refuse, which I don't think he will, wouldn't that be better than suffering and wondering how things might have turned out?''

Sophie said she wasn't sure, and Lauren had run out of time.

''Do it,'' Lauren urged. Then, impulsively, she kissed her cheek.

Grabbing her carry-on bag, Lauren hurried toward the loading gate and did not look back.

Only when she was on board, her seat belt fastened, did she allow the tears to fall.

It was over.

Chapter Seventeen

Midge pointed at Lauren's sandwich. "If you aren't going to eat that, can I have it? No need to waste food or money, I always say."

"Sure. Go ahead." Lauren pushed the plate towards her.

They were having lunch in a restaurant across the street from the new dental clinic, where Lauren had been working for nearly three weeks. She had gone by the day after returning from California and been hired on the spot.

"So…" Midge said around a bite of tomato, "Let's hear it."

"Well, I really like it. My salary is the same, but the patients seem nicer." She smiled. "At least nobody has bitten me yet."

Midge shook a pickle at her. "I don't mean your new job, and you know it. You've told me all that. Several times, in fact. I asked you to lunch today to hear about what you were doing all those weeks you dropped off the face of the earth, and you're not leaving this booth till you tell me, and I mean it.'' She bit down on the pickle with a loud crunch.

Lauren teased, ''Actually, I don't think you'll leave till the restaurant runs out of food…which could happen, the way you've been eating. What's wrong with you, anyway? First you gobble down a cheeseburger and fries, and now you're attacking my sandwich like a piranha. I've never seen you like this.''

Midge swallowed and took a big gulp of her soda before confiding, ''I've never felt this way before, either.''

''What way?''

''Hungry all the time.''

''Maybe it's being married. You aren't worrying about your figure now that you've hooked your man.''

''Oh, I worry all right, but there's no need. Not now.'' With a grin, Midge announced, ''I'm pregnant.''

At first, Lauren could only stare at her as she fought a sudden wave of envy. Then, eyes misting, she said, ''A baby. Oh, Midge, that's wonderful. I'm so happy for you. What does Scott say?''

''He is absolutely over the moon. You know, we really didn't plan on having a baby this soon, but I must have missed a pill or two. I'm almost three months along.''

Lauren gasped. ''And you haven't told me till now? Your very best friend?''

''I've wanted to tell you,'' Midge said with a shrug. ''I was just going to use it as bargaining power. You know— you tell me your secret, and I'll tell you mine. But I let it slip, so now it's your turn.''

Lauren played dumb. ''To do what?''

Midge tossed a French fry at her, and Lauren ducked. ''Your secret, darn it. Something is bugging you. You've lost weight. You don't eat. You're depressed. I've got a feeling it has to have something to do with that mysterious job you had. And besides, you told me the reason you took it was because it paid well and you needed the money to change careers, but the minute you're back in town all you do is change dental offices. It doesn't make sense.''

Lauren nibbled on a potato chip. ''I suppose it doesn't, and I know you're hurt because I won't tell you about it, but I just can't. I promised I wouldn't tell anybody.''

''So what about the money? Didn't you get paid?''

Lauren thought about the cashier's check. It was in her jewelry box at home. She'd not been able to make herself cash it, because to do so seemed so final. And that was silly, because it *was* final. She had changed her phone number to unlisted. The few people at Dr. Brockworth's clinic who knew where she'd gone to work had crossed their hearts and hoped to die ten thousand times over if they breathed a word to anyone about it. She had found a new apartment near her office, everything was packed, and come Saturday, a truck would be there to move her out. She didn't plan on leaving a forwarding address. There was no way Sam could track her down—even if he tried.

Midge reached across the table to wave her hand in front of Lauren's face. ''Hello. Anybody there? Earth to Lauren. Earth to Lauren.''

Lauren pushed her hand away and managed a laugh despite her gloomy mood.

''*What is wrong?*'' Midge demanded. She snapped her fingers. ''I know. You fell in love with that guy that hired you to do whatever it is you're too ashamed to talk about.''

Lauren lifted her chin. ''I am not ashamed of anything. I told you—I made a promise.''

Midge held up her hands in surrender. ''Okay, okay. I'm sorry. I didn't mean to imply anything. I just care about you, and I want to help.''

''I'll be fine, really. Don't worry about me. Now, then,'' she said brightly, anxious to take the focus from her, ''Let's talk about the baby. Have you had an ultrasound yet? Do you want to know if you're having a boy or a girl?''

Midge said she'd like to know but explained Scott was

against it. "He says it's sort of like opening a present before Christmas. It spoils the fun on Christmas morning."

She chattered on about what they might name the baby, their plans to decorate the nursery, and her ebullience made her forget her curiosity about Lauren for the moment.

Lauren listened, but Midge's enthusiasm over impending motherhood was like a knife to her heart, painfully reminding of how she had been a mommy, too...if only for a little while.

Her mind drifted as she recalled so many precious memories—bathing Jamie, feeding him, the way his fist curled around her finger when she was giving him his bottle. He had even begun to clap his hands in delight and laugh out loud every time he saw her. And when he had reached out for her with his little fat arms, wanting her to take him and hold him, it had melted her heart.

She thought, too, of the wonderful nights of splendor in Sam's arms. Together they had touched the stars and soared through the heavens.

But they had also shared glorious times that had nothing to do with sex. There had been picnics, and walks, and bike rides, and splashing in the pool. They had worked in the yard, washed dishes and even cleaned house a few times. They had fun together, real fun.

And, oh, how she missed him.

"Lauren?"

She glanced up but had to stop and think where she was, for her musings had taken her far, far away.

Midge was frowning. "You haven't heard a word I've said. What were you thinking about?"

Lauren glanced at her watch. "I was thinking how I've got to get back to work. I'm ten minutes late."

She reached for the check, but Midge caught her hand. "No. It's my treat. I invited you." She made a face. "But it was a waste of money, because you wouldn't tell me anything."

Lauren reached over and gave her cheek a playful pinch. "Now how can you say that? You ate both lunches, fatty."

"Oh, you—" Midge sputtered, laughing.

"But I'll pay, anyway." Lauren snatched the check away from her. "Be sure to remind Scott he promised to help me move Saturday. See you."

The afternoon seemed endless, but Lauren did not care. She had nowhere to go except home, and nothing waited for her there. Even the geranium she'd left with a neighbor had died.

It was as though her life no longer had any meaning or purpose. She got up in the morning and went to work. When a patient left her chair, another took his place. She went home to nuke a frozen dinner, which she hardly touched. A few hours of mindless TV, then it was time to crawl into bed to toss and turn...and cry...and do it all over again the next day.

She wondered how long the misery would last. When she was not thinking of Sam and how much she loved him, then the image of a dimpled smile and coos and gurgles filled her mind.

Her heart bled for two lost loves.

And the anguish was unbearable.

Finally, another routine day at work ended, and Lauren made the long trek across town, grateful that after the weekend she would no longer have so long to commute. The new apartment was only a ten-minute walk from the clinic.

She groaned when she walked in the front door, to see the stack of empty boxes waiting. It was going to be a long night, because she had to finish packing everything so Scott could begin moving the small things in his car the following evening. How on earth, she wondered, had she managed to accumulate so much junk?

After changing clothes, she plunged right in without bothering to make supper. Midge was right. She had lost weight. But she didn't care about food anymore. She didn't care about anything.

Taking her time, she sorted junk from what she wanted to take with her. It was nearly two in the morning when she finished.

Exhausted, she fell across the bed, grateful to be too tired to think.

Perhaps it would be a night without dreams…about blue eyes…and dimpled smiles.

She heard the sound from far, far away, past the velvet shroud that had taken her to peaceful oblivion.

She struggled to awaken, but she was sleeping so deeply that she stirred, moaned, then burrowed her head under the pillow.

The sound grew louder, more persistent.

Then it dawned on her that it was actually someone banging the brass knocker on her front door.

She looked at the clock. It was not yet 6:00 a.m. Outside, the wind howled, rattling the windows. It was almost the end of February, and she was freezing after collapsing on top of the blankets.

The rapping continued.

"Oh, hold your horses," she muttered grumpily as she got up, thinking that whoever it was had better have a good reason for banging on her door at such an ungodly hour.

"Who's there?" she yelled.

There was no answer, and the banging had stopped. Evidently they had given up and left. Still, she was curious.

Switching on the porch light, she peered through the peephole but did not see anyone.

She unfastened the dead bolt and eased the door open.

No one was there.

With a yawn, she started to close the door but froze to hear a soft, cooing sound coming from…*the porch floor.*

Looking down, Lauren gasped, sure she was seeing things, sure that all the hours spent pining away had taken their toll and damaged her brain, because…

She thought she was looking at Jamie.

He was snuggled in a baby carrier, blankets tucked about

him, but he had recognized her and now kicked his arms and legs in his way of telling her he wanted her to pick him up. His contented coos were fast turning to indignant squawks, and she knelt to unfasten the straps holding him down.

If it was a dream, then she would enjoy it as long as it lasted, by God.

And that was when she saw the note pinned to his blanket.

With pounding heart, she knelt down and read:

I need a mommy.
Do you need a baby?
I come complete with diapers—
and a daddy.

Lips trembling, tears filling her eyes, Lauren looked up to see that Sam had stepped from the shadows.

And he was holding his arms open wide.

She did not remember standing up, did not know how Jamie wound up crushed between the two of them. All Lauren knew was that her dream of dreams had come true, and Sam was holding her and kissing her.

"Lauren, my darling," he whispered fervently, "I never knew it was possible to love someone so much. Say you'll be my bride for real...my wife, forever."

"Yes, oh, yes," she cried without hesitation when she could find her voice. "But I can't believe you're here. I can't believe any of this."

"And I can't believe you're saying you'll marry me. I was convinced you'd sworn off men forever, but—"

"I was...till you came along, only I was scared to tell you, because you said over and over it was strictly business, nothing more."

He kissed the tip of her nose. "It wasn't business when we made love. It was magic."

She felt a familiar warm rush sweep from head to toe. "It was, wasn't it? And now I know it was because we were falling in love. But I couldn't say anything. I was too afraid of having my heart smashed again. Remember what I said about three strikes?" She laughed softly. Oh, it was good to be happy again.

"Yes, but you had forgotten that even when a ball player swings three times and goes out, there's always another time up at bat."

"I know that now, and I wish I'd thought that way sooner, because now I feel like I've hit a home run, and, oh, Sam—" She shook her head wildly, laughing and crying at the same time. "I just love you so much."

"I was as scared as you were, but Sophie made me realize I had to take a chance."

"Sophie? I don't understand."

"She admitted how she'd been putting off telling me she'd made her decision so she could gather the courage to ask if she could see Jamie from time to time. I told her of course she could and how I was surprised she'd ever have thought otherwise. That's when she said she had you to thank for finally coming forward—that you made her see that she had to ask, because too many lives are ruined when people are afraid to take a chance, fearing disappointment or humiliation. Their pride stands in the way.

"When she said that," he rushed on to explain, "I knew I had to do the same thing—ask how you felt, even if you laughed in my face. And oh, darling, how glad I am that I did."

They hugged some more, and kissed some more, and then remembered how cold it was and got Jamie inside the house.

When he was fed and sleeping contentedly in Lauren's arms, Sam told her how he'd tried to find her at work, tried to call, of course, and finally decided to show up on her doorstep.

Lauren would not let herself think of how things might have turned out had he waited any longer.

"But there's one more thing," he said, a twinkle in his eye.

"Anything." She felt as though she were going to burst with her joy.

"I've got another note to deliver." He drew a piece of paper from his pocket and held it out for her to read.

I need a great-grandma.
Do you need a baby?
I come complete with diapers—
and a mommy and daddy.

"As soon as we can afford it," Sam explained, "I want us to fly to California and knock on her door and do the same thing I just did to you. Who knows? She might even want to move to Atlanta. There's nothing to keep her in California. So as soon as we can—"

Lauren silenced him with a kiss, then asked coyly, "How would it be if we asked to have our wedding in her rose garden? She might like that."

"Wedding?" He blinked. "Then she'd know that we lied about being married."

"She won't care. She'll be so happy to know she's really going to be a part of our family. Besides, she's not the narrow-minded person we thought she was. All she ever really cared about was Jamie's welfare and happiness."

"True," he said with a thoughtful nod, "but I'd hoped we could get married right away, and it'll be a while before we can afford—"

Again, she silenced him with a kiss, then said, "Do you think ten thousand dollars will be enough for our tickets if we squeeze into coach class and dream about better service?"

"You didn't cash the check."

"No, I didn't. I was waiting for you to show up to help spend it," she teased.

"No," he said, lifting Jamie from her arms and putting him back into his carrier. "You were waiting for this...and so was I."

He folded her in his arms, and, with a sigh, Lauren melted against him.

She was where she belonged and always had, for it was the moment, the life, she had dreamed of.

And no longer was she a make-believe mom or make-believe wife.

She would, gratefully and happily, be playing both roles for real.

Epilogue

The sun shone down through silver-tinged clouds, and a gentle breeze blew in from the Pacific Ocean to kiss the dazzled faces of the bride and groom.

Lauren, elegantly beautiful in a simple gown of white satin, with fresh rosebuds from Sophie's garden adorning her hair, smiled all the way from her very soul as Sam took his place beside her.

He looked breathtaking in a white tux, with a rosebud in his lapel. His eyes smoldered with the love radiating from his heart.

The day was perfect...as perfect as they both knew their marriage, their life, would be.

The setting was Sophie's rose garden, the air permeated with sweetness to take the breath away.

The minister began the ceremony, and they spoke their vows, gazes locked in quiet contemplation and affirmation of a love that would truly last till death did they part.

And at the end, when they were pronounced man and

wife, there was an unexpected movement behind them, and they turned, startled, then broke into wide grins and laughter as Sophie, carrying Jamie, handed him to his daddy...and his new mommy.

They were a threesome.

A family.

Sophie stepped away, only to have Sam reach out to draw her within the circle.

"Now we're a *real* family." He smiled.

Lauren nodded to affirm and whispered, "Truly, we are."

"I love you," Sam whispered to her then, shutting out the world in that crystallized moment of intimate affirmation of devotion for all time.

"And I love you," Lauren avowed. "And I always will."

They kissed, with Jamie squirming between them, and then Sophie laughed and said, "Come on in for cake and champagne, everyone. The bride's not for hire anymore. She's got a full-time job now."

Sam winked. "That's for sure."

And Lauren could only smile and firmly declare, "Darling, I wouldn't have it any other way."

* * * * *

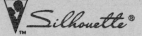
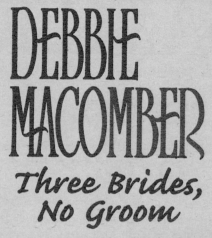

National Bestselling Author

MARY LYNN BAXTER

"Ms. Baxter's writing…strikes every chord within the
female spirit."
—Sandra Brown

LONE STAR Heat

SHE is Juliana Reed, a prominent broadcast journalist whose
television show is about to be syndicated. Until the murder…

HE is Gates O'Brien, a high-ranking member of the
Texas Rangers, determined to forget about his ex-wife. He's
onto something bad….

Juliana and Gates are ex-spouses, unwillingly involved in an
explosive circle of political corruption, blackmail and murder.

In order to survive, they must overcome the pain of the past…and
the very demons that drove them apart.

Available in September 1997 at your favorite retail outlet.

MIRA The brightest star in women's fiction   MMLBLSH

Look us up on-line at:http://www.romance.net

DIANA WHITNEY

**Continues the twelve-book
series 36 HOURS in
September 1997
with Book Three**

OOH BABY, BABY

In the back of a cab, in the midst of a disastrous storm,
Travis Stockwell delivered Peggy Saxon's two precious babies
and, for a moment, they felt like a family. But Travis was a
wandering cowboy, and a fine woman like Peggy was better off
without him. Still, she and her adorable twins had tugged on
his heartstrings, until now he wasn't so sure that *he* was
better off without *her*.

For Travis and Peggy and *all* the residents of Grand Springs,
Colorado, the storm-induced blackout was just the beginning
of 36 Hours that changed *everything!* You won't want to miss a
single book.

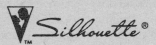

Look us up on-line at: http://www.romance.net   36HRS3

Silhouette is proud to introduce
the newest compelling miniseries by
award-winning author

SUSAN MALLERY

TRIPLE TROUBLE

Kayla, Elissa and Fallon—three identical triplet sisters
are all grown up and ready to take on the world!

✳✳✳✳✳✳✳✳✳✳✳✳✳✳✳✳✳✳✳

In August: **THE GIRL OF HIS DREAMS
(SE#1118)**

Could it be Prince Charming was right in front of her
all along? But how was Kayla going to convince her
best friend that she was the girl of his dreams?

In September: **THE SECRET WIFE
(SE#1123)**

That Special Woman Elissa wasn't ready to throw in
the towel on her marriage, and she set out to show
her husband just how good love could be the second
time around!

In October: **THE MYSTERIOUS STRANGER
(SE#1130)**

When an accident causes her to wash up on shore,
the handsome man who finds her has no choice but to
take in this mysterious woman without a memory!

Don't miss these exciting novels...only from

Silhouette®SPECIAL EDITION®

Daniel MacGregor is at it again...

New York Times bestselling author

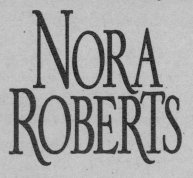

NORA ROBERTS

introduces us to a new generation of MacGregors
as the lovable patriarch of the illustrious MacGregor
clan plays matchmaker again, this time to his three
gorgeous granddaughters in

THE MACGREGOR BRIDES

From Silhouette Books

Don't miss this brand-new continuation of Nora Roberts's
enormously popular *MacGregor* miniseries.

Available November 1997 at your favorite retail outlet.

▼ Silhouette®
TM

Look us up on-line at: http://www.romance.net

NRMB-S